From the Nancy Drew Files

THE CASE: *Track down the person stalking handsome TV star Rick Arlen.*

CONTACT: *Actress* Mattie Jensen, *Rick's beautiful co-star on the soap opera "Danner's Dream"—and his ex-girlfriend.*

SUSPECTS: William Pappas, *the hot-tempered director who will do anything to keep Rick from leaving the show.*

Lillian Weiss, *assistant director and another of Rick's ex-girlfriends. She's jealous of his other romantic involvements.*

Dwayne Casper, *Rick's former agent, who still has a grudge against his ungrateful client.*

A crazed fan—*Rick's adoring public sometimes gets out of control.*

COMPLICATIONS: *Nancy's friend Bess has fallen head over heels for the gorgeous TV actor—even though she's putting herself in terrible danger.*

D0552752

Nancy Drew Files™ available in Armada

THE NANCY DREW FILES™

Case 17

Stay Tuned for Danger

Carolyn Keene

ARMADA

First published in the USA in 1987 by
Simon & Schuster Inc.
First published in Great Britain
in Armada in 1991

Armada is an imprint of
the Children's Division of
HarperCollins Publishers Ltd,
77/85 Fulham Palace Road, London W6 8JB

Printed and bound in Great Britain by
William Collins Sons & Co. Ltd, Glasgow

Stay Tuned for Danger

Chapter

One

Nancy, you're driving me nuts! Would you please finish that sundae? Our plane leaves in an hour!" Bess Marvin looked longingly at her friend's dessert. Then she pulled a pink beret over her straw blond hair and reached for the matching pink jacket that was hanging on the back of her chair.

Nancy Drew looked at Bess, her blue eyes sparkling with amusement. "Take it easy, Bess. We're five minutes from the airport. George'll get us there in plenty of time."

Nancy and Bess were flying to New York City to visit Nancy's aunt, Eloise Drew, and

1

George was dropping them off. It was early, so they had decided to stop for ice cream near the airport.

"Admit it, Bess," George Fayne said with a laugh, throwing an arm around her cousin's shoulders. "You're just jealous because Nancy's eating that fantastic, splendiferous, mouth-watering—"

"Mmmm. And it's so-o-o good," Nancy said, licking her lips.

"Quit teasing, you guys," Bess muttered. "I swear I gain weight just looking at something that fattening."

"It does look good," George said, wistfully agreeing. She and Bess were cousins as well as best friends, but they couldn't have been more different. With her tall, athletic figure, her dark hair and eyes, and her levelheaded approach to life, George was her cousin's opposite in every way.

"When you two get back from New York, we've got to come here again," George said. "You can fill me in on your trip, and by then I'll be able to order something disgustingly rich and gooey. Just like those banana splits we had at that wonderful restaurant, Rumpelmayer's." George sighed. "I wish I were going with you."

"I'll never understand you," said Bess. "How can you pass up a chance to go to New York, the most glamorous city in the world, just so you can run in some stupid race? What's the big deal?"

"Don't be dumb, Bess. I've been training for this race for months. It may only be the River Heights marathon, but it's important to me."

"Yummm," Nancy savored one last mouthful of ice cream before putting down her spoon. "Okay, I'm ready," she said with a toss of her reddish gold hair.

Bess eyed the remains of Nancy's sundae hungrily. "No," she told herself, "I refuse to blow my diet before we even get to New York. I mean, you never know who I might meet," she said, looking at her friends. "In New York, anything's possible."

Nancy and George exchanged knowing smiles. Bess was sure to find cute guys in the Big Apple, just as she did in River Heights.

"Well, if I know Nancy," George said, "you two will probably wind up in the middle of an adventure. Remember the last time we were in New York? We didn't even have time to go shopping!"

George was right. Intrigue and mystery seemed to find Nancy wherever she went. At eighteen, she was already a rising star in the world of detectives.

"No way," Nancy protested. "This time I'm just going to be a tourist. I'm going to spend some time with my aunt, Eloise, do some shopping, see a Broadway show——"

"*A* Broadway show? Are you kidding? There are at least six that I'm dying to see!" Bess exclaimed.

"Hey, you two," Nancy declared, looking at her watch. "Now we had better hurry."

And with that, the three girls paid their bill and filed out of the ice cream shop.

"Here we are," Bess said, staring up at the elegant old apartment building. "This street always looks like a movie set of 'old New York' to me. Like it's a hundred years old, at least."

It was true, Nancy thought. The street had old-world charm, from the tall gingko trees with their fanlike leaves to the old-fashioned gas lamps along the sidewalk that fronted the many brownstone buildings.

"Did I tell you my aunt bought her apartment last year when— Oh, look, there she is!" Nancy cried, waving to her aunt, who was coming out the front door. Tall and elegant, Eloise Drew was a female version of Nancy's father, Carson. They had the same lustrous brown hair and aristocratic features.

"Nancy!" Eloise cried, hugging her niece warmly and planting a kiss on her cheek. "I'm so happy to see you! And Bess," she said, taking Nancy's friend warmly by the hand. "How good it is to see you again. How was your trip?" Eloise asked as they entered the building.

"Kind of boring," Bess admitted with a smile.

"Wonderfully uneventful is more like it," Nancy said in the elevator up to Eloise's second-floor apartment. "I've been so busy lately that it was great just to sit down and leaf through a magazine."

"Well, here we are!" Eloise said, pushing open the door to her apartment. "I've redecorated a bit since you were here the last time."

The apartment was spacious and homey. Bright sunlight splashed across the walls, which were papered in a dainty flowery print.

"I love what you've done!" Bess exclaimed enthusiastically as they were passing through the living room. She paused to look out the window. "I had forgotten there were trees in the backyard!"

"In New York we call it a courtyard. Unfortunately, though, as you probably remember, your room faces the street." Nancy's aunt led them across a small hallway to a cozy bedroom. "Don't worry, the street is usually pretty quiet."

Just then a fire engine came careening down the block, its siren blasting. Eloise waited for it to pass before adding, "Quiet for the city, that is."

The room was all ready for the two girls. Both beds were freshly made with light blue comforters, and two sets of fluffy white towels were neatly folded on top of the modern oak bureau. Eloise slid open a pair of white louvered doors, revealing a nearly empty closet.

"Here you are, ladies," she announced. "And after you've unpacked, we'll have a snack. For dinner, I thought we could go to my favorite Chinese restaurant."

"Super," Nancy said, looking over at Bess, who seemed enthusiastic. "As long as there's no mystery involved, I'm game for anything."

"Well—" Nancy's aunt said hesitantly. "I wouldn't go so far as to say 'no mystery,' Nancy. I was going to save it for later, but since you brought it up . . ."

"Oh, no! I don't want to hear another word. I'm here for a week's vacation, and that's that!" Nancy flung herself on the bed and covered her head with a pillow.

"Okay, okay." Eloise shrugged. "I only thought you'd be interested because it has to do with a TV show. . . ." She stared absently at the ceiling, showing no emotion.

"What TV show?" Bess asked. Nancy's aunt didn't answer. "Come on, Nancy, ask her. I've got to know!"

Nancy peeked out from under her pillow, looking back and forth from Bess to Eloise. "Okay, Aunt Eloise," she muttered. "I give in. What show?"

"Well, let me start at the beginning," the older woman replied, sitting down next to

Nancy. "Yesterday, I happened to tell my downstairs neighbor you were coming to stay with me. Her name is Mattie Jensen, and she's an—"

"*The* Mattie Jensen? Of 'Danner's Dream'?"

Eloise nodded, and Bess nearly fainted with excitement.

"I don't believe it! Mattie Jensen is your neighbor! Is she as beautiful in real life as she is on TV? Is she anything like Serena Livingstone?"

"Hey, wait." Nancy propped herself up on one elbow, looking bewildered. "You guys are way ahead of me! Who's Serena Livingstone?"

Bess looked at Nancy as if she had just arrived from Mars. "That's Mattie Jensen's character on 'Danner's Dream.' Gosh, Nancy, you're really out of it. You at least know who Rory Danner is, don't you?"

Nancy shook her head.

"His real name is Rick Arlen. He and Mattie are the stars of the show," Eloise explained. "Anyway, I told her that you're a detective, and she got very excited."

"Well, is she?" Bess persisted. Nancy and Eloise looked at her, puzzled. "As beautiful in real life, I mean. And as together as Serena?"

"Oh!" Eloise laughed. "Well, let's see. If anything, I'd say she's more beautiful in person. As for together—well, Mattie's a sweet

7

girl, but she's very emotional. I guess you could say she has an artistic temperament."

Eloise turned back to her niece. "Anyway, she was really hoping you would stop by the set. It seems some strange things have been happening to Rick Arlen. She said she could get both of you guest passes for tomorrow morning. If you're willing, that is."

"*If* we're willing? Of course we are!" Bess declared. "I can't believe I'm going to visit the set of 'Danner's Dream'! Wait till George hears about this! She's as crazy about Rick Arlen as I am."

"Don't tell me George watches 'Danner's Dream,' too," Nancy cried in surprise. George was always either training for some athletic event or lost in the pages of a book. How could she have time to watch daytime TV?

"Her mother tapes it for her," Bess explained. "Everybody watches Serena and Rory. They're the hottest couple on the soaps!"

"I think I have heard of them, actually. He was featured in *Chatter* magazine last month, right?" Nancy asked.

Bess nodded. "Blond hair, dazzling blue eyes, muscles out to here," she said, indicating large biceps. "Need I say more?"

"I get the picture," Nancy replied. "But I promised myself—*no mysteries.*"

"Oh, come on, Nancy. How many chances do you get to meet real stars?"

"Well, it would be kind of interesting to see how a television show is put together—"

"Interesting?" Bess cried. "It'll be fantastic! I'll die if we don't go!"

"Then I guess I *can't* say no, can I?" She turned to her aunt. "Okay, you can tell your neighbor we're on."

"Great," said Eloise. "Mattie said you could show up at the studio around ten."

"All right!" Bess exclaimed, her light blue eyes dancing. "Now, I've just got to decide what to wear tomorrow."

"I'd rather check out that snack you were talking about, Aunt Eloise."

"Wait a minute!" cried Bess. "I'm coming, I'm coming. I'll pick out my clothes later."

Nancy had to laugh. Bess was so excited. She just hoped that Mattie Jensen was as prone to exaggeration as Aunt Eloise had said she was. If so, how much of a mystery could there really be?

"Are you sure this skirt fits?" Bess asked. She and Nancy had just walked through the huge glass doors of Worldwide Broadcasting.

"You look fabulous," Nancy assured her friend. All morning Bess had been fussing in front of the mirror, getting ready for their visit to the set of "Danner's Dream." And the results were definitely worth the work. In her soft suede skirt, tights, and ankle boots, Bess looked like a star herself.

"Okay, people," a voice behind them shouted. "We go in here! Make sure your guest pass is visible."

Nancy turned and saw a group of about thirty people push through the same glass doors she and Bess had just entered.

"It's okay, Harry," the tour guide in a navy blue uniform called to the security guard. "They're with me."

"Where you going? 'Danner's Dream'?" the guard asked.

"You guessed it," replied the tour guide.

"It's going to be a zoo in there today," the guard muttered. "But whatever— Management must know what they're doing. Take them into studio one, Joe."

"Well, if I were Serena, I'd kill him," Nancy heard a woman in the tour group say. "I mean, who does that Rory Danner think he is?"

"They may *have* to kill him," her companion replied. "I heard he's leaving the show at the end of the season."

"No!"

"Yes! Didn't you read the *Star Sentinel* last week? He wants to break his contract to make a movie."

"Well, if you ask me, Rick Arlen has gotten

too big for his britches," the first woman said. "We fans count, you know."

At the rear of the group was a large man in an old sweatshirt. He was shifting from foot to foot and muttering, "You'll find out, Rory. You're not that great."

At last they all disappeared through a set of swinging doors. "Boy, they sure seem angry," Nancy remarked.

"That's nothing," the security guard said. "Ever since Arlen decided he was leaving the show, seems like everybody hates him. I wouldn't want to be him right now, no siree." He shook his head. "Can I help you girls?" he finally asked.

"We're here to see Mattie Jensen," Nancy said politely. "She's expecting us."

The guard checked his book. "Miss Drew and Miss Marvin?" he asked. "Let's see—ten o'clock . . . she's probably just going into makeup. It's down the hall and around to your right. First left after the producer's office."

Thanking him, the girls made their way through the set of swinging doors that led into a long hallway. The noisy tour group had gone directly onto the set, but Nancy and Bess continued on, looking for the makeup room.

"This must be the hall he means," said Nancy.

"Maybe we'll pass the casting director's office," Bess whispered, following her.

Just then, two young secretaries stepped into the hall ahead of them. "Well, I think he has a good point!" one was saying to the other.

"He may have a point, but that's still no way to talk to people. Even if he is the producer!"

Feelings seem to be running high everywhere, Nancy thought. Suddenly she grabbed Bess by the wrist and signaled for her to be quiet.

They stopped by an open door with a sign that read William Pappas, Producer. They couldn't see in or be seen. Inside, a man was shouting, probably into a phone since no one responded to him. "I've told you before, he can't do this to me! I don't care if he *is* Rick Arlen. If he leaves this show, he'll never work again! Nobody—*nobody*—breaks a contract with me. I'll kill him before I let him work for someone else!"

Chapter

Two

I CAN'T BELIEVE he feels that strongly about Rick Arlen," Bess whispered angrily.

Nancy peered into the office, taking care to remain hidden. William Pappas's face was flushed with anger as he stared at the phone he had just slammed down. He fumbled in his pocket for a cigar.

"Actors! They're all alike! No class—none at all," he muttered to himself. Then he rose and shouted to a timid-looking girl in an inner adjacent office. "Get the writers on the phone and tell them I want a Rory Danner death scene—the more realistic the better. That idiot doesn't deserve to live after what he's put me through! And where's my Danish? You know I can't think before I've had my second coffee."

"Come on!" Nancy said in Bess's ear. "Let's get out of here." They hurried down the long hallway without looking back.

"Gosh, Nancy," Bess announced after they'd rounded a corner and were safely out of sight, "I'll bet he's the one who's causing all the trouble."

"I don't know, Bess. Maybe he has an artistic temperament, too. Remember what my aunt said about Mattie Jensen?"

Bess's attention, however, was caught by something else. "'Makeup.' Here we are." Bess placed her hand over her heart. "I can't believe I'm about to walk through that door and meet Mattie Jensen! How do I look? Are you sure this skirt is okay?"

Nancy couldn't help laughing. "You're too much," she said teasingly. "It *still* looks great, but if you're so uncomfortable why did you wear it?"

"Because it looks great—you just said so yourself!" Taking a deep breath, Bess knocked on the door.

"Come in," someone called out. Bess immediately recognized the voice of her favorite soap opera character.

Inside, Mattie Jensen was sitting in a large, barber-style chair. Her famous auburn curls were wrapped in purple curlers, and her porcelain skin was scrubbed clean. Not a hint of makeup anywhere. But she still looked incredibly beautiful, and her green eyes sparkled.

"Mattie J-Jensen," Bess sputtered.

"You must be Nancy Drew," Mattie replied. She held out a manicured hand and gave Bess a warm smile.

"No, I'm Bess Marvin. She's Nancy."

"Oh, of course," Mattie corrected herself, taking Nancy's hand. "It's great to meet both of you."

"Thanks, same here," Nancy answered.

"Nancy, Bess, I'd like you to meet Kay Wills. She's our makeup artist and one of the great ones. Without her, I'd be lost."

"Come on, Mattie, don't be so modest." Kay rolled her eyes at the girls and began dotting ivory base on Mattie's forehead. "With looks like yours, you'll never be lost."

"Well, looks aren't everything, are they?" Mattie sighed, holding her head still as Kay blended in the foundation.

"Try telling that to your leading man," Kay sniffed, continuing to work.

"Poor Rick," Mattie murmured. "He's so misunderstood. And now all this awful stuff is happening to him. Nancy, maybe you'll be able to help."

Nancy leaned against the wall. "To be honest, Ms. Jensen, I'm in New York on vacation.

I really don't want to get involved in anything complicated."

"Please, call me Mattie. And you've got to help him, Nancy! It's a matter of life and death!"

"You know, you're a lot more upset than he is, Mattie," Kay put in. "As far as I can tell, he loves the attention, no matter how negative it is."

Nancy was puzzled. "If you tell me what's going on, maybe I could give you a few suggestions," she offered. After all, she told herself, giving advice was different from actually getting involved.

"Didn't Eloise tell you?" Mattie asked frantically, her luminous eyes filling with tears. "Someone is trying to kill Rick!"

"Don't cry," Kay ordered, dabbing Mattie's eyes with a tissue. "You'll ruin your makeup."

"Sorry. It's just so upsetting."

"Maybe you should start at the beginning," Nancy said, taking an empty chair next to Mattie.

"It began with the chocolate," Mattie explained, leaning forward. Kay chased after her face with a powder puff. "A box of it came in with the rest of the fan mail one day. Rick is a maniac for chocolate, so he opened the box and ate one right away. It was so bitter that for a minute he thought he'd been poisoned. After a while, though, when he didn't keel over, he figured it was just a practical joke. We all did. But then a letter arrived. It said something like, 'Scared you, didn't I? Good, because this was just a dress rehearsal.' About two days later, a watch came in the mail. It was set at five to midnight, and there was a note attached that said, 'Your time's running out.' You see? Somebody is trying to kill him!"

Mattie was practically standing up in her chair. Kay gently pushed her back down and began working on her eyes. "Take it easy, hon," she said matter-of-factly.

"Maybe this is a stupid question," Nancy ventured, "but has anybody called the police?"

Kay laughed. "If we called the police every time we got a nasty letter around here, we'd be calling them every day! You should see some of the fan mail."

Mattie wheeled around in her chair. "But this is different! These aren't just nasty letters, they're real threats! The trouble is, nobody is taking them seriously!"

"Not even Rick?" Nancy asked.

"Especially not Rick," Mattie said huffily. "He thinks nothing will ever hurt him. As far as he's concerned, the whole thing is the work of a single loony fan out for kicks. I'm the only one who's really worried, and that's why I need your help."

"She'll help you, won't you, Nancy?" Bess

said, not really asking the question. "We'll stay here as long as it takes!"

Nancy smiled wryly. Bess would have promised anything if it meant she could spend more time with her idols.

"But, Bess," she said, protesting. "We have a lot of sightseeing planned, and—"

Just then, the door flew open and Rick Arlen burst in. Bess gasped. He really was even more gorgeous in person. A lock of blond hair had fallen over his forehead, and he impatiently brushed it away. He was holding up a black-and-white glossy photograph of himself. The photo had been scratched almost beyond recognition.

"Mattie," he said, thrusting the picture into her hands, "it's happened again! Look at this!"

Mattie looked at the photo, and at the message scrawled beneath it. "'If you won't be mine, you won't be anybody's,'" she read. She looked up at Nancy. "You see what I mean?"

"At least it's an old picture," Rick said, trying to make a joke. "It's not even very good, actually."

Bess was standing, absolutely frozen, staring moronically at Rick. Noticing her obvious interest, Mattie hastily introduced the girls to Rick, but it was clear that his mind was on other things. He hardly noticed them.

"Whoever did this has some nerve," he was

saying. "Imagine, tearing up my face like that."

"Please, Rick," Mattie begged, "if you won't call the police, will you at least tell security about this?"

"Come on, now," he said, waving away her concern. "What are they going to do about it? Shake their heads and wring their hands, that's what. Anyhow, it's probably just old man Pappas trying to scare me."

"Rick!" Mattie gasped. "You don't really think—"

"I don't know what to think," he muttered with a shrug. "All I know is that we're scheduled to be on the set in five minutes for dress rehearsal, and I haven't got time for nonsense like this." Rick turned toward the door. Jaw set, eyes ablaze, he was the picture of that perfect romantic rebel, Rory Danner. "See you on the set, Mattie. Oh, and nice meeting you, girls."

He gave Bess and Nancy a cursory nod as he left the room. "What a hunk!" Bess whispered hoarsely. "Oh, Nancy, you've just got to take this case! Just think what might happen to Rick if you don't."

"Bess, sick as it might be, sending hate mail is not a felony."

"Please," Mattie said, breaking in. "Something's very wrong here, I'm sure of it. I'd feel so much better if you'd at least stay and watch this morning's dress rehearsal.''

Nancy looked from Mattie to Bess and back again. There was no way they would let her say no. Besides, she reasoned, watching a soap rehearsal was kind of like sightseeing, wasn't it? "Okay, we'll stay," she agreed.

"Oh, Nancy!" Mattie cried happily. "You won't regret this! I promise!"

Nancy hoped not. But she couldn't get rid of the depressing feeling that for the hundredth time, a relaxing vacation was about to be ruined.

On their way to the set, Nancy filled Mattie in on what she and Bess had overheard outside Pappas's office.

"Those two are really on the outs these days," Mattie said. "Ever since Rick got that film deal and gave his notice, it's as though a war has been declared between them. I can't really blame Mr. Pappas, though. The show's ratings depend on Rick. If he goes, 'Danner's Dream' could be in big trouble, and that means trouble for all of us."

"Hmmm." Nancy thought for a moment. "So it's not just Mr. Pappas who's down on Rick."

"Oh, no. In fact, lately it's been Rick against the world." She stopped. "Well, here we are."

Mattie pushed against a vacuum-sealed door. With a *whoosh,* it opened, and the three of them walked onto the set.

Nancy and Bess gazed around the massive studio. In straight rows, rooms that had three walls but no ceilings were set up. Rows of klieg lights hung on suspended bars. Above the lights was a narrow catwalk, and above that, total darkness.

On the ground level, the activity was incredible. Hundreds of cables wound across the floor, and several huge cameras were mounted on dollies. Each one was surrounded by people. On the set of the Danner living room, where the first scene was about to be shot, set dressers were putting the final touches on the scenery. And in the middle of it all stood Rick Arlen. Kay was fussing over his makeup, and he was going over his lines with a script girl. But in case he or anyone forgot a line, a teleprompter stood in either corner of the room. All an actor had to do was cast a glance at one of them and read his lines from the screen.

Nancy and Bess were struck by the strangeness and complexity of it all. They looked dazed as Mattie motioned them to a spot on the floor where they could watch the rehearsal and still be out of the way. Then she disappeared behind the walls of a set.

"Can you believe this?" Bess whispered excitedly.

"Could somebody tell Rick to get on the set, please?" A beautiful black-haired woman barked impatiently into a small megaphone.

"I'm right here, Lillian, dear," Rick purred sarcastically. "What would you like?"

"I hope you bothered to memorize your lines," she snapped.

"Yes, love, I did," he cooed.

"That's what you always say," she said, trying too hard to keep the anger out of her voice. "You shouldn't need a teleprompter, Rick. You're a big boy and a professional."

"If you're referring to that one small incident, Lillian, you'll also recall that I received a death threat that morning. It wasn't exactly my best day."

Suddenly a voice boomed over the set's sound system. "Lillian, back off, will you?"

"Who's that?" Nancy wondered out loud.

A bearded stagehand who was walking by with a line of cables answered her. "That's Luther Parks, the director. He's up there." The stagehand pointed to a Plexiglas booth above the door at the back of the room. "He watches the rehearsal on a bank of TVs up there, and then chooses which camera shots they'll use."

"And who's Lillian?" Nancy asked.

"Ready to roll, ladies and gentlemen," the

director's voice interrupted them. "Let's have quiet on the set, please."

"Places, everyone!" the stage manager yelled. "Charlie, are we locked up?" The man at the door nodded. A bright red light went on above him.

"That light means we're shooting," the same stagehand explained in a soft whisper. With a quick smile, he was gone.

In the silence of the huge studio, Nancy could feel the crackling of tension. For a split second no one moved. Then Rick appeared on the set and sat down on the beige sofa in the Danner living room. With his head in his hands and his elbows on his knees, he looked just like the tortured Rory Danner, brooding over his life. Then Mattie, playing the cool and dignified Serena, appeared in the living room doorway.

"Rory?" she called out softly. "May I come in?"

Rick looked up, but then dropped his head back into his hands. "I don't want to see you, Serena," he growled. "Just get out and leave me alone!"

Mattie stood by the door, cold as ice. "Rory, I have to talk to you—right now." The cameras rolled in for a closeup.

Just then, Nancy noticed a faint shadow moving back and forth on the back wall of the set. She glanced up to see what was causing it. High overhead, she saw a klieg light wobbling wildly on its track. Horrified, Nancy watched as it broke off the bar with a sickening snap and hurtled downward. It was heading right for Rick!

Chapter

Three

NANCY STOOD UP and dove across the set, landing on top of Rick. The sofa beneath them toppled over backward. Everyone watched in frozen terror as the heavy lamp hit the floor where the couch had been, shattering into a thousand pieces.

Moments later pandemonium broke out as the cast and crew gathered around the scene of the disaster. Mattie rushed up to Nancy and Rick, who were still in a heap on the floor, gasping for breath.

"Rick! You could've been killed!" Mattie cried. The stage manager was calling for everyone to remain calm on the set, and Bess tried to push her way through a group of stage-hands. She stretched, looking to see if Nancy and Rick were okay.

"What in the world is going on around here?" William Pappas hurried onto the set, pushing people aside as he went. "This is all I need! Our insurance rates are high enough as it is!" he muttered angrily. "Is anybody hurt?"

"Nope," Rick replied from his position on the floor. "I was just rescued by this beautiful creature." He looked up at Nancy with a grateful smile. "Hello, gorgeous. Where have you been all my life?"

Nancy turned red to the roots of her hair as she scrambled off Rick and onto her feet. Brushing herself off, she started to push her way through the crowd of onlookers. She had to find Bess.

"Wait!" Rick called after her. "Don't leave me now!" With that, a group of stagehands who were standing nearby broke out in nervous laughter.

Just then Nancy felt a hand on her shoulder. It was Mattie. "Thank heavens you were here. If you hadn't gotten to Rick so quickly . . ." She shivered. Turning to the crowd, she called out, "Everyone, I'd like you to meet Nancy Drew. She's my guest today." Everyone clapped, and Mattie smiled weakly. "And now

I'm going to call security. Maybe they'll believe that someone really is after Rick!" And with a toss of her pretty head, she stepped off the set, headed for the intercom behind the scenery.

"Well, dear, that's one way to meet a star," Lillian observed caustically, glaring at Nancy.

"Wait just a minute—" Nancy began. But then she decided it would be better not to say anything. Lillian might not be the friendliest person she'd ever met, but the last thing Nancy wanted was to make an enemy at the beginning.

Beginning of what? Nancy asked herself. An investigation? Was there really anything to investigate? After all, she reasoned, accidents do happen.

Dodging Lillian's pointed remark, Nancy excused herself and made her way over to the corner of the set. Rick was there, chatting with Bess.

"Ah, my savior!" he said when he saw Nancy. But her quick frown made it clear that she wasn't going to fall for his lines.

"Hey, girls," Rick suggested, "why don't the three of us go back to my dressing room? We can have a soda and get to know each other a little better while they're cleaning up this mess."

"Oh, we'd *love* to!" crooned Bess. Elbowing

Nancy in the ribs, she prompted her friend. "Wouldn't we?"

"I guess that would be all right," Nancy shrugged. Until security had finished looking around, no one would be allowed near the scene of the accident anyway. And maybe she could use the time to find out a little more about Rick Arlen.

"By the way, who was that woman—Lillian somebody—who was so angry at you earlier?" Nancy asked him as they headed down the empty corridor.

"Her name is Lillian Weiss," he hissed, making the name sound snakelike. "She's the assistant director. While Luther is up in the booth playing God, she's his watchdog."

"Sounds like she's not your favorite person."

"She's not. But then, Lillian's just a nobody around here. I don't let her get to me—she's not worth even thinking about."

Just then they came to a door with a polished brass star on it and Rick's name above the star. "Come into my parlor, said the spider to the fly," he quipped lightly. He ushered them in and closed the door quietly behind them.

The bright lights in the dressing room blinded Nancy for a moment when she stepped in.

"I love this room—it's so warm and bright. This is the place I go to get away from the craziness out there." He pointed toward the door. "Let's see, now," he mumbled. "I'd offer you a chocolate, but I'm afraid they're a little bitter. But can I get you something to drink?" Rick opened a small refrigerator.

Bess pushed a lock of blond hair behind her ear before she said, "Okay. Um, a diet soda for me."

"*Pour vous?*" he asked, turning to Nancy.

"The same, thanks."

"You're a very smart girl. And brave, too. Would you care to marry me?" Rick had taken Nancy's hand gently in his own, and now he offered her a bouquet of imaginary flowers with the other.

Nancy pulled her hand away and looked at him. "I have a boyfriend. Sorry," she said, apologizing.

"Ah—I'm crushed. Well, then," he purred, instantly turning to Bess and taking her hand. "How about you? Would you marry me?"

Bess's eyes twinkled mischievously. "Okay, you're on."

"Oh, you only like me for my looks," Rick complained. Nancy saw him catch a quick glimpse of himself in the mirror before he gazed back at Bess appreciatively. "But then, you're not too bad yourself."

29

Bess blushed. She seemed to melt into the dressing table as Rick stared at her.

Rick Arlen obviously knew how to flirt, Nancy observed. And Bess was definitely being taken in.

"Well," said Nancy, trying to break the spell, "for a guy who just barely escaped a terrible accident, you're in an incredibly good mood."

"Of course! Of course I am!" Rick said agreeably as he poured the sodas. "I was lucky. That's the best way to be if you're going to be in an accident. Don't you agree? But then, I've always been a lucky guy. I mean, I just met you two, didn't I?"

"Some people don't think the things that have been happening to you lately are accidents," Nancy said.

Rick sank into a plush chair and looked at her impatiently. "Some people are also frightened of their own shadows. Look, when you're a TV star, you have to expect a little craziness. It comes with the territory. Along with a lot of good things, too. Has anyone ever told you that you're beautiful," he added offhandedly to Bess. She almost swooned into his costume rack.

She's really eating this up, Nancy thought. Bess actually seemed to take Rick's baloney seriously.

"Look, I'd better get back to the set," Nancy said, putting down her soda. "Security should have had a good look around by now, and I want to find out exactly what happened. Are you coming, Bess?" she asked.

"Is it okay if I meet you back there in a little while?" Bess responded.

"Don't worry about Bess here," Rick put in with a grin. "I'll take care of her."

That was just what Nancy was afraid of.

Pushing through the thick, soundproof door, Nancy stepped back onto the set. Immediately she saw Mattie trying to break up a fight. One of the men was William Pappas. Nancy hadn't seen the other man before. He was slim, handsome, and at that moment his eyes were ablaze with anger.

"It was an accident!" Pappas was shouting. "Technicians are only human. Now, if you'll get off my back, I'll find out who was responsible and deal with that person. I can't do anything if you're going to stand here and scream at me all day!"

"You *still* don't get it, do you?" the other man shouted back. "Mattie could have been *killed* in there! And I promise you, if so much as a hair on my client's head is ever hurt, your network will be facing the biggest lawsuit the world has ever seen! Come on, Mattie!" He grabbed Mattie's arm and marched toward the door. Nancy ducked behind a piece of scenery and continued to watch.

"Dwayne, please, calm down!" Mattie protested. "No one was trying to hurt me! I was nowhere near the accident!"

"It's the network's responsibility to protect you from things like this, Mattie. Look at those shards of glass! What if one of them had cut your face? Your career would be ruined."

"Nobody is going to get hurt, Dwayne," Pappas said, calmer now. "This is never going to happen again. Now, will you please get out of here so we can clean up this mess and get on with the show?"

As Dwayne stalked off, Nancy heard Pappas remark to Mattie, "It's just my luck that that idiot agent was here today. The last thing I need is a nervous Nellie on the set the day the roof falls in. No offense, Mattie, but the man is a complete fool. Excuse me, please, will you?"

As Pappas breezed by her, Nancy grabbed Mattie's elbow, and they followed him. The producer walked immediately over to the chief of security and began asking questions. Nancy and Mattie got as close as they could without being noticed and listened intently.

"It looks like an accident, plain and simple, Mr. Pappas," the security man was saying.

"Thank you," Pappas muttered. Then he strode directly over to where the lighting technicians were gathered. "Which one of you was responsible for checking the lights this week?" he asked.

"I was," admitted one of the men unhappily. It was the man with the beard who had talked to Nancy and Bess earlier. "But they checked out fine. In fact, just this morning—"

"What's your name?" asked Pappas darkly.

"Uh, MacPherson, Mr. Pappas, but—"

"You're fired, MacPherson. Stop by the front office and pick up your severance pay. I don't ever want to see you around here again, understand?" Before the man could say another word, Pappas was gone.

Mattie and Nancy looked at each other. "You've got to believe me," Mattie whispered urgently. "That was no accident, I'm sure of it!"

Nancy sighed. If security thought it was an accident, it probably was. Still . . . "I think I'll take a look around myself. You never know."

There wasn't much to see. All the glass from the broken light had been swept into a pile in the corner, and the light itself was in pieces against the wall. Each piece had been tagged for reference. Security seemed to have done a thorough job.

Nancy was about to give up and go back to Rick's dressing room but decided to take a last look around. As she walked over to the back wall of the living room, a flash of something metallic caught her eye, and she bent to the floor. There, almost completely hidden from view, was a piece of metal with a bolt attached. One edge of the metal was shiny, as if it had been scraped or cut.

Nancy walked over to the lighting technician, who was gloomily gathering his things together. "Excuse me," she said, "but—could I ask you a question?"

The man turned around and looked at her for a moment. "Oh, hi, I remember you. You're the girl who saved Rick's life," he said with a smile. "I guess I should thank you. I'd have been in *real* trouble if he'd gotten hurt."

"You don't have to thank me," Nancy waved him off. "But you could tell me what this is." She showed him the bolt she'd found.

"Why, that's a C-clamp. They're used to hold the lights on the bar."

"Does it look odd to you? Is there anything strange about it?"

MacPherson studied the clamp briefly. "One end's been sawed," he gasped. "Almost clean through. The rest looks like it snapped off. This must be— But if—"

"Just what I was thinking," Nancy said, agreeing. "That was no accident this morning. The light was rigged so it would fall. Somebody tried to kill Rick Arlen—and almost succeeded!"

Chapter

Four

Do you believe me *now?*" Mattie was on the verge of tears as she pleaded with the chief of security. She and Nancy had just shown him the broken clamp. "I've been telling people for weeks that someone was after Rick, but nobody believed me. You've got to believe me now!"

"Now, Mattie," Pappas said, patting his leading lady on the arm. "Let's not get hysterical and blow this out of proportion."

"Well, I'll be," the security man muttered as he examined the C-clamp. "Where exactly did you say you found this, young lady?"

"By the back wall of the set," Nancy replied.

"Well, it proves the light was sabotaged. No doubt about it."

"This is just what I need," Pappas muttered in frustration. "I don't have enough problems without someone sabotaging my show!"

"Mr. Pappas, who actually has access to this stage?" the chief wanted to know.

"Well, the crew and the actors, of course. Nobody else, really. Maybe an occasional guest, but they all register at the front desk."

"Wasn't there a tour group in here earlier today?" Nancy asked.

Pappas snapped his fingers. "Right!"

"And some of them were mad at Rory Danner, too," Nancy said.

"You don't suppose some crazy fan could have—" Pappas shook his head.

"There're a lot of nuts out there, Mr. Pappas," the chief said. "All it takes is one person who can't tell fantasy from reality."

"That settles it!" Pappas exclaimed. "From now on this set is closed to anyone not directly involved in the show." Yelling across the studio, Pappas repeated his order for everyone to hear. "That means no guests, no agents, no mothers, fathers, sisters, or brothers. I want this set sealed tighter than a pharaoh's tomb!

"Now, we'll take a couple-hour break and then back to work. If you need anything, I'll be in my office."

After Pappas walked away, Nancy turned toward Mattie.

"Thank goodness he gave us a break," she told Nancy. "I've got to go rest." Rubbing her eyes, she added, "See you later. And thanks again for saving Rick's life." Flashing Nancy a grateful smile, Mattie walked off the set.

Since the set was closed to guests, Nancy and Bess had to leave. Nancy began to make her way back toward Rick's dressing room to collect Bess. But she soon realized she must have gone through the wrong door or made a wrong turn somewhere. One long corridor led to another, and for a moment Nancy didn't know which way to turn. Then the sound of a door slowly opening caught her attention. Instinctively knowing that she shouldn't be there, Nancy moved back into a recessed doorway and waited silently.

Nancy could just see Lillian Weiss nervously looking both ways before stepping into the hall. Once the door was closed behind her, Lillian seemed to relax. Nancy's heart was in her throat as she realized Lillian was heading straight for her. Nancy opened the door behind her and slammed it, making it sound as if she had just come through that door. She stepped out into the corridor.

"Well, well," Lillian said, greeting Nancy with a snarl. "Is our fair rescuer lost and helpless?"

"Yes, I guess I am. I was looking for Rick's dressing room, actually," Nancy told her. Well, it was almost the truth.

"Continue down this corridor and make your first left," Lillian snapped. "And by the way, it was nice knowing you. I'm sure now that Pappas has closed the set, you won't be around anymore. Too bad. I'm sure you were Rick's favorite little bodyguard." With a smug smile, Lillian continued down the hall and disappeared around a corner.

The room that Lillian had come out of turned out to be the prop room. After making sure she was alone, Nancy ventured inside.

At first she was overwhelmed by what she saw. The room was huge, with several long aisles. Stacked from floor to ceiling, making an incredible clutter, were thousands upon thousands of items—anything that could ever possibly be needed on the set of the show. As organized as the room seemed to be, with everything numbered and labeled, there was no way to keep it all neat. Dust covered some of the items that hadn't been used recently, and Nancy felt her nose begin to itch.

There seemed to be nobody there, but when Nancy sneezed, she heard a rustling in a far corner. A copy of the *Daily News* moved, and a grizzled head poked out from under it. The old man had a mop of unruly white hair flowing out from an ancient orange cap.

"Who's there?" a crackly voice called. "I'm awake, I'm awake. On the job all the time, yessir! What can I do for you?"

Nancy couldn't help smiling at the wizened old man. He wore red suspenders, which held up a pair of baggy gray pants, and he was covered with as much dust as everything else in the room. Nancy would have almost believed that he had been sleeping there uninterrupted for years.

"Sorry, I must have opened the wrong door," she said, apologizing.

"Oh, it's good to have a little company," the man said. "This week has been just kitchen stuff and living room knickknacks, day after day. I've been sitting here reading my paper all week without seeing a soul."

"But wasn't the assistant director in here just a moment ago?" Nancy said.

"Who? Lillian? Nah, haven't seen Lillian in ages. The only time she ever came into the prop room was to complain that a butcher knife didn't look sharp enough. I had to put a little oil on it to give it that threatening gleam when the camera panned in on it. That's an old prop man's trick, you know."

"Achoo!" Nancy couldn't help sneezing again. "Are you sure no one was in here earlier?" she asked again, persisting.

"Absolutely one hundred percent, young lady. And nobody gets anything by me."

That's what you think, Nancy thought as she said goodbye to the prop man. As she stepped back into the corridor and made her way to Rick's dressing room, Nancy's mind was in a whirl. Maybe one of the fans from the tour group *had* tampered with the klieg light. She supposed it was possible. But even so, something funny was definitely going on. What had Lillian been doing in the prop room? And why was she so hostile? Nancy was determined to find out. And that meant she had to get onto the set again the next day and do some more checking around.

Here I am, she said to herself as she turned a corner and saw the familiar door with the star on it. Wait till I tell Bess what I found!

A moment later, after a quick knock, she threw open the door, smiling broadly. What she saw made her stop dead. Bess was in Rick's arms, and they looked about a split second away from a kiss too steamy for TV!

Chapter

Five

"Nancy!" Bess cried, awkwardly trying to disentangle herself from Rick's embrace.

Nancy looked from a blushing Bess to Rick and back, "I'm sorry to interrupt, but—"

"It's not what you think!" Bess said, interrupting her as she tossed her blond hair over her shoulder and straightened her collar. "Rick just asked me to help him rehearse, that's all."

"She's very talented," Rick said, putting his arm around Bess's waist and drawing her closer.

"Well, I just came to tell you that Pappas

closed the set to all visitors," Nancy said, looking at Bess.

But Bess wasn't about to let anything ruin her day. "Nancy, you'll never guess what Rick has offered to do!"

"It's really nothing," Rick said, protesting.

"Nothing?" Bess replied, her eyes dancing with excitement. "You call taking me all over the city in a limousine nothing?"

"Well, I already have the limousine." Rick shrugged modestly.

"He's going to give me a personal tour of the city on Saturday! Would you believe he's never been on top of the Empire State Building?"

"How can you live in New York and not visit the Empire State Building?" Nancy asked.

"Actually, a lot of New Yorkers have never been there," he explained. "We always say we're going to go someday, but somehow we never get around to it. It'll be a real treat for me."

Bess continued to gaze at the handsome TV star. Nancy couldn't help worrying that her friend might be getting in over her head.

"Bess, aren't you forgetting that Rick might be in danger? I don't know if it's such a great idea for you to be alone with him, you know."

"Don't be silly!" Rick laughed, wiping his makeup off with a thick cloth. "I can take care of both of us. Listen, I've got an even better idea—why don't you come, too? I'm sure I could round up a friend for you."

"That's great!" Bess cried happily, turning to Nancy.

"Okay, count me in," Nancy agreed. Spending the day with Rick was one way to keep an eye on him. And on Bess.

"Come on, Bess," she said, taking her friend by the elbow. "We'd better leave the set. Nice meeting you, Rick." Nancy turned to the door, but Bess wasn't quite finished talking to Rick.

"Well, I'm sorry we have to go so soon, but we're definitely on for Saturday, aren't we?" she asked.

"I can hardly wait, love," he replied, blowing her a kiss. "Till then, 'Parting is such sweet sorrow.'"

As soon as she closed the door, Bess stood stock-still for a moment. Then she leaned on the wall in a daze. "Did you hear? He called me 'love.'"

"I heard," Nancy replied uneasily.

"Oh, Nancy," Bess cooed, "he's so wonderful! Not at all conceited like some big stars probably are. Just think, I have a date with *the* Rick Arlen. Me—Bess Marvin, regular person! Do you know how many girls would kill for a date with the star of 'Danner's Dream'?"

"Yeah—" Nancy said, only half paying attention. She was wondering who was trying to kill Rick Arlen—and why?

"We were standing there, watching this intense scene. I mean, it was so quiet you could hear your heart beating!" Bess was going over the whole day as Nancy's aunt emptied a package of white mushrooms into her food processor. "And then, well, the light just snapped! Right in front of our eyes! Right, Nancy?"

Nancy looked up from the microwave, where she was getting ready to bake three potatoes. "Uh-huh," she agreed.

"And Nancy saved the day. You should have seen her," Bess said, continuing. "I don't know how she reacted so fast. The light only missed him by a few inches. And Rick is amazing. He wasn't even afraid! He said it was all in a day's work. Can you believe it?"

Eloise's eyes clouded over with worry. "I'm not sure I want you two poking around in a place where they have accidents like that," she said, shaking her head.

Nancy looked over at Bess and put her finger on her lips, but Bess didn't pick up on it.

"Oh, no!" Bess went on. "It *wasn't* an accident! Nancy found the evidence—somebody tampered with the light!"

"Nancy!" Aunt Eloise exclaimed. "Do you mean to say Mattie was right to suspect some-

45

thing was wrong? Oh, dear, please be careful! I don't want you getting hurt."

Bess laughed and shook her head. "Don't worry, Rick says it's just some crazy fan trying to scare him. Now that they've closed the set, I'm sure there won't be any more trouble."

Just then the phone rang.

"Hello?" Eloise answered. "Oh, yes, Mattie, we're here. Come on up." Replacing the receiver, she said, "I hope it's all right if Mattie joins us. I should have asked you first."

"It's fine with me!" Bess cried happily.

Nancy went to the vegetable bin and took out another potato. After rinsing it, she popped it into the microwave.

"That's it," Eloise said. "Dinner in ten minutes."

In a few minutes there was a knock on the door, and Nancy went to open it.

"Hi, everybody!" Mattie called as she breezed into the apartment with a bouquet of spring flowers. Nancy was amazed at how carefree Mattie seemed. "Oh, I'm so happy you're on the case," she cried, embracing Nancy warmly. "I know nothing bad can happen to Rick now."

Nancy frowned slightly. Everyone seemed to think Rick Arlen was safe, including Rick himself. She wasn't at all convinced.

"Did you hear about your niece, this morning's heroine?" Mattie said, going over to kiss

Eloise and hand her the flowers. "You weren't exaggerating when you told me how brave she was."

Eloise reddened and looked over at Nancy. "Don't get the wrong idea," she warned. "I'm proud of you, but that doesn't mean I approve of your taking unnecessary risks. Please be careful."

"I will," Nancy promised.

Dinner was ready, and the four of them gathered around the large oak table in the dining area.

"Marinated steak. Smells great, and I don't mind saying so myself," Eloise remarked. "I may not be the greatest cook, but every once in a while I do all right."

"I can testify personally that she's a fantastic cook," Mattie said with a laugh. After they ate and chatted for a while, Mattie turned more serious and asked, "So, Nancy, what do you think? Was it someone from the tour group who tampered with the light?"

"Well, some people seem to think that," Nancy answered. "But from what I can tell, his fans aren't the only ones who're angry at Rick. There are other people—people who see him every day. Pappas, for instance. Or Lillian Weiss. Maybe others, too."

"Hah! You don't know the half of it," Mattie said. "There isn't a person on that set who Rick hasn't alienated at one time or another."

"Really? Why?" Nancy wondered.

"Oh, Rick's just— He's talented, handsome, and rich. Some people would hate him just for that, but he's also walked over a lot of people to get where he is. He's used a lot of people, broken a lot of hearts—" She sighed deeply.

Was one of those broken hearts Mattie's? Nancy wondered. The actress seemed so fragile and sad when she talked about Rick.

"I wish I could point to just one person and say, 'That's the one,' but Rick has made a lot of enemies." Mattie shook her head and reached for her glass of mineral water.

"People resent his success," Bess commented. "He was telling me about that today, about how jealous people are of him. How they all want something from him."

"Oh," Mattie said, turning to face Bess. "You two were talking together?"

"Uh-huh!" Bess said happily. "We found out we have a lot in common."

"I see," Mattie said, looking down at her plate.

"Wait a minute," Bess said slowly. "You two aren't going out or anything, are you?"

"Oh, no," Mattie quickly replied. "That is, not anymore."

So, Mattie *was* one of those broken hearts! Nancy thought.

"Oh, phew." Bess breathed a sigh of relief.

"I wouldn't want to steal somebody else's boyfriend or anything. You see, he's asked me out for Saturday."

"He—he asked you out?" Mattie whispered. Her eyes grew incredibly wide, and her mouth fell open.

"Yes," Nancy interjected soothingly. "And I'm going along, too. It's perfect, don't you think? That way I can keep an eye on Rick."

"I see." Mattie looked somewhat calmed by Nancy's explanation. Still, she turned to Bess with a sudden, compelling stare. "Just be careful, please," she said, warning her. "You don't know Rick the way I do—you don't know how dangerous he can be."

Chapter

Six

Listen, Bess—" Mattie relaxed her stare a bit, trying hard not to look so severe. "I really don't want to upset you, but, honestly, Rick can really love them and leave them. Maybe it's because deep down inside, he's very unsure of himself. Or maybe he's become too successful too fast, and— Sometimes I wonder if he can really handle it."

"Rick? Unsure of himself?" Bess shook her head in disbelief. "I'm sorry, Mattie. I don't think you know the real Rick."

"Maybe not, but I've known him a long time. We did summer stock together years ago.

He was different then, warm and sincere. In the past few years, he's really changed. He can be so cold now, even cruel."

"Well, maybe he just hasn't met the right girl yet," Bess suggested.

"Wait a minute," Nancy interrupted. "Mattie, why are you so concerned about a man you've just told us is cold, cruel, and steps on people?"

"Oh, I don't know," Mattie answered softly. "I guess I still think of him as a friend, even if it didn't work out between us." Looking over at Nancy imploringly, she added, "Rick would never admit it, but I'm sure that way down deep he's scared. I'd just feel so much better if you were on the set tomorrow."

Bess rolled her eyes and got up from the table. Nancy watched her go. She hoped Bess knew what she was doing where Rick was concerned.

"I'd like to be there myself," Nancy replied, turning back to Mattie. "But now that the set's closed to visitors—"

"Wait a minute!" Mattie cried. Her eyes shimmered with excitement. "I just got a brilliant idea! We're shooting a hospital scene tomorrow, and I'll bet I could get you and Bess jobs as extras! What do you think? Will you do it?"

Across the kitchen, Bess couldn't help jumping up and down with excitement. "That would be fantastic!"

Nancy thought for a moment. "Are you sure you could do it?"

"Almost sure. Here, let me call the casting director. Eloise, do you have a phone book handy?"

Nancy's aunt brought the book over as Bess loaded the dishwasher. "Just imagine, Nancy, appearing on my favorite soap!"

"We're in luck!" Mattie announced, hanging up the phone a few minutes later. "She says you two can be nurses. Just report to the studio at seven sharp, and go straight to the costume room as soon as you get there."

"But what if people recognize us?" Nancy wondered out loud.

"Oh, they won't recognize you." Mattie laughed and stood up to leave. "No one ever looks at the extras. Besides, when you're on camera you'll probably have wigs and uniforms on. You probably won't even recognize yourselves."

"You know, Nancy," Bess said after Mattie had gone. "No matter what anyone says, I've read that a lot of big stars started out as extras. You never know—this could be my lucky break!"

Bess and Nancy had reported to the studio at seven the next morning. After the dry blocking, in which they learned what they were to do, they reported to makeup and wardrobe. Now, standing on pedestals as two wardrobe people finished their final fittings for the dress rehearsal, Bess and Nancy couldn't help giggling.

"You're really a knockout as a brunette, Nancy!" Bess said.

Nancy looked over at her friend, who was wearing an identical uniform. She had a white nurse's cap over her bright red wig, and Nancy had never seen her look more excited.

"Your dress rehearsal will be third, ladies," a production assistant told them. "After the big love scene, which is the second, report to Lillian. You know where to stand and what to do from the first rehearsal. So, break a leg. Oh, if you want to catch Rick and Mattie in rehearsal, you can. Rory and Serena are going to have a big scene. It's supposed to be pretty hot stuff."

Bess immediately dashed down the corridor to the set, determined not to miss a word of Mattie and Rick's scene. It was all Nancy could do to keep up with her.

Watching the cast and crew gather around the set of Serena Livingstone's living room, Nancy could feel their edginess. The near-disaster of the day before had obviously gotten to everyone. Even though the set was closed to outsiders, Nancy could tell that nobody felt truly safe.

The only person who seemed at ease was Rick. Flashing a smile at Bess as he walked onto the set, he looked as if he were on top of the world.

He took his place in the middle of the set, and slowly Rick Arlen seemed to fade away. When the director finally called "Action," he had become Rory Danner.

In the scene, Rory was supposed to tell Serena that he'd be hers forever, if she would have him. Even though it was an intense scene, Nancy noticed that Rick was reading nearly all his lines from the teleprompter. But then, with all the excitement the day before, she reasoned, he probably hadn't had time to memorize them.

Mattie was having trouble with her lines, too. She had excused herself early the night before to go home and work, but obviously she didn't remember much. Although she was really throwing herself into the scene, Nancy noticed that she, too, kept glancing over at her teleprompter to check her lines.

"Should I leave, Serena? Is that what you want?" Rick asked, pacing in front of Mattie nervously.

"No, Rory, don't go. I love you," Serena said. Her voice was quivering, and her emerald eyes were full of tears. "I've always loved you, even when you didn't want me."

"Cut!" came the director's voice. "Mattie, I need you to cool it a little. If you start the scene at such a high emotional pitch, we won't have anywhere to go."

"Right, Luther." Mattie nodded up to the director's booth.

"Okay, everyone, take it from 'Should I leave,'" Lillian ordered.

"Should I leave, Serena? Is that what you want?" Rick said.

"No, Rory, don't go. I love you! I've always loved you, even when you didn't want me."

They were into it by then. Mattie and Rick were utterly convincing, making everyone who was watching really believe they were desperately in love. Bess had tears in her eyes as she watched them move slowly toward each other. Finally, Serena collapsed in Rory's arms.

"Here comes her big speech," Lillian muttered under her breath to nobody in particular. "Watch her screw it up."

"Oh, Rory, I want to do so many things with you," Mattie whispered hoarsely. "I want to take walks in the rain with you, I want to sit with you under the stars on a deserted beach. I want to dance with you, to sing with you, to—"

Mattie suddenly fell silent. She stood as if frozen, her eyes fixed on the teleprompter, her beautiful face a terrible white. Then, as everyone looked on in horror, she let out a blood-curdling scream and slumped slowly to the floor.

Chapter

Seven

"Mattie! Mattie!"

"What happened?"

"Is she all right?"

"Don't touch her!"

Everyone gathered around Mattie, who was lying on the floor. After what seemed forever, her eyes began to flutter open. She looked dazed. Mattie struggled to her feet with Rick's help. The look in her eyes only grew wilder.

"Look!" she cried, pointing to the teleprompter.

Her monologue had been changed. It read:

"I WANT TO DANCE WITH YOU, TO SING WITH YOU,

TO MURDER YOU. YES, YOUR TIME IS UP, RICK ARLEN. I'M GOING TO KILL YOU. I'M GOING TO WATCH YOU DIE A HORRIBLE DEATH, AND I'M GOING TO LAUGH."

"What in the name of— What is this?" Pappas yelled. "Get me the teleprompter operator! I want to talk to her right now!"

"I'm here, Mr. Pappas." A short red-haired girl spoke up.

"Would you care to explain this?" he asked, arching his eyebrows.

"Well, sir, I, uh—I really can't explain it," the girl stammered. "I got here early to type in the scene, and I was at the keyboard all morning. The only time I left was to take a phone call. And I know I wasn't gone for more than a minute because when I picked up the phone, there was no one there. I—I didn't think—"

"Exactly, you didn't think." Pappas shot the operator a harsh look. "You're fired. And whoever's job it was to keep strangers off this set, you're fired, too." Then, to the frightened cast and crew he said, "I'll fire every last one of you if I have to. This nonsense has got to stop!"

Nancy watched the producer from the sidelines. He seemed genuinely concerned, but what if it was all an act? What if beneath all his theatrics, there was something completely different going on, something much more calculated—and sinister?

She noticed Lillian Weiss, too. Lillian was off in a corner, trying to be inconspicuous, but nothing could hide the pleased look on her face. She was loving every minute of all this.

"Okay, everybody," Luther's voice boomed from the director's booth. "Lunch break. And when we come back, let's try to get this show back on schedule, shall we?"

"Calm down, Mattie! You're not going to let some practical joker ruin your day, are you?" Rick opened the front door of the studio for them, and Mattie, Bess, and Nancy filed past him onto the sidewalk.

"Come on," he added with a grin. "Let me treat you all to lunch—while I'm still alive, that is."

"Stop it! Stop pretending everything's fine!" Mattie turned on him, her green eyes flashing. "You've got to be terrified! Why don't you just come out and admit it?"

"Me? Terrified? Don't be ridiculous—they can't kill me. The world needs me! Besides, it'd spoil the ratings if I died."

"Oh, I could just punch you," Mattie growled. "And I'll pay for my own lunch, thank you."

"Whatever you say." Rick shrugged. "I'll just have to treat Bess—and Nancy, of course. Right, ladies?"

Bess and Nancy said nothing, embarrassed

by the way Rick was taunting Mattie. Nancy started to walk off by herself.

"Hey, look who's here!" said Rick, his attention caught by a man at the studio door. "It's the president of the losers' league himself. Hi, Dwayne."

Dwayne Casper, Mattie's agent, rushed up to them, pointedly ignoring Rick's remark. Nancy stopped and observed the scene at a short distance from the others. "Mattie!" he cried, throwing his arms around her. "I was bringing some of your new head shots to the front office and I heard what happened. It's absolutely outrageous! Are you all right, darling?"

"Oh, I suppose so," Mattie replied softly, shaking free of his embrace. "It was awfully upsetting, but—"

"But nothing," Dwayne said, interrupting. "You're in danger, and I won't have it!"

"Keep your shirt on, Casper," Rick said, with a scornful laugh. "This nut is supposedly after me, not Mattie. Why don't you leave us alone and go hover over some of your other clients. If you have any, that is."

"Rick!" Mattie cried sharply.

"It's all right, Mattie, he doesn't bother me. As long as you're all right—"

"I'm fine, Dwayne. Please don't worry about me." Mattie smiled at him warmly. "Honest."

"Yeah, don't worry, old buddy. I'll take care of Mattie," Rick said, trying to assure him.

"Oh, I'm sure you will." Dwayne sneered. Then he turned to Mattie and took her by the hand, looking deeply into her eyes. "I want you to promise to call me if there's any more trouble on the set."

Mattie nodded, then Dwayne walked off, throwing a nasty look over his shoulder at Rick.

"For pete's sake, Mattie," Rick muttered before Dwayne was out of earshot, "when are you going to dump that jerk and get yourself a real agent!"

"Oh, Dwayne's not so bad," Mattie answered, watching the man disappear. "Remember, he took me on as a client when nobody else would even give me an interview."

"But you've come a long way since then. You're a star now. You should have a major agency representing you," he said as they started walking to catch up with Nancy.

"I don't know. Somehow I'd feel like a rat if I left Dwayne."

"All I know is, a major agency could get you a lot more work and more money. And a girl with your talent deserves the best." Seeing he was getting nowhere, Rick threw up his hands. "All right, I won't say another word. You know how I feel, though." He stopped in front of an expensive-looking restaurant. "Here we are. Serena, Nurse Sanford, Nurse Johnson, would you care to have lunch with me?" he said, opening the restaurant door for them.

"It's Saturday morning and time for another edition of 'Soap Opera Weekly,' where we bring you the latest on your favorite shows and introduce you to the stars," the television announcer was saying as Bess shook Nancy's shoulder.

"Wake up, Nancy Drew!" Bess said, mimicking the announcer. "Come on. The alarm went off ten minutes ago! Your aunt's still sleeping so I wheeled the TV in here. Rick's going to be on 'Soap Opera Weekly' this morning. We can watch while we get dressed."

"Mumpfh—" Nancy mumbled, burying her head under the pillow. Was it really morning already?

She and Bess and her aunt Eloise had had such a great time the night before. They'd gone to see *Soft Shoe,* the Broadway musical smash of the season. The show was wonderful, but they'd stopped for a bite to eat afterward. By the time they got home, it was almost one in the morning.

Flipping over and squinting at the TV, Nancy saw shots of different soap opera stars as the upbeat theme song played in the background.

"Our special 'Soap Opera Weekly' guest today is the star of 'Danner's Dream'!" the announcer said. "Will he and Serena Livingstone finally tie the knot this time? Mr. Sex Appeal himself, Rick Arlen, will be here with us in just a few minutes! But first—"

The commercial came on, and Nancy realized there was no way she was going to get back to sleep. Not with Bess rummaging around the room, tossing one outfit after another on the bed and saying things like, "What do you think, Nancy? The pink or the yellow?"

Pulling herself up onto her elbows, Nancy yawned and looked out the window. It was a glorious day outside—warm and sunny. A perfect day for seeing the sights, she thought happily.

"He's on! He's on!" Bess shouted a few minutes later. Nancy turned from the closet and saw Rick. He was seated casually across from the interviewer, waving and nodding as the audience clapped and cheered.

Cleverly refusing to give away any of the show's carefully guarded secrets, Rick did admit that he was considering leaving the show at the end of the season to star in a movie. The audience groaned, then applauded.

"Tell us about the real Rick Arlen," the interviewer prompted. "Could we be hearing wedding bells soon?"

Laughing, Rick made an old joke about the gossip columns having him engaged to three different girls. "But then, you never can tell," he added slyly, blowing a kiss to a "special lady out there."

"He means me!" Bess cried happily.

"I don't think so. That's just talk, Bess. He could mean anybody—or nobody."

Bess shot her friend an angry scowl, and Nancy decided to back off.

After the interview with Rick, the show moved on to an update of that network's daytime and evening soap operas. Bess snapped the TV off then.

"He said he'd be here in an hour. I can't wait!" Bess scooped up her makeup and headed for the bathroom. "Hey, I wonder who he'll bring for you, Nancy. I mean, any friend of Rick's is probably cute, but I wonder what he'll be like."

An hour later the apartment intercom buzzed, signaling the arrival of Rick and his limousine.

Bess checked herself in the mirror one last time. She looked terrific in an oversize cotton cardigan and flowing skirt and flats. "Not bad," she pronounced. "Come on, Nancy!" With that, she flew down the steps of the brownstone to the waiting limousine.

"Not bad at all," Nancy admitted, looking admiringly at Rick's limo. The uniformed driver ushered them into the backseat, where Rick was waiting.

"Good morning, girls!" he said brightly. "Welcome to my abode on the road."

The first order of business was to pick up Rick's friend, a guy named Gilbert Frost. "He's an old pal from acting school," Rick explained. "You'll love him."

Bess threw Nancy a meaningful look, but Nancy just sighed and looked out the window. There was no way that she was going to fall for any of Rick Arlen's friends—not when she was in love with Ned Nickerson. Of course, Ned would understand her being on this date —she had to go. Someone's life was in jeopardy.

At the corner of Twenty-third Street and Park Avenue South, she noticed a skinny guy in jeans and running shoes, leaning against a streetlight. He looked totally normal, except that he was wearing big black-rimmed glasses and a false nose.

"What?" Nancy mumbled as the limo stopped in front of him. The man swept down in a low courtly bow.

"Hey there, Gil!" Rick laughed, opening the door. "Girls, I'd like you to meet Gilbert Frost. Say hello, Gilbert."

"Hello, Gilbert!" the guy mimicked, sliding into the plush limo.

Bess was giggling uncontrollably, and Nancy

couldn't help smiling as Rick's friend took off his glasses, revealing another pair underneath.

Finally, they pulled back into traffic and Nancy got a good look at Gilbert. Without his getup on, he was pretty cute. He had glossy black hair and warm brown eyes that twinkled with laughter.

"Gil is going to be the next host at the Comedy Basement," Rick said. "He does stand-up."

"I also do sit up and grow up," Gil announced. Everyone groaned.

Throwing a proprietary arm around Bess's shoulder, Rick instructed the driver to take them to Forty-second Street and the Hudson River.

"Today we're going to do all those corny things you see in old movies about New York," Rick said. "Like go on a boat trip around Manhattan and to the top of the Empire State Building. Bess is a very old-fashioned girl," he explained to his friend.

"Rick Arlen! I am *not!*" Bess protested. Secretly, though, she was flattered by his remark.

By the time they got to the West Side pier, the four of them were relaxed and having a great time. Before leaving the limo, Rick put on sunglasses and an old hat. That way, most of his face was covered. "Just normal precautions," he insisted. "These go everywhere with me. Otherwise, the fans—well, I'm sure you can imagine."

"I think you look adorable like that," Gilbert said. Rick punched his friend lightly on the arm, and they all piled out of the car.

"So, Gil, how did you get involved in show business?" Nancy asked while they waited on deck for the cruise to start.

"Oh, now we're going way back—to the day little Freddie Gilbert was born in Illinois in a log cabin— No, no, just kidding. How did I get involved in show business, you ask. Thank goodness someone cares besides my mother."

In spite of his nonstop chatter and putdown humor, Nancy decided she liked Gil. He seemed a little lonely, somehow, and afraid to be just himself, but instinct told her he had a good heart.

"You see, my real name is Fred Gilbert. I had to change it after I got to New York. There already was a Fred Gilbert out there in the show business stratosphere. And so Gilbert Frost was born. But he had the wrong nose. So I changed that, too. And then I had to darken my hair. By the time I was finished, the same club owners who used to tell me to get lost were dying to sign me. What can I tell you? It's a crazy business. Maybe someday I'll even make enough to pay my rent. And if I'm really lucky, I might even hit it big like old Rick here."

"I'm sure you will," Nancy said, looking up.

The view from the boat was spectacular —the skyline sparkled in the noon sun.

But as the boat trip continued and they finally circled the northern tip of Manhattan, Nancy couldn't help feeling that something was wrong. All through the ride, she had been keeping an eye on Rick. And she noticed other people were watching him, too. Nancy saw two women look at him, jab each other, and whisper. And a child tugged on his father's sleeve and pointed toward Rick. A portly man was also watching him, although he pretended to be looking at something else.

As the boat swung into the final leg of the tour, Nancy recognized the portly man. He had been the one cursing Rory Danner on the tour of the set just two days before.

"Attention, ladies and gentlemen. We will be docking in a few minutes. Please disembark via the white stairs on the port side of the boat. That's the left, to all you landlubbers," the tour guide instructed.

"That's him! That's Rick Arlen!" a young woman suddenly shrieked.

An excited murmur went through the crowd, and everyone turned to look at Rick.

"Take the hat off, Rory! We know it's you!" a woman called out good-naturedly. The group laughed, and Rick cooperated.

"Ah, my fans." He smiled and waved.

"You're the greatest—all of you! I love you madly!"

"Rick, may I have your autograph?" a woman cried happily. Everyone crowded around him and began rifling through their bags for pens, too.

"Write one for my niece, Rick!"

"Oh, Mr. Arlen, thank you!"

Rick was standing by the guardrail signing the backs of envelopes, napkins, address books, and matchbook covers. Suddenly, the man who had been on the studio tour lunged forward, his eyes wild, his voice like thunder. "You killed Jill Rowan, and now you want to destroy Serena Livingstone. Well, I won't let you! I'm not going to let filth like you near her! You're going to die, Rory Danner—right now!"

With that, the man lunged for Rick, sending him halfway over the rail. He was about to plunge into the river!

Chapter

Eight

LEAPING FOR RICK, Nancy and Gilbert
grabbed him just in time and pulled him safely
back over the rail. Nancy felt a pair of hamlike
hands on her shoulders. She turned to face the
assailant and delivered a swift kick to his left
shin. Then she seized his hand and flipped him
head over heels onto the deck. The ship's crew
then held him pinned against the deck until
the ship had docked and the police arrived,
followed by a couple of reporters.

"Okay, fella, let's go," a police officer said,
leading the man to a patrol car. "You'll feel a
lot better after a nice long rest."

"I killed Rory Danner and the world will be a better place for it!" the man exclaimed. "He was filth! Filth!"

"Sure, sure," another police officer said, agreeing. "You can tell the doctor all about·it."

As their limo pulled out of the parking lot, the crowd cheered Rick. He was leaning out the window, smiling and waving.

"Thank you, everyone!" he called. He slipped back into the car. "Well, thank goodness that's over. And thank you, Gil. And Nancy." Turning to Bess, he added, "You certainly know how to pick your friends, love."

Gil still seemed a bit shaken. "You know, Rick, the way you were hanging over the edge there, I thought you were history." He shuddered. "I'm going to sign up for karate lessons next week. I want to be prepared for fame."

"Let's just put the whole thing behind us, okay? Now it's time to celebrate!" Rick grinned devilishly. "Why not go for the best! Driver—take us to Trump Tower!"

Later, riding up the escalator from the lobby of the brass-and-marble palace, Bess and Nancy looked around in wonder. The place was amazing!

"This makes the River Heights mall look

like a mom-and-pop store," Nancy whispered. She looked all around her as they rose ever higher through the glittering atrium.

"Tell me about it!" Bess said enthusiastically. "Rick, I can't believe people actually *live* in this building."

"They do," he assured her. "There are apartments here that sell for millions."

"Seriously?" Bess couldn't believe it. "What do they have, solid gold faucets?"

"Almost," Gil replied. "You'd be amazed at what people spend their money on."

"Cappuccino, anyone?" Rick broke in cheerfully. They had just come to an attractive café on an upper level.

Soon they were all sitting around a table sipping cups of the strong Italian coffee.

"You know what being here makes me realize?" Bess was saying. "I've realized that I'd make a great millionaire."

"I think you'd make a lovely one, too," Rick said, flirting. "In fact, I saw something in a shop across the way that I think you should have. Be right back."

A minute later Rick came back to the table, holding a silk scarf printed in pastel geometric shapes. It matched Bess's outfit perfectly.

"Oh, Rick!" she exclaimed. "It's beautiful!"

"Wear it and think of me," he murmured. "So, everyone, are you ready to scale the heights? It's such a clear beautiful day—what do you say we catch the view from the Empire State Building?"

"Sounds great!" Bess was beaming. Anything Rick said would have sounded great to her.

"I used to sell souvenirs at the observatory," Gil threw in. "That was when I still *worked* for a living." He straightened up and helped Nancy from her chair. "Madame?" he said. "Your chariot awaits. That is, *Rick's* chariot awaits," he said, correcting himself.

By the time they reached Thirty-fourth Street and made their way up to the top, the sun had slipped much closer to the horizon. Rick and Bess, their arms around each other's waists, stood at the observatory's edge, gazing into the distance. Gil had stopped to chat with his old coworkers at the souvenir shop, so Nancy wandered off by herself.

Up that high, the wind cut like a knife, seeming to come from all directions. It blew Nancy's hair wildly around her as she stared down at the magical city. The noise from the street sounded like a low moan up there, almost human and full of sadness. It made Nancy shudder for a moment.

As she looked out over the city below her, she felt a growing sense of dread. The police had arrested the deranged fan that afternoon, but she was still worried. In the late afternoon sun, Nancy had a sudden, powerful feeling that someone *else* was after Rick. Someone who was not only crazy, but also clever, determined, and deadly. Nancy felt an icy shiver go through her. Someone was waiting down on the street—she was sure of it—waiting to end Rick Arlen's life.

Bess scooped up one last mouthful of chocolate mousse pie and sighed contentedly. "What a dinner! I'm in heaven."

"Not bad," Gil agreed, glancing around at the glass walls of Tavern on the Green. Positioned on the edge of Central Park, the view out the windows of the restaurant was of trees decorated with tiny white lights. The park looked like an enchanted fairyland, in direct contrast to the city around it.

When the check came, Rick picked it up. "What's money for if not to treat friends?" he asked, placing a gold credit card on the small black lacquered tray the waiter had brought.

"What a day!" Bess remarked happily. "What a night, too! I've had such a fabulous time today, Rick . . . thanks to you."

Rick looked genuinely pleased as he took her hand in his. "There's just one more thing I'd like to do. I could use a little exercise after this dinner, and it's such a great night—why don't we take a walk beside the park?"

Bess's eyes were twinkling with delight. Rick

seemed to be having a hard time saying good night to her!

"A walk sounds wonderful," Nancy said.

"Good, we're on!" Gil agreed.

Stepping out onto the sidewalk along the park, Rick and Bess linked arms. They were completely caught up in each other as they giggled and joked, walking ahead of the other two. Nancy watched them carefully as she half listened to Gil, who was telling her the rest of his life story.

"Then I realized I had to change my material," he was saying. "Nobody goes for rubber-chicken jokes anymore. So I began writing myself a whole new act. . . ."

Nancy couldn't help worrying about Bess. She was heading for trouble, Nancy was sure of that. Even if Rick was sincere, how could it last? They lived miles from each other. And a broken heart was the last thing Bess needed.

The sound of a speeding car made Nancy spin around. A taxicab jumped its lane and screeched diagonally across the street. Suddenly a broken heart was the least of Bess's troubles. The out-of-control cab was headed onto the sidewalk, aimed straight at Rick —and Bess!

Chapter

Nine

WATCH OUT!" NANCY screamed. Racing up to pull Bess away from the oncoming taxi, she managed to get just close enough to grab her friend's arm as the taxi swerved onto the sidewalk. It barely missed the stunned Bess before jumping the curb back onto the street and careening away.

Bess stood absolutely still in the middle of the sidewalk. "Nancy? Am I okay?" she asked in a dazed voice.

"Your shirt is torn, but I think you're fine."

Suddenly Bess looked around frantically. "Rick! Where's Rick?"

"Right here," he answered. They all turned

and saw Rick's head poking out from behind a tree. "See? I told you it would take a silver bullet to get me! Not even a scratch," he added, proudly showing them his arms and legs.

"Don't tell m-me that was just an accident," Gil stammered, running a hand nervously through his hair. "He never even hit the brakes."

"He's right, Rick." Bess seemed quite shaken now. "Maybe there's more than one crazy fan after you."

Nancy bit her lip and thought for a moment. This latest incident confirmed her worst fears. She knew now that the crude attempt on Rick's life on the boat trip was just a sideshow. The main event was still to come.

Gil was still shaking. "Well, I don't know about you folks," he said, "but I've had about all the excitement I can take for one day. Next time we get together, Rick, remind me to take out extra insurance."

"Hey, calm down. It's the price of life in the fast lane, that's all." Rick laughed nervously. "Come on, I'll give you a lift home on my way downtown. Bess?" Turning to Bess, he pulled her gently to him and gave her a lingering kiss.

They walked back to the limo, and Nancy and Gil climbed in. Nancy turned her head away, embarrassed, while Bess and Rick stood on the sidewalk. They were whispering, probably about what had just happened.

Nancy frowned. Things looked bad, very bad indeed. It was as if Bess hadn't even noticed that she and Rick had almost been killed!

"It's just a feeling I get, Ned, but it's a strong one. Something's very wrong here." Nancy flung herself down on the dark blue sofa and filled her boyfriend, Ned Nickerson, in on everything that had happened since she'd arrived in New York. "I only wish you weren't so far away." She sighed wistfully.

"Same here," Ned agreed. "I miss you."

"I miss you, too. And I could really use your help on this case."

"Can I do anything from here?"

"Honestly, I don't think so. Except share a little of your wonderful insight. I'm completely baffled by the whole thing right now."

"Sounds like you need some on-the-scene help. I'd be on the next flight, but I have a big paper due. I do want you to promise not to take any unnecessary chances, though."

"Come on, Ned, you know me. I'm always very careful," Nancy said, teasing him.

"Yes, I know. That's why I want you to keep a low profile. I want you to be in one piece the next time I see you."

Nancy blew a kiss into the phone and said goodbye. After she hung up, she smiled sadly. If only Ned were able to meet her in New York . . .

Just then, the front doorbell rang. Nancy went to open it, and before her stood Mattie Jensen. Her rich auburn hair was pulled up in a ponytail, and she was wearing jeans and a sweatshirt. She looked almost as young as Nancy.

"Hiya, kiddo!" the actress said, bubbling. "Eloise told me she was going to the ballet tonight, so I thought you guys might want a little company."

How could anyone as beautiful and successful as Mattie Jensen be all alone at ten o'clock on a Saturday night? Nancy wondered. It didn't seem possible. But there she was. She's lonely! Nancy realized.

"Sure. Come on in," she said. "Bess is in the shower."

"Hey, I read about what happened to you today on the boat trip. After everything he's been through, Rick must be glad they caught the guy. They said the man tried to throw him overboard."

"Hmm-hmm," Nancy replied, wishing she could have shared Mattie's sense of relief.

"They said the guy was released from a mental institution a few weeks ago."

"I didn't hear that, but from the way he was acting . . ." Nancy's voice trailed off.

"Oh, Nancy, I'm so relieved. Now I'll finally be able to sleep at night!" Mattie smiled softly, but Nancy just turned away. "What's the matter, Nancy? Are you still upset?"

Nancy heaved an enormous sigh. "Mattie, I hate to say this. I know you're not going to like it, but I don't think the man they arrested today is the person we're after."

"But—but they said he'd been stalking Rick for weeks."

"He may have been, but I don't think he's the one who tampered with the light, and sent the chocolates."

Mattie gazed at Nancy in amazement. Then she nodded. "Okay. Tell me why you think it isn't the same person."

"Two reasons. For starters, someone tried to run Rick over tonight."

"No!" Mattie exclaimed.

"I'm afraid so. Don't try to tell Rick that —he insists it was a hit-and-run accident. But I was there, Mattie. The cab never blew its horn, never slowed down—and the license plate was covered over with mud. This all may be circumstantial evidence, but still . . ."

Mattie was silent, taking it all in. "And then," Nancy said, continuing, "there's the photograph of Rick, the one that was all scratched up. It wasn't just a publicity shot, the kind he might autograph for a fan. There was a résumé of all the shows he's been in stapled to the back of it. Correct me if I'm wrong, but actors don't just give out their résumés to the general public, do they?"

"No, of course not. But lots of people would have them."

"Like who? A producer?"

"Sure. When an actor auditions for a job, he always brings a picture and résumé," she said, sitting down. "Pappas would have them. So would the director, and Lillian, of course. His agent would have hundreds. I suppose even Dwayne might have a few left, unless he cleaned out his files recently." Mattie stared at the wall with a faraway look. "But Dwayne is harmless. I'm sure—"

"Wait. Why Dwayne? I thought Rick said he was with International Management."

"Yes, but when Rick was first in New York, Dwayne was his agent. The summer I first met both of them, we were in an acting company doing Shakespeare in Oregon. We were so sure of ourselves," she mused. "Anyway, that fall, we set out for New York and the 'big time.' Rick and I did all right, but Dwayne, who was trying to make it as an actor still, ran into trouble getting parts. He was the wrong type somehow. So, he decided to open a talent agency instead. He really got our careers moving, too."

Just then Bess stepped into the room, a terry bathrobe wrapped around her. "I thought I heard somebody! Hi, Mattie," she chirped. "Did Nancy tell you about our day? Kind of wild, huh?"

"I read about part of it in the paper," Mattie said. "It was—" The telephone rang, interrupting her.

"That's probably for me!" Bess said as she dove for the phone. "Oh, hi!" she purred into the receiver. "Yes, I thought you might— Really? Hmmm—" Suddenly Bess turned a deep crimson and let out a wild giggle. "Umm, just a minute," she said. "I think I'll take this in the other room."

Carefully putting the receiver on its side, Bess gestured wildly at Nancy and then the phone. "It's Rick!" she whispered excitedly. "Hang up for me, okay?" With that, she ran into the bedroom.

Nancy turned to Mattie. She was pale and her glamorous face was drawn tight. Staring vacantly toward the bedroom, her enormous eyes began to fill with tears.

Nancy replaced the receiver. "Mattie . . ." she murmured gently, "you still love him, don't you?"

Mattie collapsed back into her chair. "Yes, I do. Heaven knows why," she answered. "Just a habit, I guess. I've loved him since I first saw him. We've been through a lot together."

Nancy put her hand comfortingly on Mattie's arm. As they listened to Bess giggling happily in the other room, Nancy could feel Mattie's grief. If a girl were talking with Ned like that, she'd be crushed, too.

"But then," Mattie said with a sad smile, "Rick obviously doesn't feel the same way. Well, I'd better go. I might as well get some sleep. We're still having brunch tomorrow morning, right?"

Nancy nodded and walked Mattie to the door, watching as she went down the stairs to her garden apartment. Just as the actress was about to disappear, Nancy remembered what she had been thinking before the phone rang.

"Mattie! Wait!" she called.

The actress looked up from the stairwell. "Yes?"

"How could I get into Dwayne Casper's office? I'd just like to take a look around."

"Well," said Mattie, her brow wrinkling as she thought, "I suppose you could set up an appointment and say you were an aspiring actress. You could even say we did a show together once."

"That might work. I don't think he ever noticed me before. Whenever I saw him I wasn't near you or him. But I don't have any pictures or résumés," she reminded Mattie.

"Oh, that's okay," Mattie assured her. "Just tell him you're new in town. Ask him for advice—he loves that. Dwayne's really good with newcomers, and he'll be flattered that you came to him for guidance. If you call first thing Monday morning and say I told you to call, I guarantee you'll get in. But I promise you, Dwayne is harmless. I should know—we've been friends for years."

"I hope you're right. But if Dwayne's got anything to do with this, I've got to find out. And, Mattie," she said softly, "don't worry about Bess. I know her. She falls in and out of love all the time. She'll get over Rick as soon as she gets back home, you'll see."

Mattie stared into the distance, trying to hide her feelings. "Maybe," she murmured softly. Giving Nancy a strange look, she disappeared down the stairwell to her apartment. Nancy could hear her door close behind her.

That night, tossing and turning in her bed, Nancy couldn't sleep. Her eyes kept popping open, and she'd lie still and stare at the ceiling while her mind was in high gear and she worked through detail after detail. If only they added up.

Rick Arlen. She could picture his handsome face with that winning grin of his, and those sparkling azure eyes. Someone wanted him dead, but who? Rick might not win any popularity contests among the people who knew him best, but only one person hated him enough to want him dead.

It took a very clever person to conceal such powerful hatred so successfully. Nancy tried to imagine who it might be, but there were so many people wishing him ill: Pappas, Casper, Lillian Weiss, and who knows how many others there were just on the set alone. Nancy had had cases this difficult before, and she'd solved them successfully. But this time there were so many possibilities; which one should she investigate first?

As she drifted to sleep, the shadowy figure of Rick came back into her mind. He was signing autographs for a crowd of fans. A monstrous figure walked toward him, slowly stalking him. Nancy tried to cry out, but her voice was caught in her throat. The figure turned toward her, seeing her for the first time. Eyes of indescribable evil glowed at her, paralyzing her with fear.

Then the figure drew a long and sharp knife that glinted in the dim light. Nancy tried to scream, but nothing happened. The shadowy figure was getting closer and closer—

Nancy awoke with a gasp and sat up in bed. The clock-radio by her bed read 5:05 A.M. It was only a dream, thank goodness! she thought, her heart racing. But it was so real.

Sighing with relief, she turned over, ready to

go back to sleep. That's when she noticed that Bess's bed was empty.

In an instant, Nancy was up and out of bed. She hurried into the kitchen—no Bess. She checked the bathroom, the living room, then ran back to the bedroom. Nothing. It couldn't be, but it was.

Bess was gone!

Chapter

Ten

THE SOUND OF a car pulling up in front of the building sent Nancy to the window. Opening it and leaning out, she saw a shiny black limousine gleaming in the light of a streetlamp.

A second later Bess stepped out onto the sidewalk. She was followed by Rick, who wrapped his arm around her shoulder. "You won't mind if I don't walk you to the door, will you?" he asked, just loud enough for Nancy to hear.

Bess twirled around and leaned closer into his arms. "Of course not," she said. "I had a great time. It was fun, zipping around the city,

THE NANCY DREW FILES

just the two of us. Thanks." They fell into a
kiss that seemed as if it would never end.

Standing at the window, Nancy was
alarmed. As flighty as Bess could be, it wasn't
like her to sneak off in the middle of the night.
Rick had gone to Bess's head like bubbly
champagne. Nancy could only hope her friend
wasn't in for a nasty "hangover" when it was
all over.

"Nancy!" Bess called out in surprise when
she saw her friend waiting for her at the door
to the apartment. "What are you doing up?"

"Excuse me," Nancy answered in a low
voice, careful not to wake her aunt. "But what
are *you* doing up is the question."

Bess's eyes were sparkling. "Oh, Nancy,"
she said breathily. "New York is so *wonderful!*
I've never really noticed before how incredible
it is. I just have to live here someday. *Soon.*"
Turning to her friend, Bess continued, "We
went everywhere. We rode around Wall Street
and went to the South Street Seaport and then
to this incredible disco, Le Grandine. Absolutely everyone there knew Rick. And he likes
me. I mean, he really likes *me!* This could be
it! This could be the man I've been looking for
all my life!"

"Bess," Nancy began as gently as she could,
"didn't you think it might be just a little
dangerous to be going out with Rick in the

middle of the night when someone is trying to kill him?"

Bess looked annoyed. "Don't spoil this for me, okay?" She walked past Nancy into the apartment and went to their room.

Nancy glared at her friend as she disappeared down the hall. Bess could be so irritating sometimes. Earlier that day she had narrowly missed getting herself killed, and here she was laughing in the face of danger. "You think I'm being silly?" Nancy asked, following after her.

"Of course I do! They arrested the guy, didn't they? Rick convinced me that the runaway cab was only an accident. Besides, nobody would mess with Rick. You should feel his muscles—they're like steel!"

Bess slipped out of her satiny dress and kicked off the slingbacks she had worn to go dancing. Too tired to change into a nightgown, she fell back on the bed in her lacy pink slip.

"Oh, Nancy," she murmured excitedly. "He's so wonderful—and so cute." Reaching over, she snapped off the light between their beds. "Am I going to have happy dreams tonight!"

As Nancy lay in her bed, watching the light of dawn brighten the room, she couldn't help worrying about Bess. This was obviously more than just a schoolgirl crush. And Nancy was more convinced than ever that this fairy-tale romance was not going to have a happy ending.

The clock by Nancy's bed read 9:04 A.M. Bess was still asleep, a contented smile on her lips. Nancy figured she'd be out for a few more hours.

The apartment was quiet. Looking out the window, Nancy saw only one person on the street. The whole city seemed to still be asleep. At eleven, she'd be going out to brunch with her aunt and Mattie, but that was still two hours away.

After pulling on her favorite jeans and slipping her new yellow sweater over her head, Nancy decided that a walk might be just what she needed to help her think and unwind.

Stepping out onto the street, Nancy took a deep breath of the fresh spring air. The birds were singing, and the golden-green leaves on the trees swayed in the morning breeze. On this quiet Sunday morning, with church bells ringing in the distance, New York seemed like a small nineteenth-century town. Nancy loved it. As she walked, she imagined she was part of that older, simpler time.

After a while she came to a tiny park tucked between two buildings. The morning sun was just beginning to warm the benches, and a few people were out with their children, pushing them on swings and watching as they ran and played. Nancy couldn't help herself; she sat down on a bench and let the sun warm her face, relaxing for the first time in days.

A minute later the touch of a hand on her shoulder made Nancy jump. Glancing around, she found herself looking into the dark eyes of Lillian Weiss.

"Well, if it isn't our fair rescuer," Lillian smirked. "Fancy meeting you here."

Nancy was puzzled. New York was a huge city. The odds of running into someone that she knew were small, to say the least.

"Mind if I sit down?" Lillian asked casually. "I'm dead tired. Haven't slept all night."

Nancy moved over to make room for her. She felt uncomfortable in the company of such an unpleasant person, but she didn't want to be impolite.

"Are you still trying to save Rick Arlen's life?" Lillian asked suddenly, looking right into Nancy's eyes.

She certainly is blunt, Nancy thought. Well, I might as well be blunt right back. Whoever was trying to kill Rick already knew that she was on the case. "Still trying," she admitted.

"You really shouldn't bother," Lillian said. She looked down at her feet, so Nancy couldn't read her expression.

"I don't understand," said Nancy, prompting her.

Lillian looked at her curiously, as if she were sizing Nancy up. After what seemed an eternity, she fixed her eyes on Nancy. "Rick is going to die, and there's nothing you can do about it. And I'll tell you something else—whatever happens to him, he has coming. He got where he is by stepping on a lot of people, but he made one mistake. Along the way he stepped on the *wrong* person, and he's going to pay for it."

Nancy couldn't believe what she was hearing. Was this a confession? A warning? She wasn't sure how to take Lillian's statement.

As suddenly as she had appeared, Lillian stood up to leave. "Well," she said, fingering the hem of her purple lamb's-wool sweater, "nice running into you." She gazed at Nancy with a tight smile. "I'll say one thing for you—you've got guts."

Nancy watched as the strange young woman walked away. She was sure now that Lillian had deliberately arranged to run into her. But why? Nancy was more in the dark than ever.

"The restaurant we're going to isn't far away, Nancy. We'll just ring for Mattie on our way out." Eloise was standing in front of the hall mirror, fussing with a teal blue silk scarf. "Is Bess ready yet?"

"Bess!" Nancy called as she knocked on the

door of the room where her friend lay sleeping. "Don't you want to have brunch with us?"

The answer was muffled, so Nancy opened the door. "Leave the address," was all Bess could manage. "I'll meet you there." With that, she flopped over and buried her face in the pillow.

Nancy closed the door. Eloise waited by the main door of the apartment while Nancy wrote down the address and left it on the telephone table. "Ah, youth," Eloise said, smiling wistfully. "I used to be able to sleep like that on weekend mornings. Now I'm always up at the crack of dawn!"

With a wink, Eloise tugged on Nancy's arm. "Shall we? If I wait for my morning coffee much longer, I won't be worth knowing."

As they sat in the restaurant eating eggs Benedict, Nancy couldn't stop thinking of her conversation with Lillian Weiss. The look in her eyes had been so intense. Could it be that Lillian was the one who was trying to kill Rick? Or maybe she was just hiding the identity of the person who really was.

Nancy decided not to mention running into her. Still, she had to know what Lillian's personal situation regarding Rick was. "Mattie," she began offhandedly, "tell me more about Lillian Weiss. I know you said lots of people hate Rick, but she seems to hate him more than most."

Mattie looked up, amazed. "You don't think she's behind it all, do you?"

"I don't really know," Nancy replied. "But I'd like to know more about her."

"Lillian's the one Rick broke up with me for," Mattie blurted out. She looked down at her plate unhappily. "I couldn't believe it when he told me. I mean, I'd stuck by him through all the bad times. When he finally made it, he just dropped me. It was so—" she paused for a moment, unable to go on "—so humiliating." She took out her handkerchief and blew her nose. Suddenly Mattie laughed. "But that's Rick for you. They were only together for two months. He stuck with her till she introduced him to the film people she knew, then he dumped her. I really can't blame Lillian for hating him. I just wish she'd get on with her life. She's just—I don't know —the kind of person who nurses a grudge. The kind that never lets go of anything, know what I mean?"

"Yes," said Nancy thoughtfully. "I think I do."

"Oh, do I dare try one of these?" Eloise was asking with a smile as the waiter held up a plate of miniature pastries.

"Oh, go ahead, Eloise," Mattie said with a

grin, trying to put all thoughts of Rick and Lillian behind her.

Eloise looked at the pastries and thought for a moment. "Why not?" she quipped, lifting a small one onto her plate.

Just then, the manager came up to the table. "Excuse me, ladies. Is there a Nancy Drew at this table?"

"Why, yes," Eloise answered, looking at her niece.

"Ms. Drew, you have a phone call," the manager said. "You can pick it up at the main desk by the coatrack."

"It must be Bess," Eloise guessed. "She probably woke up and realized she'd never be able to make it here after all."

Nancy thanked the manager and made her way to the phone.

"Hi, Bess," she said into the receiver.

But it wasn't Bess. A raspy electronic voice warned her, "Stay away from Rick Arlen, Nancy Drew! And tell your little friend she'd better stay away, too!" With that, the phone line went dead in Nancy's trembling hand.

Chapter

Eleven

B Y APPOINTMENT ONLY!" "Put Your Picture And Résumé Under The Door!" "Do Not Ring Buzzer Without An Appointment!"

Nancy read the signs and gulped. Although she'd called earlier and left a message on Dwayne's answering machine, Nancy felt she'd have a better chance of seeing him if she went in person. But getting inside Dwayne Casper's office wasn't exactly going to be easy.

With a sigh and a deep breath, she pressed the buzzer. For a moment it was so quiet that she wondered whether anybody was in the office at all. Then, crisp footsteps sounded on the other side of the door.

"Do you have an appointment?" Dwayne's voice was all business.

"Well, no," Nancy replied. "Not exactly."

"In that case, I suggest you learn to read!"

"But, Mr. Casper!" Nancy said in her most polite voice. "I left a message on your machine. Mattie Jensen said you would talk to me. My name is Diane Elliot. . . ."

Nancy heard a click as he unlocked the door. It swung open, and a smiling Dwayne Casper greeted her. "Well, why didn't you just say you're a friend of Mattie's?" he asked. "Come in! You must understand that if I opened the door to every struggling actor in this town, I'd never be able to get any work done."

"Oh, thank you, Mr. Casper," Nancy said, sounding grateful. In the front reception area was a large empty desk. No receptionist, Nancy noted.

"Right this way," Dwayne said with a sugary smile. He led her into his plush office. "How do you know Mattie?"

"Oh, well, I was an extra on 'Danner's Dream,' and she was kind enough to talk to me. She did say she'd call you about me. But I guess she got busy." That much was true Nancy thought.

Dwayne settled into his chair and looked at her appraisingly. "So you know Luther Parks too?"

"Well, no. Not personally, that is."

"I see. Has Mattie ever seen your work? Apart from extra work, that is."

Here we go, Nancy thought. Time to start lying—and lying big. "Oh, yes," she assured him. "We did a production of *The Sound of Music* together in the Midwest. Mattie played the oldest daughter, and I played one of the younger children."

An amused look passed over Dwayne's face. "That must have been at least eight years ago. Mattie wasn't more than a kid herself back then. Unfortunately, I couldn't see that production."

I know, Nancy thought. That's what Mattie told me.

Dwayne leaned back in his swivel chair. He seemed warm now, even friendly. "So, let me guess, you've come to the big city because you want to be a real actress."

Delighted that the agent had bought her story, Nancy threw herself into her real-life acting role. "Yes, sir," she answered breathlessly.

"Well, well, well— What shall we do about that?" Dwayne pursed his lips, thinking. Then he stood up, walked to the door, and locked it. "So we won't be disturbed," he explained.

A sudden chill made its way down Nancy's spine. If the electronic voice on the phone yesterday had been Dwayne's, she was now trapped.

"What did you say your name was?" Dwayne had a pen poised over a small pink index card.

"Diane Elliot," Nancy said, looking the agent squarely in the eye. "With two *L*s and one *T.*"

"That's a good name for an actress. You're lucky." He smiled. "Now tell me, Diane, why did you come to me? There are hundreds of agents in this city."

"Well, Mattie spoke so highly of you, Mr. Casper," Nancy began. Dwayne's face grew pink with pleasure. "And I know you once represented Rick Arlen—"

At the mention of Rick's name, the agent's face clouded over. "Ah, yes, the irrepressible Mr. A."

"He's not with you anymore, is he?" Nancy was being bolder than she liked to be, but she had to lead Dwayne on.

"Rick? His real name is Richard Aburtuski, by the way. No, he's no longer one of my clients. I don't deal with failures, Ms. Elliot."

Nancy looked genuinely surprised. Dwayne laughed derisively. "You think I'm being ridiculous—after all, he's at the height of success! But I can tell you with certainty that leaving this agency is the biggest mistake Arlen ever made—except for his decision to be an actor, of course. The man can't act his way out of a paper bag. He depends on his looks to get him by, but he'll learn. They all learn eventually that the biggest factor in success is loyalty. And he has none."

Dwayne's face was red with anger. He wasn't through on the subject of Rick Arlen, but just then the buzzer rang. "Whoever it is will go away," he said. "I have no appointments scheduled today."

The buzzer rang through the office once again, and then again and again. Finally Dwayne couldn't stand it anymore. He bolted from his chair and unlocked the door. "I'm going to tell this idiot to go away. Do you have an appointment?" he yelled, hurrying through the reception area. "Because if you don't, you'd better learn to read!"

"But, Mr. Casper! You *must* see me!" Bess's voice was muffled through the door, but her sense of urgency came through loud and clear. "I'm a really great actress and I need an agent! Let me read for you, Mr. Casper, and you can judge for yourself!"

Laughing bitterly, Dwayne called through the door. "Young lady, I'm a very busy man, and I don't handle street performers. Please leave me alone."

"But I'm an *actress!* Just listen." Bess began to recite a passage from *Romeo and Juliet.*

Good old Bess, Nancy thought with a smile. She really was quite an actress when she had to be. They had devised a plan: After Nancy was able to get inside Dwayne's office, Bess would divert his attention so that Nancy could search it. As soon as Dwayne was out of sight in the reception area, Nancy began to rummage through the papers on his desk. The longer Bess was able to divert his attention from Nancy, the more Nancy would be able to find out. And from the sound of things, Nancy thought she just might have all day.

"And I sing, too! Just listen to this, Mr. Casper." Bess launched into a well-known show tune in a loud, off-key voice.

"Please, young woman!" Dwayne begged. "Why don't you go sing in the park or something? You're giving me a headache!"

Aha! Nancy's eyes opened wide as she looked at the papers in front of her. An eviction notice—and several large bills from creditors. Searching further, she found warnings from collection agencies, even threats. Dwayne Casper's talent agency was obviously in desperate trouble.

"But, Mr. Casper, I'm the next Mattie Jensen! Everyone says I look just like her, except I'm prettier."

"What?" Dwayne exploded. *"Nobody,* but *nobody,* ever was, is, or will be prettier than Mattie Jensen! Mattie is one of a kind —absolutely unique!"

Nancy cocked her head to listen. It was clear to her that, where Mattie was concerned, Dwayne's interest was more than just professional.

"Well, I'm unique, too, Mr. Casper— terribly unique and incredibly talented!"

"My dear young woman"—Dwayne was practically screaming now—"if you don't leave at once, I'll call the police. And may I say in parting that with your nerve, you'll probably go far in this business!"

Quickly Nancy put everything back in the desk exactly where she'd found it. When Dwayne returned, he was trying hard to calm down.

"I'm sorry. Now, where were we before that ghastly woman interrupted us?"

Nancy shifted uncomfortably in her seat. Dwayne's eyes had a wild look in them, and having found what she'd come for, all she wanted to do was get out as quickly as she could.

"You know, Mr. Casper, I feel like such a fool, but I just remembered—I've got an appointment with a photographer in fifteen minutes! He's going to take head shots of me."

"Oh, I see," Dwayne replied, still smiling. "Well, is he any good? Maybe I know him. What's his name?"

"His name? Uh—" Nancy panicked for a

moment. What could she say? Finally she blurted out, "Ned Nickerson. He's new in town—just got in from L.A. But Mattie says he's good."

"Hmmm." Dwayne frowned. "Never heard of him. Well, Diane, come and see me when you've got your pictures. I'll see what I can do for you." He extended his hand for her to shake. His grip was firm, like iron, and his eyes searched hers intently.

"Come to think of it, have we met before? You look a bit familiar," Dwayne said.

"Well, we've never actually met," she replied, "but as I said before, I did do extra work on 'Danner's Dream'."

"That must be it, then," he said. "You'd better get going if you don't want to be late for your shoot. Look forward to seeing you again, Ms. Elliot."

"Thank you so much. You've been a great help!" Nancy said and left the office.

Down in the lobby, Bess was munching on a candy bar and smiling broadly. "How'd I do?" she mumbled, her mouth full of chocolate.

"Bravo!" Nancy applauded, laughing. "I especially loved your rendition of 'Tonight.' It was—different, very different."

"You really think so?" asked Bess, fluffing her hair and winking.

"And wait till I tell you what I found!" Nancy said, grabbing her friend by the arm. "But we'd better get over to 'Danner's Dream' right away. I want Mattie to hear this, too."

The crisp spring air whirled around them as they walked briskly up Broadway toward Columbus Avenue.

"He's really in bad shape, huh?" Bess asked incredulously after Nancy filled her in.

"Everybody in the world is after him. And when people are that desperate, it can make them pretty crazy. I want to keep a close eye on Dwayne Casper, Bess. I think he may be our man."

Pushing through the glass doors of Worldwide Broadcasting, Nancy and Bess beamed at the security guard.

"Hi!" Nancy called out. "We're back again."

"Why, hello, girls. You heard the set was closed, didn't you?" the man asked. "They've been having a little trouble in there and Pappas sent down the order. I can't let anybody in, not even you two."

"I know," Nancy told him. "But could you call Mattie Jensen? We just need to talk to her for a few minutes."

The security guard ran his finger down the list of telephone extensions on his desk. "Sure thing. Mattie, let's see— Ah! Here it is."

But before he had a chance to pick up the

intercom, he was interrupted by the boom of a powerful explosion. The sound of shattering glass tore through the air, followed by a blood-curdling scream.

"Nancy!" gasped Bess in terror. "That was Rick!"

Chapter

Twelve

WITHOUT WAITING FOR permission, Nancy and Bess followed the security guard backstage. Losing themselves in a mob of people, the girls made their way toward Rick's dressing room.

The lighting designer had been the first to reach the room itself. "Call an ambulance!" he bellowed frantically.

Nancy and Bess arrived a minute later and watched in shock as Kay Wills, the makeup artist, staggered down the hall toward them. Her skin was ashen, and she was trembling all over. Choking back tears, she turned around and sobbed, "It's bad—really bad."

Nancy stood on tiptoe and craned her neck to see inside Rick's dressing room. The first thing that caught her eye was the wide mirror over the makeup table. It had been shattered into a thousand pieces!

An emergency medical team had arrived, and they were on their way up the hall now, pushing aside the crowd of onlookers. "Make room!" Nancy called, flattening herself against the wall.

"Rick! Oh, where is he?" Bess cried frantically. She bit the back of her hand as she strained to get a good look. Just then, Rick appeared in the doorway. He had a stunned look on his face. His blond hair had been blown every which way, and the white towel around his shoulders was stained bright red. Looking down, Nancy gasped—Rick's hands were bleeding!

As soon as the paramedics saw him, they broke into a run. Gathering around him, they picked him up and laid him on a stretcher. They began pulling slivers of glass out of his hands as Rick winced in pain.

"Back off, everybody!" one of the paramedics shouted as the crowd began to press in on them again. In what seemed like just a few seconds, they had finished their immediate task and lifted the stretcher. They carried the wounded star down the hall, out of the building, and into a waiting ambulance.

Once Rick was gone, the bystanders milled around, not knowing what to do. The police arrived and began inspecting the scene, interviewing people, and collecting evidence.

Nancy walked over to Kay, who was now sitting on the floor in a corner of the hall. She still looked pale as a ghost.

"What happened, Kay?" Nancy asked gently, crouching down beside her.

"He was w-wiping off h-his cold cream—" Kay stammered, staring off into space. "And the mirror just exploded! Thank God he had that towel over his face. He'd be blind —worse, maybe. And I was just on my way in there—it could have been me, too!"

A few minutes later, while police combed the area for clues, Pappas assembled the cast and crew.

"Listen up! I have a report from the hospital about Rick." The excited buzzing died down as the producer's voice boomed out into the vast studio.

"He's going to be okay. They said it looked a lot worse than it really was, and that they're going to release him tonight. His hands will be bandaged for a while, of course, but we can work around that. I've already contacted our writers to come up with some material that'll explain his bandaged hands. If we can't work this into the story line somehow, Luther will just stick to closeups. In any case, we're not going to let this shut us down. As far as I'm concerned, you're all still under contract, and that includes Rick. I want everybody back here tomorrow at seven sharp!"

Just then the police officer who had been examining Rick's dressing room let out a long low whistle. "Hey, chief! Look what we found!"

The policeman held up a small metal object. "It's a twenty-four-hour timer. Whoever set this up must have done it yesterday."

Pappas, standing a few feet away, nearly choked. "That's impossible! This set is closed down tight on Sunday. I even hired extra security. My own mother couldn't have gotten in here!"

"Which means," said the chief, "that it was probably an inside job."

Now Nancy finally had a definite lead. She could rule out Dwayne Casper. He couldn't have gotten onto the set to plant the bomb.

But that left her with only two other suspects—Pappas and Lillian. Their faces floated in front of her tightly shut eyes as she leaned against the wall, trying to concentrate amid the confusion.

Nancy shook her head and opened her eyes. She was back at square one with a dangerous killer still on the loose right under her nose!

I've got to get out of here, she suddenly realized.

Quickly, Nancy sprang up and elbowed her way through a group of technicians hovering by the studio door. "Come on," she shouted to Bess. "We've got to go!"

Pulling her friend by the arm, Nancy made straight for the front exit. But she stopped short when she saw Lillian standing directly in front of her, a smug smile on her face. "I'm way ahead of you, Miss Teen Detective," she said, smirking. "Way ahead."

"What's wrong with her?" Bess wanted to know as they hailed a taxi on the corner. "She gives me the creeps."

Nancy didn't answer. She told the cab driver the name of the hospital as they piled in. "And hurry," she added.

Stepping off the elevator on the fifth floor, Nancy and Bess had no trouble finding Rick's room. It was the one with the two police officers in front of it.

Oh, well, thought Nancy, at least he's safe in there. Still, she couldn't help feeling as though she had failed miserably. The police were in on the case now, so there wasn't much point in continuing her investigation. And besides, she hadn't managed to come up with very much, had she?

"Sorry, miss. You can't go in this room,"

one of the officers told Bess when she tried to enter.

"I must see Rick," Bess said frantically.

"A Miss Jensen's in there with Mr. Arlen now."

Bess froze. "Oh. I see—" she finally managed to say. "Has she been there very long?"

"Ever since we got here, miss. About half an hour." He cracked open the door to look inside. "Seems like she might be awhile longer, too."

Bess stepped back, staring anxiously at the half-open door. Through it, she could hear Rick's voice. And it was not the voice of a confident TV star.

"Mattie! Oh, Mattie, I'm so scared. Someone really is trying to kill me!"

"Don't worry, my darling," she replied in a soft voice. "The police are here. They'll protect you."

"You know, Mattie, you were right all along. You were the only one who saw the truth. Mattie, if I come out of this mess alive, I swear I'm going to make everything up to you. I need you, Mattie, I need you so badly—no one else ever meant a thing to me. You're the only one I've ever loved!"

"I've heard enough!" Bess turned and ran down the hall, covering her mouth with her hands.

"Bess! Bess, wait!" Nancy called after her.

"Leave me alone!" She was fighting back her tears but losing the battle. "I can't believe it," she sobbed. "I just can't believe it!"

Nancy started to go after Bess but thought better of it. Right then Bess needed to work this out on her own. But Nancy wondered about the force of her friend's reaction. What was it about this guy that caused women to fall instantly in love with him?

Mattie and Rick had stopped talking, and the police officer silently closed the door again. No sense waiting around, Nancy decided.

Out on the sidewalk, Nancy found Bess. Her eyes were brimming over with tears, and her mascara was smeared all over her face. She looked utterly forlorn.

"Come on, Bess. Let's go home," Nancy suggested, gently taking her friend's hand. Bess nodded listlessly, allowing herself to be led.

The two friends were silent all the way back to Eloise's apartment. Looking over at Bess, Nancy wished she could comfort her somehow. She knew that Bess really hurt. Bess's brave hero had turned out to be not so brave after all. And worse than that, he was in love with someone else.

As they got out of the cab, Nancy caught sight of her aunt Eloise entering the building. "Hi, Aunt Eloise," she called as she hurried up to greet her.

"Hi, Nancy—Bess," she said as they entered the building. "Did you have a nice day?"

"You're never going to believe what happened today," Bess said in a soft voice. She had finally gotten control of herself.

"Well, as soon as we get upstairs, let's kick off our shoes and relax, and you can tell me all about it," Eloise replied, moving toward the mailboxes.

The three were in the mail alcove when Eloise looked down and spotted a small box wrapped in brown paper on the package table. She glanced at it and scooped it up. "Nancy, it's addressed to you," she said, noticing it had no stamps.

As she started to hand it to Nancy, she froze.

The box was ticking!

Chapter

Thirteen

NANCY SPRANG INTO action. "Bess, get on the house phone and get someone to call the police."

While Bess was contacting a neighbor, Nancy and Eloise examined the package. "I think the ticking sounds different now," Nancy's aunt said in a frightened whisper. She was still holding the box, but now in trembling hands. "Let's take it outside."

Slowly and calmly, the two went out of the building and walked to the curb. As soon as they had stopped and put the box down, two police bomb-squad officers arrived. It didn't take them long to discover that the box contained an ordinary, harmless alarm clock.

"I've never been so happy to see an alarm clock in my entire life." Nancy's aunt smiled with relief and clasped her hands together to stop them from shaking.

"Somebody went to a lot of trouble to scare your niece, ma'am. And from the sound of this note, that person is serious."

"'Last warning, Nancy Drew, leave town *now,*'" the officer read.

"Nancy, I think maybe we *should* get back to River Heights today." Bess had rejoined them and stood listening as the note was read.

"Bess is right, Nancy. This is serious. Your father would never forgive me if anything happened to you while you were here. Worse, I would never forgive myself. In fact, after the officers leave, I'm calling the airport."

Eloise, Nancy, and Bess thanked the men, and they turned and headed back into the building and up to Eloise's apartment.

Nancy bit her lip. "Wait a minute, Aunt Eloise," she said, trying to stop her aunt from calling the airport. She knew her aunt was only trying to protect her, but how could she leave New York while a dangerous killer was still after Rick? Even if he wasn't the greatest guy in the world, he didn't deserve to die. And obviously, the killer was getting closer and closer. Next time he might succeed.

"Our tickets are for the day after tomorrow," she called out as her aunt was about to lift the phone. "Maybe I can solve the case before then."

"Forget it, Nancy. I'm not going to let you risk your life—not even for a couple more days." Eloise sounded definite. "And besides, the police are on the case now."

"She's probably right, Nancy," Bess agreed.

"Wait a minute, everybody." Nancy was groping for the right words. "You can't ask me to just walk away from this! A man's life is in danger!"

They looked back at her with questioning stares, unconvinced.

"How about this—I promise that if I don't come up with any answers by tomorrow, I'll go straight back to River Heights as we planned originally. But honestly, I could never live with myself if I knew I'd walked away when I could have helped."

Eloise looked down at the floor. Nancy had gotten to her. Bess, despite everything, had to smile. Sleuthing was in Nancy's blood.

"All right, Nancy," Eloise said reluctantly. "I do have only myself to blame—I did introduce you to Mattie."

"Thanks, Aunt Eloise," Nancy cried warmly, throwing her arms around the older woman's shoulders. "You're a peach, you know that?"

"Some peach. I invite you to New York for a vacation, and you wind up running all over town, tracking down a murderer. And getting bomb threats delivered to your door!"

"He or she is *not* a murderer—not yet, anyway," Nancy said. "Nobody's been killed, and I hope we can keep it that way. Now, if you'll excuse me, there's something I've got to take care of right away."

"Who's there?" came Mattie's surprised voice in response to Nancy's knock.

"It's me. May I come in?"

"Oh, Nancy," Mattie said when she opened the door. "Wasn't it awful?" Mattie looked exhausted. Obviously, she had just been through quite an ordeal. "Come on in," she added distractedly. "Sorry the place is such a mess. I just got back from the hospital."

"How's Rick doing?" Nancy asked.

"He's going to be okay. But—oh, Nancy, his hands! They hurt him terribly. I just can't believe he's actually going to do the show tomorrow."

"What?" she gasped. "Tomorrow?"

Nancy was truly amazed—he had sounded so frightened at the hospital. I have to give him a lot of credit, she thought. He really was brave.

"Pappas showed up at the hospital. He just burst in past the guards. I was there for the

117

whole thing. He couldn't stop apologizing for this and all the other things that have been happening on the set lately. He even promised to hire Rick a bodyguard and to get some plainclothes detectives to be at the studio until this whole thing is over. But Rick said something about loyalty to his fellow actors, and just shrugged it off and told Pappas he'd be back at work tomorrow. As shaken up as Rick was, he just couldn't say no." She sighed miserably.

"I don't know how I'm going to get through tomorrow," she said. "I'm so worried about him. Oh, Nancy, what am I going to do? If he's killed, I'll just—I'll—oh, I don't know what I'll do!" Mattie seemed to be on the brink of hysteria.

"Hold on, Mattie. It's going to be okay," said Nancy, trying to comfort her. "I'm still here, and I've got one more day in town. I haven't given up yet."

Mattie looked into Nancy's eyes, and a glimmer of hope showed on her face. "You —you mean it?"

"Mmm-hmm. Maybe I'm not exactly closer to solving this case, but I sure know a lot more than when I started. And I'll do my best for you until it's time for me to leave," Nancy assured her. "Please don't worry."

But what Nancy didn't tell Mattie was that

she was hoping the criminal would try again and this time make a mistake—the kind of mistake he or she had managed to avoid until then. Her experience showed that most criminals tripped themselves up sooner or later.

"Oh, I hope you're right," Mattie said with a nervous laugh. "I guess I'd better get you and Bess hired on as extras again, huh?"

When it was all arranged, Mattie went back to the hospital to get Rick, and Nancy went back upstairs for a quiet dinner with her aunt and Bess.

Just before turning in, she went into the empty living room, picked up the phone, and dialed. She was in luck.

"Twice in one week?" came Ned's familiar voice. "What's going on, Nancy? Could this be true love?"

Nancy giggled, with a wave of warm feeling passing over her. Good old Ned. He was just what she needed right then—the voice of sanity. "You know I love you," she said with a laugh. "But thanks for trying to be funny. I can use a little humor right now."

"Things aren't going too well there, are they?"

"That's putting it mildly," she said, and told him the latest developments in the case.

119

Ned tried to sound comforting. "Look, Nancy, I've known you for a long time, right?"

"Forever," she replied.

"And in all that time, I've never seen you blow a case. So just hang in there. You'll figure it out."

"But, Ned, I have only one more day!" she protested.

"Something will happen, and the pieces will all fall into place. You'll solve this one, I know you will, Detective Drew."

"Well, I'm glad somebody thinks so." She sighed, not really convinced. "I appreciate the vote of confidence, though."

"And, Nancy . . ."

"Yes, Ned?"

"Be careful, okay? I'd hate to have anything happen to you."

Once again, the girls were slated to play nurses. Rick's injuries had been written into the script. In the *new* story line, Rory, in a fit of despair, would try to throw himself out a window. He would be rescued, but not before he had cut his hands to pieces and had to be taken to the hospital.

"Nancy! How do I look?" Bess asked later that day. Twirling around in her nurse's uniform, she fluffed her red wig carefully so the pert white nurse's cap wouldn't fall off. Her heart didn't seem half as badly broken since she had found out she'd be working on "Danner's Dream" again that day. She even had a "silent bit"—she was the nurse who would greet Serena when she arrived at the hospital.

"I called my mother to make sure she'd tape the program," Bess said excitedly. "Then I can take it around to casting directors and stuff."

Nancy smiled at her friend. Even in the middle of all this craziness, she was still managing to have a good time. Of course, her fun was tempered by her feelings for Rick. Whenever she saw him on the set, she turned and purposely avoided him.

"Oh, and you know what? I found out that that lady with glasses and clipboard over there is the casting director," Bess whispered, pulling Nancy by the arm. "I'm going to go hang around her for a while. You never can tell, Nancy, this could be *it*. And won't Rick feel like a fool when I become a bigger star than he ever was!"

Nancy sighed and looked at her friend. "Bess, as a friend, I've got to tell you this: You are totally insane!" Then pushing her friend playfully, she whispered, "But go for it. I hope she notices you. I'll see you when it's time for our scene, okay? I want to check out Rick's new dressing room."

Rick was dressing and being made up in an improvised area across the hall from the costume room. He sat staring listlessly into space, still stunned by what had happened the day before. Kay was with him.

"So, Rick," she was saying, trying to cheer him up, "are you going to give me a hand here, or do I have to do this all myself?"

But Rick didn't move. He seemed so scared —as though there was a voice inside his head telling him over and over again that someone was trying to kill him. And that he or she might very well succeed.

Nancy leaned up against a wall and watched as Kay put some warm water into the sink. "No mirrors in here, I hope you've noticed," she said, trying to make a joke. When she saw she wasn't getting through to Rick even a little bit, she sighed wearily and picked up a stick of makeup.

"Okay, here we go," she said, uncapping it. Then, "Oops!" she cried as the stick slipped out of her hands and fell into the wet sink.

"Clumsy me," she said to herself, shaking her head. Suddenly, there was a hissing noise. The water in the sink began bubbling furiously.

"What the—?" Rick gasped. A sharp odor rose from the sink.

Nancy recognized the smell. "That's acid," she whispered.

"Oh, my God!" Kay cried, her hands on her cheeks as she watched the acid eat holes in the stainless steel sink. "Rick, that could have been your face!"

Chapter

Fourteen

THAT'S IT!" RICK exclaimed, "I've had it!"
He tried to pick up his suede jacket, but even a
simple action such as this was difficult because
of the bandages on his hands. Growling with
disgust, he stormed out of the room.

"Rick?" Kay called, following him down the
corridor. "Where are you going?"

"Forget it, Kay. I'm taking a nice long walk
and going someplace where nobody can find
me."

Just at that moment, a beet-faced William
Pappas stepped into the hallway. "What's
going on here?" he asked as the handsome
actor flew down the hall.

"I'm out of here. Off the show. I'm not taking any more chances."

"But you're under contract, Arlen! You can't just leave!"

"Oh, yeah? Watch me." With that, Rick pushed past the angry producer and made his way toward the entrance.

Pappas made a lunge for him, but a couple of crew members restrained him.

"Come on, Mr. Pappas, calm down," they urged him. "Give him a break. The guy's been under a lot of stress lately."

Pappas let the men straighten his suit as he muttered under his breath, "He's under tension? What am I—chopped liver? I'm behind schedule, and the network is breathing down my back. I have ratings to think of!"

But it was too late. Rick was out the door and gone. Nancy and Kay looked on as the producer fumed, powerless to stop him.

Seconds later Luther Parks hurried up to them, running a hand nervously through his silver hair. "Bill, someone just said Rick Arlen left! What do you want me to do?"

But Pappas was in no mood for creative solutions. "You're the director," he snarled, heading back to his office. "Think of something!"

Luther shrugged and turned to Lillian, who was standing beside him. "We'll shoot the hospital scene with Mattie," he said.

"Whatever you say," Lillian drawled, throwing a wink Nancy's way. "Report to duty, Nurse Drew. And try not to miss your cue."

Standing in the make-believe operating room as the crew adjusted the lights, Nancy's spirits sank. Rick was out on the street somewhere, unprotected. And there she was on her last day in town, about to walk around in the background of a fictional scene instead of tracking down a very real criminal.

Someone had found a way to get around the set undetected, again and again. That was the key. In spite of guards at the doors, and people everywhere, Rick's enemy had gotten in. If she only knew how! If she could only discover the method behind the madness, she felt sure the rest would fall into place. But how could she do anything now?

"Action!" came Lillian's voice. Taking her medicine tray, Nancy crossed the set, put the tray down, and walked back again, heaving a deep sigh.

Action. That's exactly what was needed. If only there was some action she could take!

"Cheer up, Nancy." Bess peered sympathetically into the mirror at her friend's reflection. Nancy wasn't used to losing and it hurt. Bess pulled a comb through her blond hair and twisted it up in one deft move. She fastened it in place, and searched for something comforting to say. "I know it's a bummer, but you win some and you lose some." Somehow those weren't the words she had been looking for.

"Well, I don't really feel like going out to dinner, that's for sure," Nancy replied listlessly. She reached for her makeup case on the bathroom counter.

"But we're going to a really great restaurant! Your aunt, Eloise, said it's one of her favorites. And I can't wait to tell her about my big scene today. The videotape editor told me he was sure I got into the shot. Can you imagine? There I am, actually handing a paper to Mattie Jensen on national TV! My mother will flip!"

Nancy lifted the collar of her mauve jacket and fastened a rhinestone pin to the lapel. "There's just so little time left and so many unanswered questions."

Suddenly the door buzzer rang. "Come on, Nancy. That's the signal. Your aunt and the cab are waiting!" Bess cried. "Be right down!" she called into the intercom.

At the restaurant the girls were seated by a lovely young hostess, who looked more like a model than a restaurant employee.

"Pierre will be your waiter," she told them.

Just then, a young man with twinkling eyes and a handlebar mustache approached the table.

"Bonsoir. Je m'appelle Pierre. Here I haf ze menu," he said in a thick French accent. Bess couldn't help giggling as he handed the menus around the table, giving each of them a seductive look. "I can tell zees table will be my favorite of ze night."

"I didn't know this place served French food," Eloise mused out loud, watching him go.

"It doesn't," Bess remarked in surprise as she looked over the menu. "A French waiter at an American restaurant. That's weird."

"Not for New York it's not," Nancy's aunt replied.

Nancy's eyes followed the waiter to the bar, where he put in an order for some other customers. "Hey, Steve," he yelled in a regular voice, "give me three mineral waters and a Coke."

Nancy looked up when the waiter returned to the table to take their order. *"Garçon—avez vous un stylo noir, peut-être?"*

"Huh?" he asked, confused. "Want to run that by me again, lady?"

"You're *not* French?" Bess exclaimed.

"Mais non, mademoiselle," the waiter admitted with a shy smile. "I mean, nope. Never even seen the place."

"I'll bet I know what's going on," Eloise ventured. "You're an actor, aren't you?"

128

The waiter looked at Eloise for a second and then laughed. "Okay, okay. I confess. I'm guilty. I am an actor, but please don't be mad."

With that, he tugged on the end of his mustache and pulled it off. "I have an audition for the part of a French waiter tomorrow, so I thought I'd get in a little practice tonight. Now, ladies, what can I get you?" He proceeded to take their orders and then left.

"Does that happen a lot around here?" Bess asked.

Eloise smiled and shook her head no. "But many of the waiters in New York are actors, Bess. And a lot of the delivery people, word processors, dog walkers . . . They do many different kinds of work just to survive between acting jobs."

Bess was sobered by the thought that an acting career could be so difficult. But Eloise's words also had a great impact on Nancy.

"Playing different roles," she murmured softly to herself. Suddenly a big piece of the puzzle had fallen into place. That's how the culprit does it, she told herself. Hadn't she herself gone anywhere on the set completely unnoticed in her nurse's uniform? No one had even looked at her twice. Of course! How could she have missed it?

129

"And when the director called 'action' I was supposed to be sorting these papers at the front desk," Bess was telling Eloise. "And Mattie walks right up to me and says, 'Excuse me. Did Rory Danner leave a message for me?' And I nod and I hand her an envelope. We must have done the scene six times, right, Nancy?" Bess didn't wait for an answer. She just went on, filling Eloise in on every little detail of her big day on "Danner's Dream." Nancy ate her dinner in silence, trying to put the final pieces of the puzzle together.

"I'm stuffed," Bess said as they climbed the stairs to Nancy's aunt's apartment. "That dessert was too much."

"After you girls leave, I'm going to have to go on a diet," Eloise said, reaching into her bag for the keys.

Just then, through the door they heard the phone ring. "Don't worry—the machine will get it," Eloise said, letting them in and flicking the lights on.

"Hello," came Eloise's recorded voice on the answering machine. "I can't come to the phone right now, but if you leave a message at the sound of the beep, I'll get back to you as soon as I can."

"This message is for Nancy Drew." A shiver

ran down Nancy's spine. It was the voice of Lillian Weiss. "It's Lillian, Nancy. There's something I have to tell you. It's a matter of life and death. Meet me on the set tomorrow morning at six o'clock, before rehearsal. I'll leave a pass for you."

Chapter

Fifteen

"Nancy, you're not thinking of going, are you?" The color drained from Eloise's face, and she sat down on the sofa. "You told me yourself that you thought this woman might be the killer. I can't allow you to put your life in danger that way, even to save someone else's. You're my niece, and you're the only child my brother has. Think how he would feel if something happened to you!"

Nancy sat down beside her aunt and took her hand. "Aunt Eloise," she said calmly, "ever since I was a little girl, I've been trying to solve mysteries. I can't quit now! It's my life, Aunt Eloise. It's what I do best. Don't ask me to give it up now, please."

Tears in her eyes, Eloise hugged her niece fiercely. "I'll be biting my nails the whole time, you know that?" she said with a resigned laugh. "But why do you have to meet at the studio?"

"Oh, you know how dramatic soap people are. Just a little added mystery. Now, come on, there's nothing to worry about," Nancy countered with a smile. "And besides, I know quite a lot of karate, remember? All those lessons ought to be good for something."

When she got to Worldwide Broadcasting, Nancy picked up her pass at the security desk, then slipped into the main corridor. Every muscle in her body was tensed. There was something wrong about all this—she knew it the moment she had heard Lillian's voice. But something drove her on, step by step, toward the studio.

As she turned down a corridor, she saw someone and ducked back around the corner. It was the janitor, mopping the floors. Not wanting to run into anyone, she went back around, taking the long way to the studio in order to avoid him.

Finally, she reached the vacuum-sealed door and pushed her way in. The set was dimly

THE NANCY DREW FILES

lit, but Nancy's eyes adjusted to the darkness. At first it seemed to be deserted, but then Nancy saw her.

Lillian was sitting on a chair on the set of the Danner kitchen, holding her head in her hands. As Nancy approached, she turned around.

"Our fair rescuer," she said under her breath. "How kind of you to come." The words were full of bravado, but the old self-assured Lillian was gone. The mocking look had disappeared, and Lillian's face was now fearful.

"Why did you ask me to come here?" Nancy demanded. "What's all this about?"

"Oh, I'm not the maniac, if that's what you're worried about. In fact, I asked you here because—" Lillian's voice wavered. "Because he's after *me* now."

Nancy crossed the room and sat down next to Lillian. Then she listened intently to every word of her story.

"When things started turning weird around here, I got curious. Actually, I was kind of hoping Rick would get what he deserved, if you get my meaning. But then I found something. It was that day I ran into you in the hall. I had just found it in a closet. I didn't want to tell anyone about it, so I hid it where no one would come across it."

"The prop room, of course!" Nancy's eyes

lit up. So that was why Lillian had acted so secretively that day!

"Right. And this little item I found made me want to find out more. So I did. I kept on finding more and more, until—" Lillian's voice was barely a whisper. "Until I got this yesterday." She handed Nancy a typewritten note. "Were you thinking of blackmail, my pet?" it read. "Not if I kill you first."

"So you see," Lillian went on, "that's why I called you here. In case anything happens to me. I mean, I knew you were on the case, and, well, you understand." She picked up a shopping bag that lay at her feet and, taking something out of it, she held it up for Nancy to look at.

"A long-haired wig, glasses, a T-shirt—" Nancy sifted through the contents, her suspicions confirmed. "It looks like a disguise. Whoever it was used it to get around the set unnoticed."

"Exactly," Lillian agreed. "And what better disguise than as a stagehand? One of those anonymous people walking around during every shoot. Everyone else is so busy doing their work, no one notices. It's perfect!"

"What else did you find?" Nancy asked.

"Oh, more of the same. Different every day. I knew immediately that it was an actor. Or an ex-actor—"

Then I was right! Nancy said to herself.

"You see," Lillian went on, "I finally put two and two together. Which, I hate to say, is more than you've done."

"I take it you have proof of the maniac's identity, then," Nancy said.

"Of course I do," she said with a wicked smile. "It is—"

Lillian didn't get a chance to finish her sentence. All of a sudden, every light in the entire studio flashed on. Shading her eyes, Nancy glanced up to the director's booth, where the lighting controls were.

There, looking down at them from behind the thick Plexiglas, was Dwayne Casper! His expression was furious, and in his hand was a gun—pointed straight at Nancy!

Chapter

Sixteen

Well, hello, you two!" Dwayne's voice boomed at them, seeming to come from every imaginable direction. He let out a monstrous laugh. "I only followed Lillian, but I've trapped both of you. How lucky! Congratulations, your death scenes will look so lovely on videotape. A videotape for my personal viewing pleasure only!"

For an instant, Dwayne relaxed his grip on the gun a bit. Nancy, seeing her chance, made a dash for the door. Just as she reached it, she heard it go *whooossshh,* and the red light above it flashed on. The door was locked—vacuum sealed.

"Are we locked up down there?" Dwayne screamed in a grotesque parody of Luther Parks. He laughed again. "A little stage fright, Ms. Elliot? Actually, I didn't know until yesterday that you and Ms. Elliot were one and the same. Very good bit of acting. Very realistic. You see, we strive for realism here—real bullets, real blood, real death." He waved his gun playfully at them.

"You two are only the first act. Rick Arlen's death will be the climax of my little soap opera. He's gotten away from me so far, thanks to you, Nancy Drew. But with you two little nuisances out of the way, I don't think he has much of a chance. Do you?"

Dwayne paused, waiting for a reply. Nancy had to think fast. This might be her only chance to save her life and Lillian's. Somehow she had to distract him, make him forget he had a gun.

"Dwayne, why? Why do you hate Rick so much? Lillian and Mattie have more reason to hate him than you do!"

Her words seemed to ignite Dwayne's fury. He exploded at her, just as he had at Bess that day in his office.

"More reason than I? What do you know about it? Keep your ignorant little mouth shut! Rick Arlen has to die, and I'll tell you why. Because he killed me, that's why. He killed Dwayne Casper."

Dwayne paused for breath. Nancy had the feeling Dwayne's story was a long one. That was good. She needed time—time to think of a way out.

"I was an actor," Dwayne cried, all the hurt and rage in him pouring out with his story. "I'd studied every aspect of my craft and was a master of Shakespeare, dialects, stage combat—everything. I was underrated and underappreciated—but brilliant. Then I met Mattie.

"We fell in love, and I was the happiest man on earth. Then—then came August. We did *Romeo and Juliet*. Mattie was Juliet, but Rick beat me out for the role of Romeo. The director was a sucker for a pretty face, and so, I soon found out, was Mattie.

"From that moment on, my life was never the same. And I never forgot what he had done to me."

As Dwayne ranted on, Nancy looked around desperately for some way out.

"I am not like some people, who fall in love every day," he rasped. "When I lost Mattie, I knew that I would never love anyone ever again. I decided that if I couldn't have her, I'd make money, lots of money. I gave up acting and became an agent instead.

"I made them stars. I did it all. And how did Rick pay me back? By leaving me, that's how. I got nothing in return for all my hard work—nothing at all. He had destroyed me again.

"Once Rick left, other clients began to leave. All I had left was Mattie. And then—" Dwayne paused, and his expression grew dark with rage. "Then he started luring Mattie away from me. That's when I decided to kill him. Which brings me back—" he raised the gun at Nancy, looking down at them "—to you two ladies."

"Dwayne!" Nancy shouted, shaking him out of his daze. "Your story sounds like a soap opera. That stuff doesn't happen in real life!"

"That shows what you know about life, Nancy Drew," Dwayne rasped into the mike. "Real life *is* a soap opera. You'll learn that. Or rather, you would have, had you lived."

"Rick didn't kill you," Nancy insisted. "You're still—"

Dwayne erupted again. "Enough!" he screamed. "It's time for the final closeup. I'm going to write you two out of the script forever."

Quickly, he disappeared from sight. Nancy guessed that he was on his way down to the set. That only gave her a few seconds to think of something.

Nancy looked frantically around. Lillian was standing, shocked, unable to help in any way. She was frozen with fear. As clever as she had been in figuring out who the criminal was, she was utterly useless right then.

In the few seconds she had left, Nancy scanned the set, looking for something —anything. Then, she saw it.

Over in the corner stood a large metal cylinder. On it were written the words "Smoke Machine." Rushing over to it, Nancy found the control switch and turned it to the Dense setting.

Not a moment too soon, either. Seemingly from nowhere, Dwayne appeared.

"Ah, there you are, my nosy little friend. Would you care to rejoin Ms. Weiss onstage?"

Nancy moved slowly back to the kitchen area, hoping that her plan would work.

"What's that hissing?" Dwayne turned and looked around nervously, but all he could see was the nearer half of the studio. The rest was hidden by a thick white fog, which was made even worse by the spotlights.

Quickly, while his back was turned, Nancy grabbed Lillian by the arm and pulled her into the protection of the fog. By the time Dwayne realized what was happening and turned around again, they were gone!

Dwayne cursed loudly as Nancy dragged Lillian into a foggy corner on the set. She left Lillian there and began to walk toward the sound of Dwayne's voice. She had to get the jump on him from behind.

Then she heard a sound that made her heart sink. It was the sound of a giant fan—the wind machine.

"Very clever, Nancy Drew," came Dwayne's voice through the diminishing fog. "But there's an antidote for every poison, or vice versa."

The fog was now down to a very small area, and Nancy knew that her time was running out. Crouching down, she took a deep breath and prepared to make a desperate dive at Dwayne. He would still have the gun, she knew. She had only one advantage—surprise.

Rearing back, Nancy flung herself through the air at Dwayne. At the last moment, he turned and saw her. The two of them fell together, toppling over each other, and Dwayne's gun emptied itself.

Chapter

Seventeen

T HOSE WERE GUNSHOTS coming from the set!"

"Quick, this way!"

When the police raced onto the set they found Dwayne Casper flat on the floor. On top of him was Nancy Drew, holding his arms in a double hammerlock.

"His gun is on the floor over there," she told the police breathlessly as they relieved her of her burden.

"Nancy!" Eloise exclaimed, rushing over to her.

"I'm fine, really, Aunt Eloise."

"Well, all the karate lessons in the world

wouldn't have helped if this bullet had come any closer!" Eloise poked at the sleeve of Nancy's jacket. In it was a charred round hole the size of a dime.

Nancy looked down at the hole, her heart skipping a beat. "Please, don't tell Dad," she begged. "And I promise I'll be more careful from now on."

Throwing her arms around her niece, Eloise sighed. "Oh, Nancy, I'm just glad you're alive!"

Bess rushed up to them and threw her arms over theirs in a three-way hug. "Thank goodness, you're all right!" she cried. "When we heard the shots—" She couldn't go on.

The police had handcuffed Dwayne, who stood there passively, a dull look in his eye.

"Do you know how close I was to paying Arlen back for all he's done to me?" he began telling the police officer, who stood impassively beside him clutching his arm. "Do you know how long I worked to get this close?" Dwayne muttered bitterly, his hands locked behind his back.

"Tell your story to the sergeant, buddy," the police officer said. "Ms. Drew, I'll need to get a statement from you and from Ms. Weiss. Would you see that she makes it down to the station house?"

"Of course," Nancy agreed. In all the commotion, she hadn't even given a thought to Lillian. Apparently, the fright had been a bit too much for her—she'd fainted.

"I *had* to call the police, Nancy," Eloise was explaining. "Something told me you weren't safe, and I had to."

At the door, Dwayne spun around suddenly. "Rick Arlen was going to die. He should have died! And I would have killed him if it hadn't been for you, Nancy Drew!"

"Whew." Bess sighed as the officer pushed Dwayne outside. "He's crazy—"

"He's in the right hands now," Nancy added soberly. "And not a moment too soon, either."

"Flight four-seventeen will be boarding at gate three in five minutes."

"That's our flight, Aunt Eloise," said Nancy, putting down her luggage so she could give her aunt a hug.

"You must promise me you'll come again soon—maybe in the fall?" Eloise asked. "And give your father my love, will you? Goodbye, Bess—I hope I'll see you again soon."

But when Nancy and Bess turned to go, they heard their names being called out.

"Nancy! Bess, wait!" A familiar voice floated down the airport corridor. Turning around, Nancy saw a radiant Mattie Jensen running toward them, her auburn curls flying around her face. "We couldn't let you leave without saying goodbye," she cried.

Beside her, Rick Arlen was cradling two large bouquets of roses in his arms. He handed the first to Nancy and said, "Thank you for saving my life, Nancy—I don't know what I would have done without you."

Then he turned to Bess, who seemed more than a little flustered. "This one is for you, love," he murmured, giving her the flowers.

"Oh, Rick, thank you," she cried, letting down her guard. For a minute, Nancy almost felt sorry that she had been thinking of him as such a heel. She was sure the flowers were his way of saying he was sorry for toying with Bess's emotions.

But the hopeful light went out of her eyes when he explained, "They're from Pappas. He asked us to give them to you."

"Pappas sent us flowers?" asked Nancy incredulously.

"Oh, he's really a teddy bear," said Mattie. "And he's on top of the world now that the show's back on track."

"He even agreed to cancel my contract with no hard feelings," Rick said, laughing. "In fact, he's already written it into the script. I'm getting killed next week, and I go to work on my feature the week after. Ironic, isn't it? Rick Arlen lives, but Rory Danner bites the dust!"

"And Pappas rehired everyone that he

fired," Mattie added. "All thanks to you, Nancy."

Nancy's eyes twinkled. Nothing beat the wonderful feeling she always had after solving a case. "I'm glad I could be of some help," was all she could say.

"But the best news of all is—" Rick flashed Mattie a million-dollar smile. "Shall I tell them, or do you want to?"

Mattie beamed. "You go ahead."

"Mattie has agreed to marry me," he announced proudly. "We're flying to her parents' house next weekend. All this made me realize that there's only one woman in the world for me." He looked somber for a moment, adding, "Thank goodness it wasn't too late."

Nancy noticed that Rick avoided Bess's eyes as he spoke. "Well," Nancy said, "that's great news, you two. Congratulations." Looking over at her friend, Nancy could tell that Bess wished she were in Mattie's shoes. "Well, we'd better get going, though," Nancy said. "See you next time we're in New York!"

With that, and a final squeeze of her aunt's hand, Nancy put her arm around Bess's shoulders and walked past the Passengers Only sign.

"I'm sorry it worked out like this, Bess," she told her friend. News like that had to hurt.

"Oh, it's okay," Bess said and sighed. "I'm just so tired."

Nancy adjusted the strap of her carry-on bag

with a weary smile. "I know what you mean. After a vacation like this, we really need a vacation!"

"So tell me," said George, leaning forward over a hot fudge sundae and crinkling her nose. "Is Rick Arlen really as gorgeous in real life as he is on TV?"

Nancy looked over at Bess, wondering how she would respond.

"Not nearly," Bess replied. "He's kind of short, and those fabulous blue eyes are really contacts."

Nancy rolled her eyes. Bess was laying it on just a little thick.

"And you actually had a date with him?" George was practically shouting. Bess just turned her face away. "I can't believe it!" George went on. "I'm so jealous! What was he like? What did you do?"

"Uh, George—she doesn't want to talk about it," Nancy warned, finally able to interrupt.

"Oh, I get it." George nodded. "Well, you did get to be on television—and on 'Danner's Dream,'" she exclaimed cheerfully.

"Yeah—" Bess sighed. "But seeing how actors and actresses really live, and how hard they work, I don't know. I've been thinking of becoming a model instead." With that, she took an enormous mouthful of strawberry ice cream.

"Oh, really?" Nancy said skeptically. "Will you go on your famous ice cream diet?"

"She's got to look her sundae best," quipped George in reply.

Bess, however, was not amused. "Lay off, you two, will you?" she said testily. "I'm depressed enough as it is."

"Sorry, Bess," said Nancy. "There'll be other guys."

"Not for me," Bess insisted, shaking her head vehemently. "I'm through with men forever." She put down her spoon and gazed out the window dejectedly.

Suddenly her attention was caught by someone passing in front of the window—someone tall, male, and very good-looking. "Hey, who is *that?*" she asked eagerly. "He must be new in town. I never would have missed someone like that."

But neither George nor Nancy could answer. Both of them were doubled up with laughter.

Same old Bess!

Nancy's next case:

The River Heights Country Club is a playground for the town's wealthier citizens. But lately those citizens have been getting ripped off!

When Nancy investigates the robbery of a be-jeweled necklace, she finds out why: The country club members love to talk about their valuable possessions; the club is the perfect place for thieves to learn what—and where—to steal.

It seems the thieves have also been hearing about Nancy Drew. Almost before she starts the case, she finds herself in danger. Can Nancy get the goods on this ring of thieves? Find out in *CIRCLE OF EVIL*, Case #18 in The Nancy Drew Files℠.

Stories of Mystery and Adventure by Enid Blyton
in Armada

Mystery Series

Secrets Series

ARMADA

Enid Blyton
Five Find-Outers
Mystery Stories
in Armada

ARMADA

Other titles by
Enid Blyton
in Armada

ARMADA

All these books are available at your local bookshop or newsagent, or can be ordered from the publisher. To order direct from the publishers just tick the title you want and fill in the form below:

Name _____

Address _____

_____

Send to: Collins Childrens Cash Sales
           PO Box 11
           Falmouth
           Cornwall
           TR10 9EN

Please enclose a cheque or postal order or debit my Visa/ Access –

Credit card no:

Expiry date:

Signature:

– to the value of the cover price plus:

UK: 80p for the first book and 20p per copy for each additional book ordered to a maximum charge of £2.00.

BFPO: 80p for the first book and 20p per copy for each additional book.

Overseas and Eire: £1.50 for the first book, £1.00 for the second book. Thereafter 30p per book.

Armada reserve the right to show new retail prices on covers which may differ from those previously advertised in the text or elsewhere.

ARMADA

A RING FOR VINCENZO'S HEIR

BY

JENNIE LUCAS

MILLS & BOON

First Published in Great Britain 2016
By Mills & Boon, an imprint of HarperCollins*Publishers*
1 London Bridge Street, London, SE1 9GF

© 2016 Jennie Lucas

ISBN: 978-0-263-91640-9

Printed and bound in Spain
by CPI, Barcelona

USA TODAY bestselling author **Jennie Lucas**'s parents owned a bookstore and she grew up surrounded by books, dreaming about faraway lands. A fourth-generation Westerner, she went east at sixteen to boarding school on scholarship, wandered the world, got married, then finally worked her way through college before happily returning to her hometown. A 2010 RITA® finalist and 2005 Golden Heart® winner, she lives in Idaho with her husband and children.

Books by Jennie Lucas

Mills & Boon Modern Romance

Nine Months to Redeem Him
Uncovering Her Nine-Month Secret
The Sheikh's Last Seduction
To Love, Honour and Betray
A Night of Living Dangerously
The Virgin's Choice
Bought: The Greek's Baby

At His Service

The Consequences of That Night

Princes Untamed

Dealing Her Final Card
A Reputation for Revenge

One Night In…

Reckless Night in Rio

Unexpected Babies

Sensible Housekeeper, Scandalously Pregnant

Visit the Author Profile page at
millsandboon.co.uk for more titles.

To Pippa Roscoe, editor extraordinaire.

CHAPTER ONE

"You have two choices, Scarlett." Her ex-boss's greedy eyes slowly traveled from her pregnant belly to the full breasts straining the fabric of her black maternity dress. "Either you sign this paperwork to give your baby away when it's born, and become my wife immediately, or..."

"Or whut?" Scarlett Ravenwood tried to move away from the papers he was pushing toward her. But the man's overmuscled bulk took up most of the backseat of the limousine.

"Or...I'll have Dr. Marston declare you insane. And have you committed." His fleshy lips curved into a pleasant smile. "For your own safety, of course. Because any sane woman would obviously wish to marry me. And then you'll lose your baby anyway, won't you?"

Scarlett stared at him, barely seeing the gleaming buildings of Manhattan passing behind him as they drove down Fifth Avenue. Blaise Falkner was handsome, rich. And a monster.

"You're joking, right?" She gave an awkward laugh. "Come on, Blaise. What century do you think we're living in?"

"The century a rich man can do whatever he wants. To whomever he wants." Reaching out, he twisted a tendril of her long red hair around a thick finger. "Who's going to stop me? You?"

Scarlett's mouth went dry. For the last two years, she'd lived in his Upper East Side mansion as nursing assistant for his dying mother, and over that time Blaise had made increasingly forceful advances. Only his imperious mother, horrified at the thought of her precious heir lowering himself to the household help, had kept him at bay.

But now Mrs. Falkner was dead, and Blaise was rich beyond imagination. While Scarlett was nothing more than an orphan who'd come to New York desperate for a job. Ever since she'd arrived, she'd been isolated in the sickroom, obeying the sharp orders of nurses and doing the worst tasks caring for a fretful, mean-spirited invalid. She had no friends in New York. No one to take her side against him.

Except...

No, she told herself desperately. *Not him.*

She couldn't. Wouldn't.

But what if Blaise was right? What if she escaped him and went to the police, and they didn't believe her? Could he and his pet psychiatrist find a way to carry through with his threat?

When he'd crassly propositioned her at the funeral that morning—literally over his mother's grave!—she'd tried to laugh it off, telling him she was leaving New York. To her surprise, he'd courteously offered a ride to the bus station. Ignoring her intuition's buzz of warning, she'd accepted.

She should have known he wouldn't give up so easily. But she'd never imagined he'd go this far. Threatening her into marriage? Trying to force her to give her baby away?

She'd made a mistake thinking of Blaise as a selfish, petulant playboy who wanted her like a spoiled child demanded a toy he couldn't have. He was actually insane.

"Well?" Blaise demanded. "What is your answer?"

"Why would you want to marry me?" Scarlett said weakly. With a deep breath, she tried to appeal to his vanity. "You're good-looking, charming, rich. Any woman would be happy to marry you." *Any woman who didn't know you*, she added silently.

"But I want you." He gripped her wrist tightly enough to make her flinch. "All this time, you've refused me. Then you get yourself knocked up by some other man and won't tell me who." He ground his teeth. "Once we're wed, I'll be the only man who can touch you. As soon as that brat is born and sent away, you'll be mine. Forever."

Scarlett tried to squelch her rising panic. As the limo moved down Fifth Avenue, she saw a famous cathedral at the end of the block. A desperate idea formed in her mind. Could she...?

Yes. She could and she would.

It hadn't been her plan. She'd intended to buy a bus ticket south, use her small savings to start a new life somewhere sunny where flowers grew year-round and raise her baby alone. But as her own father often said when she was growing up, new challenges called for new plans.

Her new plan scared her, though. Because if Blaise Falkner was a frying pan, Vincenzo Borgia was the fire.

Vin Borgia. She pictured the dark eyes of her unborn baby's father, so hot one moment, so cold the next. Pictured the ruthless edge of his jaw. The strength of his body. The force of his will.

A shiver went through her. What if he...

Don't think about it, she told herself firmly. One impossible thing at a time. Another maxim she'd learned from her father.

As the chauffeur slowed down at a red light, she knew it was now or never. She took a deep breath, then opened her eyes with a brittle smile.

"Blaise." Scarlett leaned forward as she tightened her hidden right hand into a fist. "You know what I've always wanted to do...?"

"What?" he breathed, licking his lips as he looked down at her breasts.

"This!" She gave him a hard uppercut to the jaw. His teeth snapped together as his head knocked backward, shocking him into releasing her.

Without waiting for the limo to completely stop, she yanked on her door handle and stumbled out onto the sidewalk. Kicking off her two-inch heels, she put her hand protectively over her belly and ran with all her might, feet bare against the concrete, toward the enormous cathedral.

It was a perfect day for a wedding. The first of October, and every tree in the city was decorated in yellow, orange and red. St. Swithun's Cathedral was the most famous in New York, the place where the wealthy and powerful held their christenings, weddings and funerals. Two hundred years old, it was a towering midtown edifice of gray marble, big as a city block, with soaring spires reaching boldly into the bright blue sky.

Panting as she ran, Scarlett glanced down at the peeling gold-tone watch that had once belonged to her mother. She prayed she wasn't too late.

A vintage white Rolls-Royce Corniche was parked at the curb, bedecked with ribbons and flowers. Next to it, a uniformed driver waited. Bodyguards with dark sunglasses, scowls and earpieces stood guard on the cathedral steps and around the perimeter.

The wedding had started, then. Scarlett had been trying not to think about it for the last four months, since she'd seen the announcement in the *New York Times*. But the details had been blazed in her memory, and now she was glad, because only Vin Borgia could help her.

A bodyguard blocked her with a glare. "Miss, stand back…"

Clutching her belly theatrically, Scarlett stumbled forward on the sidewalk. "Help! There's a man chasing me! He's trying to kidnap my baby!"

The bodyguard's eyes widened behind his sunglasses. "What?"

She ran past him, calling back, "Call the police!"

"Hey! You can't just—"

Scarlett ran up the cathedral's steps, gasping for air.

"Stop right there!" A second bodyguard came toward her with a thunderous expression. Then he turned when he heard the shout of his colleague as two of Blaise's bodyguards started throwing punches at him on the sidewalk below. "What the..."

Taking advantage of his distraction, she pushed open the cathedral doors and went inside.

For a moment, she blinked in the shadows.

Then her eyes adjusted, and she saw a wedding straight out of a fairy tale. Two thousand guests sat in the pews, and at the altar, beneath a profusion of white roses and lilies and orchids, was the most beautiful bride, standing next to the most devastatingly handsome man in the world.

Just seeing Vin now, for the first time since that magical night they'd created a baby, Scarlett caught her breath.

"If anyone here today has reason," the officiant intoned at the front, "why these two may not lawfully be joined..."

She heard a metallic wrenching sound behind her, then Blaise's harsh triumphant gasp as he burst through the cathedral doors.

"...speak now, or forever hold your peace."

Desperate, Scarlett stumbled to the center of the aisle. Holding up her hand, she cried, "Please! Stop!"

There was a collective gasp as two thousand people turned to stare at her. Including the bride and groom.

Scarlett put her hands to her head, feeling dizzy. It was hard to speak when she could barely catch her breath. She focused on the only person who mattered.

"Please, Vin, you have to help me—" Her voice choked off, then strengthened as she thought of the unborn child depending on her. "My boss is trying to steal our baby!"

Unlike many grooms the night before they wed, Vincenzo Borgia, Vin to his friends, had slept very well last night.

He knew what he was doing today. He was marrying the perfect woman. His courtship of Anne Dumaine had been easy, and so had their engagement. No discord. No messy emotion. No sex, even, at least not yet.

But today, their lives would be joined, as would their families—and more to the point, their companies. When Vin's SkyWorld Airways merged with her father's Air Transatlantique, Vin would gain thirty new transatlantic routes at a stroke, including the lucrative routes of New York–London and Boston–Paris. Vin's company would nearly double in size, at very advantageous terms. Why would Jacques Dumaine be anything but generous to his future son-in-law?

After today, there would be no more surprises in Vin's life. No more uncertainty or questions about the future. He liked that thought.

Yes, Vin had slept well last night, and tonight, after he finally made love to his very traditional bride, who'd insisted on remaining a virgin until they married, he expected to sleep even better. And for every other night for the rest of his well-ordered, enjoyably controllable life.

If he wasn't overwhelmingly attracted to his bride, what of it? Passion died soon after marriage, he'd been told, so perhaps it was a good thing. You couldn't miss what you'd never had.

And if he and Anne seemed to have little in common other than the wedding and the merger, well, what difference did that make? Men and women had different interests. They weren't supposed to be the same. He would cover her weaknesses. She would cover his.

Because whatever his enemies and former lovers might accuse, Vin knew he had a few. A lack of patience. A lack of empathy. In the business world, those were strengths, but once he had children, he knew greater sources of patience and empathy would be required.

He was ready to settle down. He wanted a family. Other than building his empire it was his primary reason for getting married, but not his only. After his last sexual encounter, an explosive night with a gorgeous redhead who'd given him the most amazing sex of his life, then disappeared, he decided he was fed up with unpredictable love affairs.

So, a few months later, he'd sensibly proposed to Anne Dumaine.

Born in Montreal, Anne was beautiful, with an impeccable pedigree, certain to be a good mother and corporate wife. She spoke several languages, including French and Italian, and held a degree in international business. Best of all she came with an irresistible dowry—Air Transatlantique.

Vin smiled at Anne now, standing across from him as they waited to speak their vows. She looked like Princess Grace, he thought, blonde and grave, with a modest white gown and a long lace veil that had been handmade by Belgian nuns. Flawless. A picture-perfect bride.

"If anyone here today has reason," the archbishop presiding over their marriage said solemnly, "why these two may not lawfully be joined..."

There was a scuffle, a loud bang. Footsteps. From the corner of his eye he saw heads in the audience turn. He refused to look—that would be undisciplined—but his smile grew a little strained.

"...speak now," the minister finished, "or forever hold your peace."

"Please! Stop!"

A woman's voice. Vin's jaw tightened. Who would dare interrupt their wedding? One of his despondent ex-lovers? How had she gotten past the bodyguards? Furious, he turned.

Vin froze when he saw green eyes fringed with black lashes in a lovely heart-shaped face, and vivid red hair cascading down her shoulders, bright as heart's blood. She stood in the gray stone cathedral, his dream come to life.

Scarlett. The woman who had haunted his dreams for the last eight months. The flame-haired virgin who'd shared a single night with him he could not forget, then fled the next morning before he could get her number— or even her last name! No woman had ever treated him so badly. She'd inflamed his blood, then disappeared like Cinderella, without so much as a damned glass slipper.

She was dressed completely in black. And barefoot? Her breasts overflowed the neckline of her dress. His gaze returned sharply to her belly. She couldn't be...

"Please, Vin, you have to help me," she choked out, her voice echoing against the cool gray stone. "My boss is trying to steal our baby!"

For a moment, Vin stared at her in shock, unable to comprehend her words.

Our baby?

Our?

There was a collective gasp as two thousand people turned to stare at him, waiting for his reaction.

Vin's body flashed hot, then cold as he felt all control— over the wedding, over his privacy, over his life—ripped from his grasp. Nearby, he saw the glower of Anne's redfaced father, saw her mother's shocked eyes. Fortunately he had no family of his own to disappoint.

He turned to his bride, expecting to see tears or at least agonized hurt, expecting to have to explain that he hadn't cheated on her, of course not, that this had all happened months before they'd met. But Anne's beautiful face was carefully blank.

"Excuse me," he said. "I need a moment."

"Take all the time you want."

Vin went slowly down the aisle toward Scarlett. The people watching from the pews seemed to fall away, their faces smearing into mere smudges of color.

His heart was pounding as he stopped in front of the woman he'd almost convinced himself didn't exist. Looking at her belly, he said in a low voice, "You're pregnant?"

She met his eyes. "Yes."

"The baby's mine?"

Her chin lifted. "You think I would lie?"

Vin remembered her soft gasp of pain when he'd first taken her, holding her virgin body so hot and hard and tight against his own in the darkness of his bedroom. Remembered how he'd kissed her tears away until her pain melted away to something very different…

"You couldn't have told me before now?" he bit out.

"I'm sorry," she whispered. "I didn't…" Then she glanced behind her, and her expression changed to fear.

Three men were striding up the aisle, the leader's face a mask of cold fury.

"There you are, you little…" He roughly grabbed Scarlett's wrist. "This is a private matter," he snarled at Vin, barely looking at him. "Return to your ceremony."

Vin almost did. It would have been easy to let them go. He felt the pressure of his waiting bride, of the pending merger, of her family, of the cathedral and the archbishop and the many guests, some of whom had flown around the world to be here. He could have told himself that Scarlett was lying and turned his back on her. He could have walked back to calmly speak the vows that would bind his life to Anne.

But something stopped him.

Maybe it was the man's iron-like grip on Scarlett's slender wrist. Or the way he and his two goons were dragging her back down the aisle, in spite of her helpless struggles. Maybe it was the panicked, stricken expression on her lovely face as all those wealthy, powerful guests silently watched, doing nothing to intervene.

Or maybe it was the ghost of his own memory, long repressed, of how it had once felt to be powerless and unloved, dragged from his only home against his will.

Whatever it was, Vin found himself doing something he hadn't done in a long, long time.

Getting involved.

"Stop right there," he ordered.

The other man's face snapped toward him. "Stay out of this."

Vin stalked toward him. "The lady doesn't want to leave with you."

"She's distraught. Not to mention crazy." The man, sleek and overfed as a Persian cat, yanked on her wrist. "I'm taking her to my psychiatrist. She's going to be locked away for a long, *long* time."

"No!" Scarlett whimpered. She looked up at Vin, her eyes shining with tears. "I'm not crazy. He used to be my boss. He's trying to force me to marry him and give our baby away."

Give our baby away.

The four words cut through Vin's heart like a knife. His whole body became still.

And he knew there was no way he was going to let this man take her.

His voice was ice-cold. "Let her go."

"You think you can make me?"

"Do you know my name?" Vin said quietly.

The man looked at him contemptuously. "I have no…" His voice trailed off, then he sucked in his breath. "Borgia." He exhaled the two syllables through his teeth. Vin saw the fear in the man's eyes. It was a reaction he'd grown accustomed to. "I…I didn't realize…"

Vin glanced at his own bodyguards, who'd entered the cathedral and surrounded the other men with surgical precision, ready to strike. He gave his chief of security a slight shake of his head, telling them to keep their distance. Then he looked at the man holding Scarlett. "Get. Out. Now."

He obeyed, abruptly releasing her. He turned and fled, his two bodyguards swiftly following him out of the cathedral.

Noise suddenly rose on all sides. Scarlett fell with a sob into Vin's arms, against the front of his tuxedo.

And a young man leaped up from a middle pew.

"Anne, I told you! Don't marry him! Who cares if you're disinherited?" Looking around the nave, the stranger proclaimed fiercely and loudly, "I've been sleeping with the bride for the last six months!"

Total chaos broke out then. The father of the bride started yelling, the mother of the bride wept noisily and, faced with such turmoil, the bride quietly and carefully fainted into a puffy heap of white tulle.

But Vin barely noticed. His world had shrunk to two things. Scarlett's tears as she wept in relief against his chest. And the tremble of her pregnant body, cradled beneath the protection of his arms.

CHAPTER TWO

OUT OF THE frying pan, into the fire.

Scarlett had escaped Blaise, but at what price?

For the last hour, she'd tried to calm the fearful beat of her heart as she sat in a faded floral chair next to a window overlooking a private garden. Vin had brought her to the private sitting room in the rectory behind the cathedral and told her to wait while he sorted things out. A kindly old lady—a housekeeper of some sort?—had pushed a hot cup of tea into her trembling hand.

But the tea had grown cold. She set the china cup into the saucer with a clatter.

Scarlett didn't know which scared her more. The memory of Blaise's snarling face. Or the fear of what Vin Borgia might do now to take over her future—and her baby's.

She should run.

She should run now.

Running was the only way to ensure their freedom.

Growing up, Scarlett had lived in over twenty different places, tiny towns hidden in forests and mountains, sometimes in shacks without electricity or running water. She'd rarely been able to go to school, and when she did, she'd had to dye her red hair brown and use a different name. Things that normal kids took for granted, such as having a real home, friends, going to the same school for a whole year, were luxuries Scarlett had only dreamed of. She'd never played sports, or sung in the school choir, or gone to prom. She'd never even gone on a real date.

Until she was twenty-four. The day she'd met Vin Borgia, she'd been weak, emotional, vulnerable. And he'd caught her up like a butterfly in a net.

She looked out the window with its view of the back garden, full of roses and ivy. A secret garden, surrounded by New York skyscrapers. A strangely calm, verdant place that seemed miles from the noisy traffic and honking cabs of Fifth Avenue. Rising to her feet, she started to pace.

A frosty gray afternoon last February, she'd been picking up a medicine prescription for Mrs. Falkner when she received a text from an old Boston friend of her father's with news that had staggered her.

Alan Berry had just died in an inconsequential knife fight in a Southie bar. The man who'd betrayed her father seventeen years before, who'd cut a deal for his own freedom and forced Harry Ravenwood to go on the run with his sick wife and young daughter, had died a meaningless death after a meaningless life. All for nothing.

Standing in the drugstore, Scarlett's knees had gone weak. She'd felt sick.

Five minutes later, she'd found herself at a dive bar across the street, ordering her first drink. The sharp pungent taste had made her cough.

"Let me guess." A low, amused voice had spoken from the red leather banquette in the corner. "It's your first time."

She'd turned. The man came out of the shadows slowly. Black eyes. Dark hair. Powerful broad shoulders. A black suit. Hard edges everywhere. Five-o'clock shadow. He was like a hero—or a handsome villain—from a movie, so masculine and powerful and handsome that he'd affected her even more than the vodka shot.

"I had a…bad day." Her voice trembled.

An ironic smile lifted the corners of his cruel, sensual mouth. "Why else would you be drinking in the afternoon?"

She wiped her eyes with a laugh. "For fun?"

"Fun. That's an idea." The man had come close enough to see her red-rimmed eyes and tear-streaked cheeks in the shadowy dive bar. She'd braced herself for questions, but he just slid onto the bar stool beside her and raised his hand to the bartender. "Let's see if the second shot goes down easier."

In spite of what she knew about him now, Vin Borgia still affected her like that. When Scarlett had seen him standing at the altar with his beautiful bride, all the memories had come back of their night together in February, when he'd taken her back to his elegant, Spartan, wildly expensive penthouse. He'd seduced her easily, claiming her virginity as if he owned it. He'd made her life explode with color and joy.

She'd known Vin's name, since his doorman had greeted him with the utmost respect as "Mr. Borgia." But she'd never told Vin her last name. Some habits were hard to break.

A phone call from Mrs. Falkner's nurse had woken Scarlett when Vin still slept. Only her sense of duty had forced her to wrench herself from the warmth of his bed. She'd returned to the Falkner mansion and handed over the prescription, then dreamily looked up her one and only lover online.

That had woken her up fast. She'd been horrified by what she found.

Vincenzo Borgia was a ruthless airline billionaire who'd risen from nothing and didn't give a damn who got hurt in his pursuit of world domination. She couldn't imagine why a man like that had seduced her, when he usually had liaisons with socialites and supermodels. But she was grateful she hadn't given him her last name. She wouldn't give him the chance to hurt her.

Later, when she'd discovered she was pregnant, she'd

wondered whether she'd made the right decision. But seeing Vin's engagement announcement in the paper had clinched it.

Scarlett had never expected to see Vin again. She'd planned to raise her baby alone.

She wasn't scared to be alone. She'd grown up on the run, and her fugitive father had secretly taught her skills after her mother got too sick to notice. How to pick pockets. How to pick locks. And most of all, how to be invisible and survive on almost nothing.

Compared to what she'd already lived through, raising a child as a single parent would be easy. She wasn't a fugitive. She'd never committed any crimes. She had a marketable skill as a nurse's aide. She'd even saved some money. She no longer had to hide.

Or did she?

Scarlett stopped pacing the thick rug of the cathedral rectory, staring blankly at the faded floral furniture. Did she really want to take the chance that Vin Borgia, the man she'd read such horrible things about, could be a good father? Did she dare take that risk, just because she'd loved her own father so much?

She could see the soft shimmer of dust motes through a beam of fading golden sunlight from the window. She put her hands gently on her belly.

Vin had saved her from Blaise, but rich, powerful men all had one thing in common: they wanted to be in control. And Vin Borgia was richer and more powerful than most.

She should just leave before he returned.

Right now.

Scarlett took a step, then stopped when she remembered her suitcase and handbag were still in Blaise's limo, with her money, ID, credit card, phone. When she'd fled him in terror, those had been the last thing on her mind. But now... How could she run with no money and no passport?

She looked down glumly at her bare toes snuggled into the plush rug. She didn't even have shoes!

"What's your name?"

She whirled to face the door. Vin had entered the room, his jaw like granite as he loosened his tie. Just looking at his hard-muscled body caused a physical reaction in her, made her tremble from the inside out, with a mixture of fear and desire. Even the sleekly tailored tuxedo couldn't give him the look of a man who was entirely civilized. Especially with that hard, almost savage look in his black eyes.

She swallowed. "You know my name. Scarlett."

He glowered at her. "Your *last* name."

"Smith," she tried.

Vin's jaw tightened. Turning away, he picked up a carafe of water sitting on a tray on a nearby table. He poured water into one of the glasses. "Your last name is Ravenwood."

Her lips parted in shock. "How did you—"

Reaching into his jacket pocket, he held up her wallet, his handsome face impassive.

"How did you get that?"

"Falkner sent your purse to me. And your suitcase."

"*Sent?* You mean he dumped them in the street?"

"I mean his bodyguards personally brought them to me, neatly stacked, with his compliments."

Oh, this was so much worse than she'd feared. Scarlett breathed, "The worst man I know is afraid of you?"

He smiled grimly. "It's not unusual." He held her wallet out toward her. "Here. Seventeen dollars cash and a single credit card. With an eight-hundred-dollar limit."

"Hey!" She snatched at it. Her cheeks burned. "How do you know my credit limit?"

Picking up his glass, Vin swirled the clear water thoughtfully. "I wanted to know what I was dealing with.

An orphan who never lived anywhere for long, who came to New York for a thankless live-in job, who saved every penny for two years, who made no new friends, who worked all the time and never went out." He tilted his head, looking at her with heavily lidded black eyes as he murmured, "With one memorable exception."

A flash of heat went through her, then cold. She couldn't think about that night. Not now. "You have some nerve to—"

"The Falkners barely paid minimum wage, but you saved every penny you could. Impressive work ethic, considering your jailbird father—"

"Don't you dare call him that!" she shouted. "My dad was the kindest, best man who ever lived!"

"Are you serious?" Vin's lips curved. "He was a bank robber who became a fugitive and dragged you and your mother into a life on the run. You had no money, barely went to school, and your mother died of an illness that she might perhaps have survived with proper care. What am I missing?"

"Stop judging him," she raged. "My father gave up that life when I was a baby. But a friend of his convinced him to try for one last score. After my mother found out, she gave him an ultimatum. He gave the money back to the bank!"

"Just gave it back, hmm?"

"He left the bags of money outside the police station, then tipped them off with an anonymous call."

"Why didn't he turn himself in?"

"Because he didn't want to leave my mom. Or me." Scarlett took a deep breath. "We would have been fine, except Alan Berry was caught spending his own share of the money six months later and threw my father under the bus as the supposed mastermind of the crime! After he'd tried to do the right thing—"

"The right thing would have been for your father to turn himself in at the start," Vin said mercilessly, "instead of waiting ten years to find the courage, and dragging you and your mother through such a miserable life on the run." He calmly took a sip of water. "The only truly decent thing your father ever did was die in that plane crash after he got out of prison. Giving you that tidy multimillion-dollar settlement offered by the airline."

Scarlett nearly staggered to her knees at his easy reference to the greatest loss of her life, one that still left her grief-stricken every day—her father's sudden death, along with thirty other people, in a plane crash a year and a half before, as he was coming to New York to see her, finally free after five years in a medium-security prison.

Vin looked at her curiously. "You gave all that money away." He tilted his head. "Why?"

She was so shocked, it took her a moment to find her voice. In mere minutes, Vin Borgia had casually ripped through her privacy and exposed all the secrets of her life.

"I didn't want their blood money," she whispered. "I gave it to charity."

"Yes, I know. Cancer research, legal defense for the poor and help for children of incarcerated parents. All fine causes. But I don't understand why you'd choose to be penniless."

"Like you said, maybe I'm used to it. Anyway." She clutched her wallet. "Some things matter more than money."

"Like a baby?" Vin said coldly. He put the glass down with a *thunk* on the wooden table. "You let me seduce you and take your virginity, then snuck out while I slept. You never bothered to contact me. You waited until my wedding to spring the news on me that you were pregnant."

"I had no choice—"

"There were plenty of choices." His jaw tightened. "Tell

me the truth. If Falkner hadn't threatened you today, you never would have told me about the baby, would you?"

She stared at him for a long moment, then shook her head.

"Why?" he demanded.

The warmth from the cathedral garden was failing. Scarlett glanced at the fading afternoon light, now turning gray. She didn't answer.

"You refused to even tell me your last name that night. Why?" he pressed, coming closer. "Was it because you were also encouraging Falkner's attentions?"

"I never did!" She gaped at him. "I knew he wanted me, but I never thought he'd attack me while giving me a ride from his mother's funeral!"

"Ah. That explains the black dress." He looked down at her pale pink toenails. "But why are you barefoot?"

"I kicked off my shoes running on Fifth Avenue. I knew your wedding was here today." She looked down. "I'm sorry I ruined it."

"Yes. Well." His jaw tightened as he said grudgingly, "I suppose I should thank you."

"You didn't know your bride was cheating on you?"

"She convinced me she was a virgin and wanted to wait for marriage."

A laugh rose to her lips. "You thought she was a virgin? In this day and age?"

"Why not?" he said coldly. "You were."

Their eyes met, and Scarlett's body flooded with heat. Against her will, memories filled her of that night, of being in his arms, in his bed, his body hard and hot and slick against hers. She tried to smile. "Yeah, but I'm not normal."

"Agreed." His dark gaze seared hers. "Am I really the father of your baby, Scarlett? Or were you lying just because you needed my help?"

"Of course the baby's yours!"

He bared his teeth into a smile. "I will find out if it's not true."

"You're the only man I've ever slept with, so I'm pretty sure!"

"The only man? Ever?" For a moment, something stretched between them. Then it snapped. "So what do you want from me now? Money?"

She glared at him. "Just point me in the direction of my suitcase and I'll be on my way!"

"You're not going anywhere until this is sorted."

"Look, I'm deeply grateful for your help with Blaise, and sorry if I ruined your big wedding day, but I don't appreciate you digging into my life, then assuming that I'm either a con artist or a gold digger. I'm neither. I just want to raise my baby in peace."

"There will be a DNA test," he warned. "Lawyers."

She looked at him in horror. "Lawyers? What for?"

"So we both know where we stand."

Scarlett felt a *whoosh* of panic that made her unsteady on her feet. Her voice trembled. "You mean you intend to sue me for custody?"

"That will not be necessary." She exhaled in relief, before he finished, "Because once I have proof the baby's mine, Scarlett, you will marry me."

With those words, Vin took control over the spinning chaos of the day.

He'd been wrong about Anne Dumaine. He'd convinced himself she was modest and demure when all the while she'd been cheating on him and lying to his face. To say she'd turned out to be a disappointment was an understatement.

"Sorry," she'd whispered the last time he'd seen her, when she'd pressed the ten-carat engagement ring into his palm. But she hadn't looked sorry as she'd joyfully turned to her lover—a boy of maybe twenty-three, ridiculously shabby in a sweater, and they'd fled the cathedral hand in hand, Anne's wedding veil flying behind her like a white flag.

Leaving Vin to face the annoyed glower of her father.

"If you'd bothered to show my daughter the slightest attention, she wouldn't have fallen for that nobody!"

The merger with Transatlantique was clearly off.

Vin's mistake. He'd never bothered to look beyond Anne's cool blonde exterior into her soul. Truthfully, her soul hadn't interested him. But he should have had his investigators check her more thoroughly. *Trust no one* had been his motto since he was young. Trust no one; control everything.

Scarlett Ravenwood was different. She didn't have the education or pedigree of Anne, her manners were lamentable and she had no dress sense. Her only dowry would be the child she carried inside her.

A baby. His baby. After his own awful childhood, he'd decided long ago that any child of his would always know his father, would have a stable home and feel safe and loved. Vin would never abandon his child. He'd die first.

Standing in the shabby room of the rectory, surrounded by chintzy overstuffed furniture, Vin looked at Scarlett, so vivid with her pale skin and red hair.

The dark sweeping lashes over her green eyes, the color of every spring and summer of his Italian childhood, seemed to tremble. When he'd first seen her in that bar nearly eight months ago, right before Valentine's Day, coughing over her first taste of vodka, it had been like a burst of sun after a long cold night, a sunrise as bright and red as her hair, filling him with warmth—and fire.

His mind moved rapidly. She had no fortune, but perhaps that was an advantage. No father-in-law to scream in his ear. No family to become a burden. She had nothing to offer him but their baby. And her sexy body. And the best lovemaking of his life.

He shivered just remembering that night...

It was, he reflected, not the worst way to begin a marriage. He could make of her what he wanted. She could be the perfect wife, made to his order. She had no money. She was grateful to him for saving her from that imbecile Falkner. He already had complete control.

Now she just had to realize that, as well.

"You want to marry me?" Scarlett repeated, staring at him in shock. "Seriously?"

"Yes." He waited for her to be suitably thrilled. Instead, she burst into laughter.

"Are you crazy? I'm not marrying you!"

"If the baby is mine, it is our only reasonable course of action," he said stiffly.

As if he'd told her the best joke in the world, she shook her head merrily. "You really don't want to lose your wedding deposit, do you?"

"What are you talking about?"

"Am I expected to just put on your last bride's wedding gown, and you'll let the guests know there's been a slight change in the lineup? You'll just change the color of the bride's hair on the cake topper from blond to red, and proceed as planned?"

"You think I'd marry you to avoid losing a little money?" he said incredulously.

"No?" She tilted her head, on a roll now, clearly enjoying herself. "Then what is it? Is marriage just on your schedule, and you need to check it off your to-do list before you pick up your dry cleaning and pay your electric bill?"

"Scarlett, I get the feeling you're not taking this seriously."

"I'm not!" she exploded. "Why on earth would I marry you? I barely know you!"

Vin felt irritated at her irrational response, but he reminded himself that she was pregnant, and therefore to be treated gently. "You've had a trying day," he said in the most soothing voice he could muster. "We should go to my doctor."

"Why?"

"Just to check you're doing fine. And we'll get the paternity test."

"You can't just take my word the baby's yours?"

"You could obviously be lying."

For some reason, she seemed upset by this. She glared at him. "I'm not doing some stupid paternity test, not if it causes risk to the baby "

"The doctor just draws a little blood from your arm and mine. There's no risk to the baby whatsoever."

"How do you know that?"

Vin didn't care to explain the sordid story of the one-night stand who last February had tried to claim her baby was his, even though he'd used a condom and she'd claimed to be on the pill. It had turned out the DNA test was unnecessary as she wasn't pregnant at all. She'd just hoped he would marry her and she'd get quickly pregnant—and he'd be too stupid to do the math. That experience had left him cold.

It was ironic that after confronting that one-night stand over her lies, he'd stopped for a drink in a new bar—and, meeting Scarlett, they'd ended up conceiving a child.

Looking at Scarlett now, he felt his body tighten. She had no right to look so lovely, her riotous red curls tumbling over her shoulders, her eyes so wistful and luminous, her lips so naturally full and pink. Her breasts strained the modest neckline of the simple black dress, and her large baby bump made her even more voluptuous, more sexy.

Pregnant. With his baby.

If it was true, he would devote his life to giving this baby a very different childhood than he'd had. His child would always be safe, and loved. Unlike Vin, his child would always know who his father was.

If her child was even his, he reminded himself. She could be lying. He needed proof. He held out his hand. "Let's go."

With visible reluctance, she put her hand in his. "If I go with you to the doctor, and you get proof you're the father, then what?"

"I'll have my lawyers draw up a prenuptial agreement."

"A pre-nup?" Her voice sounded surprised. "Why?"

He gave a grim smile. "I can hardly marry you without control."

"Control of what?"

"Everything," he said honestly.

He led her through the now empty cathedral, with only rapidly wilting wedding flowers and a few despondent janitors sweeping up. Her voice trembled as she asked, "What specifically would be in the pre-nup?"

"Standard things." He shrugged. "Giving me final say on schooling and religion and where we will live. Things like that. I am based in New York but have homes all over. I am often required to travel while running SkyWorld Airways, sometimes for months at a time. I would not want to be away from my children."

"*Children?* I'm not carrying twins."

"Obviously, our child will need siblings." She made a sound like a squeak, but he ignored her, continuing, "I expect you to travel with me whenever and wherever I wish."

Her forehead furrowed. "But how would I hold down a job?"

"Money will no longer be an issue. As my wife, your only requirement will be to support me. You will be in so-

ciety. You will learn to properly entertain powerful people
to promote my company's best interests. You may need
comportment lessons."

"What?"

"And, of course," he added casually, "in the event we
ever divorce, the pre-nup will simplify that process. It will
clearly spell out what happens if you cheat on me, or either of us decides to separate. You'll know what amount
of money you'll be entitled to based on years—"

"Of service?"

He smiled blandly. "Of marriage, I was going to say.
Naturally, I would automatically gain full custody of our
children."

"What?!"

"Don't worry. You would still be allowed to visit them."

"Big of you," she murmured. As they walked down the
cathedral steps to his waiting car, his bodyguards waiting
beside the large SUV behind it, Scarlett abruptly stopped.

"Before we go to your doctor and have the paternity
test, could you do me a favor?" She smiled prettily, showing a dimple in her left cheek, then waved helplessly at her
bare feet on the sidewalk. "Could we stop at a shoe store?"

Like Cinderella, Vin thought. He was surprised how
well she was taking everything. The way she was looking at him so helplessly, so prettily. She would be easy to
mold and shape into the perfect wife.

"Of course," he said almost tenderly. "I'm sorry. I
should have thought of that before." Picking her up in his
arms, he carried her. In spite of being heavily pregnant,
she seemed to weigh nothing at all. He gently set her into
the waiting car, still bedecked with flowers.

The driver's eyes were popping out of his head to see
Vin had left the church carrying a redhead, when he'd
gone in to marry a blonde. But he wisely said nothing and
just started the car.

Vin climbed into the backseat beside her. "Any preference about the shoe store?"

He expected her to name a designer store, the sorts of luxury brands that Anne had constantly yammered about, but here again Scarlett surprised him.

"Any shoes good to run in," she said demurely, her black eyelashes fluttering against her pale cheeks.

"You heard her," he told his driver.

Ten minutes later, Scarlett was trying on running shoes at an enormous athletic store on Fifty-Seventh Street. She chose her favorite pair of running shoes, along with a pair of socks, exclaiming at Vin's generosity all the while.

"Thank you," she whispered, suddenly giving him a hug. For a moment, he closed his eyes. He could smell the peppermint of her breath and breathed in the cherry blossom scent of her hair. Then she abruptly pulled back. Staring up at him wide-eyed, she bit her lip. Vin could imagine the sensual caress of those full, plump lips.

Then she smiled, and her eyes crinkled. "I'll wear the shoes starting now. Excuse me."

Vin watched her walk toward the ladies' restroom, past the displays of expensive athletic shoes and equipment. His eyes lingered appreciatively over the curve of her backside, the sway of her hips. Scarlett made even a plain black funeral dress look good.

What a wife she would make. And as for the honeymoon…he shuddered.

Determined to hurry them into the car, he turned toward the cashier. Normally his assistant would have dealt with such mundane details, but he'd left Ernest at the cathedral to handle the logistical problems of the ruined wedding—returning mailed gifts, organizing early rides to the airport for disgruntled guests, donating the expensively catered reception dinner to a local homeless shelter. So Vin himself went to pay for the shoes.

There would soon be lots of other purchases, he thought. Baby booties. A crib. A nursery. He'd have his houses baby-proofed. He'd hire a larger staff. He would buy a few more family-sized SUVs to add to his personal fleet of expensive cars. Small tasks that would distract him from building his empire, but it would be worth it to finally have a family of his own.

He'd be the parent he himself had never had. His child would never know what it felt like to be abandoned. To be used. To be neglected and alone.

Reaching into his tuxedo jacket, Vin felt for his wallet. Frowning, he looked in his pockets. Empty. Had he left it in the car, or back at the cathedral? Scowling, he motioned for one of his bodyguards to pay and told the other one to track down the wallet. Sitting down at a nearby bench, Vin called his doctor to arrange for an immediate appointment. Then he tapped his feet.

Scarlett was taking a long time.

"Go check on her," he ordered his bodyguard impatiently.

Vin paced. Checked his phone again. Stopped.

Suspicion dawned.

She couldn't. She wouldn't.

She had.

"Miss Ravenwood is nowhere to be found, boss," Larson said when he returned. "I had the bathroom checked. Empty." He hesitated. "There is a door beside it that leads to a storeroom, then out to the alley."

With a low curse, Vin strode through the sporting goods store, his two bodyguards behind him. In the back, near the ladies' restroom, he found the storeroom. Store employees shrank back at his glare as he threw open the back door with an angry bang.

Outside was an alley with graffiti-littered brick walls. Vin walked slowly past the Dumpsters to the end: busy

Madison Avenue, crowded with people and cars packed bumper to bumper. He stared around him in shock.

Scarlett Ravenwood had not only walked out on him, she'd most likely stolen his wallet. Not only that, she'd warned him first! "Shoes good to run in" indeed!

Clawing his hand back through his dark hair, he gave a single, incredulous laugh. He'd been ditched twice in one day. Lied to by two different women.

Anne's loss he could accept. That had involved only money.

Scarlett was different. He'd never stopped desiring her. And now she was carrying his baby.

Or was she? Perhaps she'd lied. He rubbed his forehead. Why would any woman run away when he'd asked her to marry him and live in luxury for the rest of her life? Unless she was afraid of the paternity test. That was the only rational explanation: the baby wasn't his. The thought caused a sick twist in his gut.

Then he remembered the angry gleam in Scarlett's green eyes.

I don't appreciate you digging into my life, then assuming that I'm either a con artist or a gold digger. I'm neither. I just want to raise my baby in peace.

Standing motionless as pedestrians rushed by him on Madison Avenue, Vin narrowed his eyes.

Either way, he had to know.

Either way, he'd find her.

And this time, she wouldn't trick him so easily. Nothing would stop him from getting what he wanted. He wouldn't listen to her excuses. Next time, he'd bend her to his will.

Barefoot, if necessary.

CHAPTER THREE

THERE WAS ONLY one thing that mattered in life, Scarlett's father had always told her as a child. Freedom.

Freedom. It was Harry Ravenwood's rallying cry every time their family had to flee in the night, tossing their belongings into black trash bags and heading blindly to a new city. At seven years old, when Scarlett accidentally left her teddy bear—her only friend—behind, she'd cried until her father comforted her with stories of Mr. Teddy backpacking around the world, climbing the Pyramids and the Pyrenees. His funny stories of her bear's adventures finally made her smile through her tears. On cold winter nights in Upstate New York, as their family shivered in unheated rooms and icy wind rattled the windows, Harry sang jaunty songs about freedom.

Freedom. Even on the bleak night when Scarlett was twelve, when her mother died in the emergency room of a hospital in a faded factory town in Pennsylvania, her father kissed Scarlett as tears streamed down his weathered face. "At least now your beautiful mother is free of pain."

Scarlett had her freedom now. From Blaise Falkner. From Vin Borgia. She and her unborn baby were free.

But it had come at a cost.

To start with, her flight two weeks ago, from Boston to London, had had a little trouble over the Atlantic.

A small fire in the cargo hold caused the plane to divert to a small airport on the west coast of Ireland. As the plane descended, she saw dark clusters of birds through her porthole window, flying rapidly past the plane. "Bird strike!" a passenger cried out, and as one flight attendant rushed toward the cockpit, another tried to murmur reassuring, unconvincing words to the passengers. Wide-eyed, Scarlett gripped her armrests as she felt the plane ominously vibrate and groan in midair.

All she'd been able to think was, she shouldn't be on this plane. Pregnant women weren't supposed to fly after their seventh month. She was nearly at eight. She'd fled from New York, with a quick stop in Boston, because she thought it was her only way to escape Vin. But now that danger seemed small when she and her child were both going to die. Just like her own father had died in that wintry plane crash a year and a half ago. *She never should have gotten on a plane.*

"Prepare for crash landing," came the pilot's terse voice over the intercom. "Brace for impact." The flight attendants repeated the words as the nose of the plane started to plummet and they rushed to buckle themselves in. "Heads down! Brace for impact! Stay down!"

Scarlett had braced herself, hugging her belly, thinking, *please don't let my baby die.*

Like a miracle, the plane had finally steadied on one engine and limped hard, landing with a heavy bang on the edge of the runway. No one was hurt, and passengers and crew alike cheered and cried and hugged each other.

Sliding off the plane on the inflatable yellow slide, Scarlett had fallen to her knees on the tarmac and burst into noisy, ugly sobs.

She never should have gotten on a plane. Any plane. After her father's death, she should have known better.

But just like when she'd accepted that limo ride from Blaise Falkner, she'd ignored her intuition and convinced herself that her fears were silly. And both she and her baby had nearly died as a result.

She'd never ignore her intuition again. From now on,

she'd listen seriously to her fears, even when they didn't make rational sense.

And above all: she would never, ever get on any plane again.

But why would Scarlett need to? She had no family in New York. No reason to ever go back. Vin Borgia had done her a huge favor, warning her in advance that he intended to rule her life and their child's with an iron fist and separate her from her baby if she ever objected or tried to leave him. She didn't feel guilty about leaving him, not at all.

She did feel guilty about stealing his wallet. Stealing was never all right, and her mother must be turning over in her grave. Scarlett told herself she'd had no choice. She'd had to cover her tracks. Vin was not only a ruthless billionaire, he owned an airline and had ridiculous connections. If she'd stepped one toe on a flight under her own name, he would have known about it.

So she'd contacted one of her father's old acquaintances in Boston to buy a fake passport. That cost money.

So she'd taken—borrowed—the money from Vin. She hadn't touched anything else in his wallet. Not his driver's license, or his credit cards, most of them in special strange colors that no doubt had eye-popping credit limits. And after she'd arrived safely in Switzerland via ferry and train from Ireland, and gotten her first paycheck at her new job, she'd mailed back Vin's wallet, returning everything as he'd left it. She'd even tossed in some extra euros as interest on the money she'd borrowed.

She'd gotten the euros from northern Italy, where she'd gone to mail back the package. She could hardly have sent Vin money in Swiss francs, letting him know where she was!

But that was all behind her now. She'd paid everything back. She and her baby were free.

Scarlett took a deep breath of the clear Alpine air. She'd been in Gstaad for over two weeks now, and finally, *finally* she was starting to relax. She just had to hope when Vin couldn't easily find her, he would forget about her and the baby, and she'd never have to worry about him again.

Scarlett passed out of the gates of the chalet, if the place could be called a chalet when it was the size of a palace, and turned her face up toward the sun.

It was mid-October, and the morning air was already frosty in the mountains around the elegant Swiss ski resort of Gstaad. The first snowfall was expected daily.

She had her own event to expect soon, too. Her hand moved over her belly, grown so large she could no longer button up her oversize jacket. Only two and a half weeks from her due date. Her body felt heavier, slower. But luckily her new job allowed plenty of opportunity for gentle morning walks.

She'd been lucky to get this job. When she'd fled the shoe store in New York, racing down the alley to hail a cab on Madison Avenue, she'd already decided exactly where to go. Her mother's best friend, Wilhelmina Stone, worked as housekeeper to a wealthy European tycoon in Switzerland. Though Scarlett hadn't seen her since her mother's funeral, she'd never forgotten the woman's hug and fierce words, "Your mother was my best friend. If you ever need anything, you come straight to me, you hear?"

Since then, she'd gotten only an occasional Christmas card. But when Scarlett had shown up uninvited and shivering at the gate of the enormous villa outside Gstaad, the plump, kindly woman had proved good as her word.

"My boss just asked me to hire a good cook for ski season. The best Southern cook in the US, he said. Can you make grits and fried chicken? Jambalaya? Dirty rice?"

Eyes wide, Scarlett shook her head. Wilhelmina sighed. "All right, he usually starts coming here in early December, after the season starts. So you've got six weeks, maybe more, to learn how to make amazing fried chicken and all the rest. I'll put you on staff payroll now. Just make sure you learn to cook for groups of ten or more, because Mr. Black always brings friends!"

For the last two weeks, Scarlett had been trying to teach herself to cook, using cookbooks and internet videos. She was still pretty bad. The security guard routinely teased her that even his dog wouldn't eat what she cooked. It was sadly true.

But she would learn. Being a specialty chef for a hard-traveling, hard-partying tycoon who was rarely around was the perfect job for any single mother with a newborn. She would be able to take a week or two off to heal after the birth, then work with her baby nearby, almost as if this were her own home.

Plus, Switzerland was the perfect place to raise a baby. Scarlett tucked her hands in her jacket pockets as she walked along the slender road. Gravel crunched beneath her soft boots as she took a deep breath of crisp mountain air smelling of sunlight and pine trees. For a brief moment, she closed her eyes, turning her face to the sun. Her heart was full of gratitude.

Then she heard a snap in the forest ahead of her.

She opened her eyes, and the smile dropped from her face.

"Scarlett," Vin greeted her coldly.

He stood ahead of her, wearing a long black coat, a sleek dark suit and a glower. She saw a sleek sports car and a black SUV parked on the road behind him. Three bodyguards lined the vehicle, an impenetrable wall of money and power.

She stumbled back from him. He was on her in seconds, grabbing her wrist.

"Don't touch me!" she cried.

His grip tightened, his eyes like black fire. "You stole from me."

"I paid all your money back—with interest!" She glanced back desperately toward the guarded gate, but it was too far. Johan would never see her. And how could one security guard take on Vin Borgia and at least three of his men?

"I wasn't just talking about the money."

She put her free hand protectively over her belly. "You're not my baby's father. I—I lied!"

"I think you're lying now."

Scarlett tried to pull her wrist from his grip. "Leave me alone!"

"I do not understand your behavior." He wrenched her closer. "Most women would find it fortunate to be pregnant by a billionaire."

"A billionaire who destroys people?" She shook her head. "You don't just take companies—you ruthlessly crush and annihilate your rivals. Their marriages, their families, their very lives!"

Silence fell in the Swiss forest. The only sound was the call of birds.

Then he spoke, his voice low and flat. "So you did some digging on the internet, did you?"

"Why do you think I never tried to contact you after our night together?" She took a deep breath. "I had a good reason to leave you that first morning. A nurse called and I was needed at the Falkner mansion. I hoped to see you again. Until I looked you up online." She glared at him. "If you think I'm going to let my precious baby be raised by a man who takes pleasure in other people's pain—"

His lip twisted contemptuously. "If you think I'm such a bastard, why did you ask for my help?"

"I was terrified of Blaise."

"And now you're terrified of me?"

"After I interrupted your wedding, I thought maybe I should give you a chance. My own father wasn't perfect, but I loved him." She narrowed her eyes. "Then you made your intentions clear."

"What are you talking about? My intention to take responsibility, marry you and be a good father?"

"If I honestly believed we could be a family, and love and trust each other, I'd marry you in a second. But I'd rather raise my baby alone than with a man who might hurt me!"

"Hurt you?" he said incredulously. "I've never hurt a woman in my life!"

"With your cold heart? I bet you've hurt plenty."

He relaxed. "Oh. You mean *emotionally*."

"Yes, emotionally," she retorted. "You don't think that counts?"

"Not really, no."

"And that's why I don't want to marry you."

He abruptly released her wrist, his eyes strangely alight. "I've never killed anyone, no matter what the rumors say. I never poisoned someone or sabotaged an engine. Nor did I hire someone else to do it. A reporter just happened to notice that during some points in my business career, some men have coincidentally had problems."

"You expect me to believe that? It was pure coincidence?"

"It's the truth. A man was discovered in an affair while doing business with me. It was hardly my fault his wife took offense and dumped poison in his morning whiskey. Another man had a heart attack from stress during my hostile takeover. He could have walked away at any time but chose to fight and take the risk. Another man chose to start a feud with his sister when she sold her shares to me. Their family was ripped apart, yes—but again, not my fault."

"Then why was Blaise so afraid of you? And you expected him to be!"

"I know the rumors about me. They're not true, but people believe them. I'd be a fool not to take advantage of it."

"And you're no fool."

"No." His jaw tightened. "So I don't appreciate that you've made me look like one. Twice."

She turned her head back again toward the distant gate of the chalet. She wished she could run. But she'd become so heavily pregnant and slow—

"I want a paternity test," Vin said coldly. "You have an appointment today with a doctor in Geneva."

"I've got my own doctor in the village, thank you."

"Dr. Schauss has a world-renowned clinic. She was obstetrician to a princess of Sweden and has delivered half the babies of the royal houses of the Persian Gulf. She's well qualified."

"I'm not gallivanting off to Geneva just because you want some extra-fancy doctor."

"The choice isn't yours to make."

"And if I refuse?"

Vin's eyes flickered. "I am acquainted with Kassius Black, the owner of this chalet." He looked up at the imposing roofline over the trees. "What would he say if I told him that your friend, his trusted housekeeper, had knowingly hired a fugitive and thief to live here, and you were both conspiring to steal from his houseguests this coming ski season?"

"You wouldn't," she gasped. "It's not true!"

He shrugged. "You are a proven thief and liar. It *could* be true. But the point is, are you willing to repay your friend's kindness in giving you a job by causing her to lose hers?"

"You are despicable."

His face hardened. "No, *cara*. You are despicable. I

have done nothing but seek to fulfill my responsibility. I am trying to do the right thing, the honorable thing. It is you who are the thief."

"I repaid every penny!"

"Yes, with interest. At an annualized interest rate of thirty percent. The money you repaid yielded a better return than many of my other investments. So it was profitable." He gave a slight, ironic bow. "Thank you for stealing my wallet."

"Oh?" she said hopefully. "So you're not—"

"Stealing my child is something else."

Scarlett's brief hope faded. What could she do? She couldn't let Wilhelmina be hurt for her loyalty and kindness.

The clinic in Geneva. That could be her escape route. Clinics had back doors. She could sneak out before her blood was even drawn.

Scarlett let her shoulders sag, scuffling her feet in the gravel, hoping she looked suitably downhearted. Her heart was beating fast. "You win."

"I always do." He gave a quick motion to the bodyguards waiting outside the black SUV with dark tinted windows, then turned back, his voice brisk. "The trip to Geneva will take two hours by car, and in your state of advanced pregnancy I am concerned this will be uncomfortable for you. I can have a helicopter here in ten minutes—"

"No!" she said a little too quickly. At his frown, she said in a calmer voice, trying to smile, "The drive will give us a chance to talk. It's so beautiful around Lake Geneva this time of year."

He stared at her for a long moment, then shrugged. "As you wish."

Five minutes later, as a bodyguard went upstairs to pack up her meager possessions, she went to the kitchen to say farewell to Wilhelmina. The older woman seemed bewildered by the sudden turn in events.

"You're quitting your job, Scarlett? Just like that?"

"I'm sorry, Wilhelmina. You came through for me, and I'm leaving you in the lurch. I'm so sorry—"

"For me it's fine. Honestly, your fried chicken still is something awful. Mr. Black would have thought I lost my mind, hiring you. You're the one I'm worried about." She looked doubtfully at Vin. "So this man is the father of your baby, but do you really want to go with him?" Her eyes narrowed in her plump face. "Or is he forcing you?"

The suspicion in the older woman's face was less than flattering to Vin, but as she was a housekeeper to Kassius Black, a man whose reputation for ferocity was even worse than his own, he could understand her lack of automatic admiration for the average billionaire. The housekeeper, like Scarlett, had obviously had enough experience with the wealthy to know the ugliness that could lie behind the glamorous lifestyle.

"I will take good care of Scarlett and her baby," he told her gravely. "I promise you."

The housekeeper stared at him, then her scowl slowly disappeared. "I believe you."

"Good." Vin gave her his most charming smile. "We intend to marry soon."

She looked accusingly at Scarlett. "You're engaged?"

Scarlett looked a little dazed. "We haven't decided anything for sure…"

"Mrs. Stone," Vin interrupted, "I appreciate your loyalty and kindness to Scarlett. Should you ever want to switch jobs, please let us know."

Handing her a card, he took Scarlett by the hand and led her out of the chalet as the bodyguards followed with her shockingly small amount of luggage: a purse and a single duffel bag. He watched as they packed it into the back of the glossy SUV. An unwelcome image floated through Vin's mind of his own meager belongings when he'd left Italy at fifteen, after his mother's devastating revelation and death, to go live in New York with an uncle he barely knew. He'd felt so alone. So hollow.

He pushed the memory away angrily. He wasn't that boy anymore. He would never feel so vulnerable again and neither would any child of his.

Vin opened the passenger door of the red sports car, then turned to Scarlett coldly. "Get in."

"You're driving us? Yourself?"

"The bodyguards will follow in the SUV. Like you said—" he gave a hard smile "—it's a beautiful day for a drive."

Once they were buckled in, he stepped on the gas, driving swiftly out of the gate and down the mountain, to the paved road that led through the expensive village of Gstaad, with its charming Alpine architecture, exclusive designer boutiques and chalets with shutters and flower boxes. The midmorning sun glowed in the blue sky above craggy forested mountains as they looped onto the Gstaadstrasse, heading west.

Vin glanced at Scarlett out of the corner of his eye. She was dressed very casually, an unbuttoned jacket over an oversize shirt, loose khaki pants and fur-lined booties. But for all that, his eyes hungrily drank in the sight of her. Her flame-red hair fell in thick curls down her shoulders. Her lustrous eyes were green as an Alpine forest. He could remember how it had felt to have those full, pink lips move against his skin, gasping in ecstasy…

He shuddered.

Why did Scarlett have such power over him?

For the last two weeks, since she'd left him standing on Madison Avenue with a stunned look on his face, he'd thought of nothing else. All of his considerable resources had been dedicated to one task: finding her.

She was in his blood. He hadn't been able to forget her. Not from the first moment he'd seen her in that bar. From the moment he'd first taken her in his arms. From the moment she'd disappeared from his bed after the best sex of his life.

From the moment she'd violently crashed his wedding and told him she was pregnant with his baby.

Scarlett Ravenwood was half angel, half demon. There was a reason he hadn't seduced any other woman for over eight months—an eternity for a man like Vin. He'd been haunted by Scarlett, haunted body and soul, driven half mad by memories of her naked in his arms.

Scarlett was the woman for him. The one he wanted. And he intended to have her.

"How did you find me in Switzerland?" she asked him quietly now.

Lifting his eyebrow, Vin focused on the road ahead. "It was a mistake for you to mail my wallet from a small Italian village. I still have connections in that country. It was easy to track down the *postino* who'd helped you. He remembered seeing your car with Swiss plates."

"He noticed my car?"

He smiled grimly. "There are surprisingly few Swiss registrations of a 1970 Plymouth Hemi Cuda convertible in pale green. The *postino* kissed his lips when he described it. *'Bella macchina.'* He remembered you, too, a pregnant redheaded woman, very beautiful but a tragic driver. He thought the car deserved better."

"I chose that car from the chalet's garage because I thought it was the oldest," she said, sounding dazed, "so figured it was the cheapest."

"They're rare and often sell for two or three million dollars."

"Oh," she said faintly. "So if I'd taken the brand-new sedan…"

"I wouldn't have found you." Gripping the steering wheel, he looked at her. "You keep wondering if I'm trustworthy. I could wonder the same about you, except I've seen the answer. You've lied to my face, stolen my wallet. Kidnapped my child—"

"Kidnapped!"

"What else would you call it?" He looked at her. "How do I know our baby will be safe with you? The criminally minded daughter of a felon?"

"Felon!" Fury filled her green eyes. "My father never should have gone to prison. If his accomplice hadn't betrayed him—"

"Spare me the excuses," Vin said, sounding bored. "He was a bank robber."

"He returned all the money. Can you say the same?"

"What are you talking about?"

"I'm talking about you and Blaise Falkner and every other billionaire—you are the real ones who should be…"

She abruptly cut herself off.

"Go on," Vin said evenly. "You were about to accuse me of something?"

Scarlett looked him straight in the eye. "Every rich man I've ever known was heartless. My dad in his worst year was less a thief than all the corporate embezzlers and Wall Street gamblers with their Ponzi schemes, wiping out people's pension funds, their savings, their hope!"

"You're comparing me to them?"

"You wouldn't sacrifice one of your platinum cuff links—" she glanced contemptuously at his wrist "—let alone risk your life or happiness, to save someone else."

"You don't know that."

"Don't I?" She lifted her chin. Through the car window he could see the gray-and-blue shimmer of Lake Geneva behind her. "You told me yourself. You don't think twice about causing emotional pain. I bet you've never loved anyone in your life. And you asked me to marry you!"

"Love isn't necessary."

"That's a screwed-up way of looking at things. That's like saying there's no point in eating things that taste good. Marriage without love, isn't that like eating gruel for the rest of your life? Why eat gruel when you can eat cake?"

"Cake is an illusion. It all turns out to be gruel in the end."

"That's the saddest thing I ever heard." She shook her head. "I feel bad for you. A billionaire who's content to eat gruel for the rest of his life."

Vin could hardly believe this penniless girl who had nothing and had once stolen his wallet actually felt sorry for him. "Better a hard truth than the sweet comfort of lies."

"No, it's worse than that. You're a cynic who claims not to believe in the existence of love." She looked up at him through dark eyelashes. "Some woman must have hurt you pretty badly."

Yes. One woman had. But it wasn't what Scarlett thought. "Then she did me a favor. Taught me the truth about life."

"Taught you wrong." She rubbed her belly, looking out the window as they drove closer to Geneva.

"Right or wrong, once the paternity test proves I'm your baby's father, we will be celebrating our marriage."

She tossed him a glance. "No, thanks. I'm no fan of gruel."

Vin ground his teeth. "Are you trying to tell me your childish, foolish dreams of love are more important than our child's welfare? A baby deserves two parents. A stable home."

Her expression changed. "Don't you think I know that?

All I ever wanted my whole childhood was to have a real home. I don't even know what it feels like to make roots, have friends, be part of a community." Her voice cracked. "But you know what? We were still happy, even on the run. Because my parents loved each other. And they loved me."

He didn't know what that felt like, Vin thought unwillingly. He'd grown up in a derelict villa in Rome, neglected and ignored by a mother who was only interested in her love affairs. Her son was valuable for one reason only: to extort money from his father.

His *so called* father.

Vin's shoulders tightened.

Anyone he loved, he lost. His mother had coldly used him as a bargaining chip to finance her lifestyle, before she violently died. Paid nannies left or were fired. His kindly grandfather had had a stroke when Vin was eight. He'd become estranged from his loving father and stepmother at fifteen. Sometimes he felt like he'd been alone his whole life. As alone as that Christmas Eve, when he was only eight and was left utterly alone in the villa, forgotten in the dark—

He shook the memory away. His own child's life would be very different. And he'd make sure his child's mother was either a loving, stable, nurturing influence—or no influence at all.

"Why did you run away from New York?" he demanded. "Because you decided to believe everything you'd read about me?"

"Are you kidding?" Scarlett looked at him in amazement. "That pre-nup."

Gripping the steering wheel, he glanced at her in surprise. "You wanted to avoid the pre-nup?"

"Did you really think I would sign papers to give you total power over not just me, but our child? Did you think

I'd be so happy to become your trophy wife, I'd trade away my freedom for the rest of my life?"

"The pre-nup has been vetted by my lawyers to be completely fair..."

"Completely fair." For the first time since he'd known her, he heard a cynical note in her voice. "When you would get to make every decision about our lives? And if we ever decided to divorce for any reason, you would automatically get full custody of our baby?"

"Divorce is not my plan," he said sharply. "But I know I could not prevent you from leaving, if you wished it. Whatever you might think, there are no dungeons in my penthouse. The prenuptial agreement is merely a tool to minimize the impact of all your potentially bad decisions on our innocent children."

"*My* bad decisions?" She shook her head almost sadly. "And that's just the stuff in the pre-nup you told me about. Who knows what would have been buried in the fine print, a requirement that I give you five blow jobs a week?"

It was a crude comment, said matter-of-factly. There was nothing sensual or suggestive about her tone. If anything, she meant to insult him, to drive him away.

But his body's reaction was instantaneous. He turned from coldly furious to burning hot in a second, blood rushing to his groin as images went through his mind of that full rose-red mouth, hot and wet, around his hardened length... He tried to clear his head of the erotic image as he shifted uncomfortably in the leather seat of the car.

"That was not my intention." Although it sure as hell was now. Vin wondered what his lawyer's expression would be if he told him to add a blow job requirement.

Scarlett continued stubbornly, "You accuse me of being childish and foolish. But in refusing to marry you, I'm protecting our baby."

"How can you say that?" As they drove through the

outskirts of Geneva, he stopped at a red light. "I can offer both you and the baby a lifestyle you could never dream of. Six houses around the world, private schools, jewels, cars. Private jets…"

She shuddered at his mention of the jets. It seemed strange to him.

"I'm protecting our baby from a man who would only want to control us," she said softly. "Not love us."

That brought Vin up short.

As they arrived at the clinic, a modern building with clean lines on the edge of the lake, he pushed his thoughts aside. Parking the car, with the dark SUV parking nearby, he got out and opened Scarlett's door. He extended his hand to assist his very pregnant future bride.

With visible reluctance, she placed her hand in his.

Vin felt an electric jolt from the contact. As they walked together toward the front door of the clinic, he wouldn't—couldn't—let her hand go. He stopped, lifting it to his lips, and gently kissed the back of her hand. Her skin was soft. He felt her tremble.

"You could never love anyone." Her voice trembled. "Because you'll never trust anyone. Just the fact you're making me take this test…"

"I believe you, Scarlett," he said softly. "I'm only insisting on a paternity test because I've been lied to about it before."

"What?"

"A woman once claimed I was the father of her nonexistent baby, trying to get me to marry her. But this time, in my heart, I already know the truth. You're carrying my baby."

"Vin…"

Reaching out, he tucked a tendril of her red hair behind her ear. Her green eyes were wide.

"I like it when you look at me like that," he murmured.

"You are so beautiful, *cara*. Your eyes are such a deep emerald. Like a forest." He gently stroked the side of her face. "Your lips," he whispered, "are red and plump and ripe as fruit. I'll never forget—" he ran the tip of his finger along the full length of her bottom lip "—how it felt to taste them…"

Her tremble became violent. She looked so vulnerable, so stricken, so caught—she, who could have had any man she wanted with her beauty! Vin realized that he, too, was shaking.

His blood was pounding with the need to take her.

Then he remembered the bodyguards watching from the parking lot, the appointment at the clinic looming overhead.

Soon, he vowed to himself. Soon, he would satiate himself with her completely.

"You're right about one thing." He cupped her cheek. "I don't believe in love. At least not the romantic kind. But I do believe," he whispered, "in desire. I never stopped wanting you. From the moment we first met."

"But you were going to marry another…"

"Because I thought you were lost to me. I thought I couldn't have you. Now… I know I will." Vin ran the pads of his fingertips lightly along the edge of her jawline, to her earlobes, to the tumbling red waves of her hair. "I will have you, Scarlett," he growled. "At any price."

CHAPTER FOUR

"THERE CAN BE no doubt, Mr. Borgia. The baby is yours."

The Swiss doctor beamed at them. She was obviously pleased to be giving them good news.

Scarlett saw a flash of emotions cross Vin's hard, handsome features—pride, relief, joy and then, as he looked at her, anger. He hadn't forgiven her for running away.

Just you wait, Scarlett thought, giving him a bland smile.

But she'd thought she'd escape before this. Certainly before they drew the blood that they'd already tested in their in-house, state-of-the-art medical lab. She'd never intended for Vin to have the actual proof he was the father of her baby, proof he could use against her in courts of law.

But he'd never given her the opportunity. From the moment they'd arrived at the medical clinic, to the hour they'd spent waiting for the results, having lunch at a nearby elegant restaurant on the lake, Vin had never let Scarlett out of his sight. Even when she'd excused herself to use the restroom, he'd waited outside in the hallway, in an apparently courteous gesture. When she needed to get her handbag from the car, he'd insisted on sending a bodyguard to collect it.

Over lunch at the Michelin-starred restaurant, as he'd enjoyed lamb and asparagus in a delicate truffle sauce and a glass of wine, he'd expounded on what he would expect of her as his wife, each detail more outrageous than the last. He expected to dictate everything in her life, from the friends she kept to the clothes she wore!

She'd tried her best to lull his suspicions, listening meekly as she ate her lunch and sipped sparkling water. But inside, she was fuming.

Vin was so sure he'd won. He thought he could bully her into giving all her rights away—being nothing more than his indentured servant, the wife he could dominate, holding power over her future and their child's! He was as bad as Blaise!

What century do you think we're living in?

The century a rich man can do whatever he wants. To whomever he wants.

Actually, Vin was more dangerous. Because from the moment she'd met him, when he'd taken her in his arms and made her feel things she'd never felt before, pleasure and joy beyond imagining, he'd made her want to surrender to his demands. And he could do it again, if she let him.

I will have you, Scarlett. At any price.

She shivered as she remembered the hunger in his black eyes. The same hunger she felt for him.

But the price was too high. She couldn't allow herself to surrender, not when it would cost her everything!

"Do you want to know the baby's sex?" Dr. Schauss asked now in slightly accented English.

Vin's eyes were wide as he looked at Scarlett. He cleared his throat and said in an unsteady voice, "Sure."

The doctor smiled. "You're having a boy!"

A boy? Scarlett's eyes filled with tears. In just a few weeks, a sweet baby boy would be in her arms!

"A boy?" Vin's face lit up, and he looked at Scarlett. His usual hard, cynical expression fell away and he looked suddenly young and joyful. Then he turned back to the doctor. "And the pregnancy? Is Scarlett well?"

If she'd loved him, or even trusted him, she might have been touched by the anxiety in his deep voice.

The doctor nodded. "Mademoiselle Ravenwood is doing well. Her blood pressure is fine and in spite of being so close to her due date, she shows no signs of imminent labor. Though that can quickly change, of course..."

"Then we have time to be married." His expression hardened as he turned to Scarlett. "My lawyer in New York has sent the prenuptial agreement. As soon as we leave here, you will sign it, and we will marry."

Scarlett's heart fell all the way to her fur-lined boots. "I..."

Holding up his hand, he pressed his phone to his ear. "Ernest, find out where we can be married quickly. Yes, I know it's more complicated in Europe. Tonight if possible, tomorrow at the latest."

Staring at him, Scarlett instantly saw her mistake.

My God, she was stupid. She never should have let him get the legal proof that he was the father of her child. She should have screamed bloody murder rather than willingly give blood for the paternity test. Running away would be ten times harder now. He'd never give up looking for her. And he'd have the law on his side.

She rose unsteadily to her feet. "Thank you for the news, Doctor." Her teeth were chattering as she glanced at Vin, who had turned away to bark questions to his assistant, about places like Gibraltar and Denmark and even, heaven help her, Las Vegas. In another moment, he'd be arranging the plane, then he'd be back to giving her his full attention. She had only seconds.

Adrenaline pumped her heart. It was now or never.

"Mademoiselle Ravenwood—" the Swiss doctor looked at her with concern in her kindly bespectacled eyes "—are you quite all right?"

"Fine, I'm great." She forced a smile. "I just need to go to the ladies' room. If you'll excuse me."

"Of course—"

Scarlett swiftly exited the brightly lit exam room. She saw Vin's eyes look up piercingly as she closed the door.

She fled down the hall, past other beaming couples holding ultrasound photos and smiling nurses and doctors in white coats. She ran down multiple hallways, looking desperately for the back exit, since she knew that Vin's bodyguards were waiting at the front entrance of the clinic.

She found the back staircase and raced down it, one hand over her heavy belly as she scrambled to think of a coherent escape plan. She'd go back to Gstaad and beg Wilhelmina to use her influence with her boss—Kassius Black—to hide her. If that failed, she'd borrow money and hop a train for somewhere Vin had no connections at all. She scrambled to think how far she'd have to go. Samarkand? Ulaanbaatar? Vladivostok?

Scarlett burst out of the steel-framed door to the sunlight and fresh air of the wide lawn behind the clinic. She saw the shining gleam of the lake, saw a local bus approaching on a distant road. She started to run across the grass—

Then came to a screeching halt.

Vin was on the grassy hill beside the clinic, his arms folded. "Going somewhere?"

Out of earshot but watching the exchange with interest, she saw his bodyguards. Her lips parted, but she couldn't find her voice. Couldn't find a single word of explanation or excuse as he came forward, his handsome, implacable face set in stone.

She stammered, "How did you—"

"I expected you to run."

"But I didn't argue with you at all!" she gasped. "I didn't even criticize the obnoxious things you said at lunch!"

"That's how I knew." His voice was almost amused.

"The fiery woman I know would never let such a thing pass."

"It was a test?" Her voice squeaked in outrage.

He shrugged. "You seemed like you were willing to come quietly for the paternity test. I was glad to let it ride. But of course I knew." He put his hands in his pockets, looking more devastatingly handsome than ever in his tailored dark suit and long black coat. He tilted his head curiously. "Actually, I'm a little disappointed in you, trying the same trick twice. I'd like to think you had a little more respect for my intelligence."

She sucked in her breath as he came closer. His dark eyes were almost feral above the hard hungry slant of his cheekbones and rough edges of his jaw, shaded with five-o'clock shadow.

"Why are you so afraid of me?" he asked softly. "You seem to think I'm a murderous villain, merely because I seek to take responsibility for my child and marry you."

She lifted her chin furiously. "You don't *wish* to marry me. You're insisting on it! You're no better than Blaise Falkner!"

He grew dangerously still. "And now you insult me?"

"He wanted me to sign papers forcing me to give the baby away, too!"

"That's not what I—"

"At least with Blaise," she interrupted, "I knew from the start he was a monster. But I liked you. I slept with you." She hated the tears that rose in her eyes. She wiped them away furiously. "But beneath your charm, you're just the same as Blaise. Selfish to the core. You're determined to force this prenuptial agreement on me. Well, guess what, I'm not going to sign it! You can't make me marry you. We're in modern-day Europe, not the Dark Ages!"

"Oh, for..." A low mutter of hard words that she guessed to be Italian curses escaped his sensual lips. He set his jaw. "I don't have time for this. I'm due in Rome in five days. The prenuptial agreement is waiting in the car. You can read it thoroughly while we're driving to the airport."

Her stomach fell. "Airport?"

"En route to our wedding in Las Vegas."

"I'm not getting on a plane!"

"Why," he jeered, "because you're afraid I will kidnap you to some shadowy place not so civilized as Switzerland? You think so little of me. Why did you let me seduce you, let me fill you with my child, if the idea of taking my name and being under my protection and letting me provide for you is so unpalatable? If you truly believe me to be such a villain, why did you give me your body?" he said softly. "Why did you grip my shoulders and cry with joy as I made love to you again and again?"

Scarlett looked up at him, hardly able to breathe. He was so close to her. "I didn't..."

"It took a week for the nail marks to disappear from my back."

She flinched, then glared at him, folding her arms. "So you're good in bed. Big deal. I didn't have the experience to fight my desire for you then, but I do now. I won't sell myself to you and I definitely won't sell my baby."

His dark eyes narrowed. "So you prefer that our son has no father? That he is raised without my name or my protection or my love, all of which I freely offer you now?"

"Your...love?"

"Of course, you think I would not love my own child?"

Oh. Of course that was what he meant. Biting back her disappointment, angry with herself for feeling it, she said, "You're not offering me anything for free. If you were, you wouldn't make me sign those horrible documents."

"You expect me to marry you without a pre-nup? Leaving you free to take half my fortune?"

Scarlett shook her head stubbornly. "Of course not. You wouldn't want to take the risk. But neither do I. So, the answer is simple. We will not marry."

Vin stared at her in the Geneva sunlight. A soft wind rustled the autumn leaves above the grassy slope, between the modern two-story clinic and the sparkling water of the lake. She heard the soft call of a bird, the distant sound of honking and noise from the city.

"Because you're hoping to marry for love." He glared at her. "You are just like my mother was, before she died. Ignoring your responsibilities to run toward some romantic fantasy."

"I'm not! I'm running *away* from a nightmare. You!"

His lips pressed together. "Perhaps once our child is born, you will run away from him, too."

"Never!" she gasped.

"How do I know?"

"I love my baby more than anything!"

"So all you want from me is child support—is that it?"

"I don't want your money."

"You'd be the first."

"Money comes with strings, as you know perfectly well. Or you wouldn't offer it."

"So how do you expect to support our baby alone?"

"Well…" She tilted her head, thinking. "If you weren't pursuing me, and I didn't have to hide from you, I might go back to Gstaad and learn to cook fried chicken."

Vin looked at her incredulously. "You mean, instead of living in the lap of luxury as my wife, you'd pursue a career as a common cook?"

"You're such a snob! Fried chicken makes the world a better place. Can you say that about what you do?"

"Owning a billion-dollar airline?"

"Yeah, stuffing passengers like cattle into economy class, in seats the size of a postage stamp!"

He ground his teeth, letting her insult slide. "I have great appreciation for fine meals and for the talented chefs who prepare them. But according to Wilhelmina Stone, that's definitely not you."

"So I'll learn." Scarlett folded her arms. "I worked my way through a year of community college to become a nursing assistant, studying at night after working all day. I can handle it. All it takes is hard work and a willingness to do without sleep, and fortunately I've had experience with both."

Vin's dark eyes glinted so dangerously, she was almost surprised she didn't burst into flames beneath the force of his glare. "So you don't want my name, you don't want my money and you won't marry me. You prefer for our child to have no father at all while you aspire to low-paying jobs and try to survive."

Scarlett looked at him uneasily. When he put it like that, he made her sound like an idiot.

Vin looked into her beautiful eyes and a realization chilled him to the bone.

He had no leverage.

No way to force Scarlett's compliance, at least not one he felt comfortable with. This wasn't the business world, where he could offer a higher price or blackmail shareholders over their secrets in order to make them comply with his requests. The standard rules of mergers and acquisitions didn't apply.

Or did they?

He'd learned enough from his investigator to realize how little Scarlett had going for her. No family. No savings. Her savings account held the same amount one might spend for a business dinner with a few bottles of wine. She had no bachelor's degree, and worst of all, thanks to Blaise Falkner, she'd have no job recommendation.

But Falkner would suffer for that. Vin's lips lifted. He'd regret treating Scarlett so badly. He'd regret threatening Vin's future wife and child.

If Scarlett ever actually became his wife.

He didn't understand why this was so hard. Why shouldn't he be able to just buy her? He'd be willing to pay quite a bit, as long as it didn't cost something he actually cared about. Like his time. Or control. Or any requirement for him to be vulnerable.

But money? He had more than he could spend. Money was confetti to him. A way to keep score. A way to buy toys. And he wanted Scarlett Ravenwood more than any toy.

Shifting his strategy, he lifted an eyebrow. "What if I sweetened the pre-nup with a million-dollar payout for every year of our marriage?"

"No."

He frowned. "Two million?"

"Vin, you can't buy me."

"Everyone says that. But everyone has a price. Ten," he said. "My final offer. Ten million dollars for every year we stay married. Think about that."

Her eyes widened. For a moment he thought he had her. Then her chin lifted. "I told you. Not for any price." Her green eyes glittered furiously. "I'm not giving you the right to order me around like a slave—and permanent custody of our baby if I ever try to fight back. Freedom is worth more than some stupid money."

Vin stared at her, then regretfully decided he believed her. Damn it. Everything about her body language spoke of stubborn sincerity. He was dealing with an idealist, with a heart as stubborn as his own.

He had mixed feelings about it. That made her different from his own mother, which would be good for his son's happiness.

But it made Scarlett a more challenging adversary for Vin. How could he gain his objective, if money wasn't enough to sway her?

Standing on the grassy hillside behind the clinic, Vin looked at the sunlight flickering across Lake Geneva.

He wanted Scarlett as his wife, as his lover. In his bed, at his beck and call.

He also wanted his son to be safe and secure and loved, raised in the same home, with the same name. He wanted his son to have siblings. Vin wanted to know exactly where his family was and that everyone was protected, and provided for, at all times.

He looked at Scarlett. "How can I change your mind?"

"You can't," she said firmly. "The only reason to marry someone is for love. And I don't love you."

"You wanted a home. I can give you six." Or more. He couldn't quite remember which ones he'd sold or bought lately.

She looked wistful, then squared her shoulders. "A home without love isn't a home at all."

"That's the most ridiculous thing I've ever heard."

But he suddenly knew his answer. He'd use her romantic heart against her.

Scarlett cared about two things: love and freedom. All he had to do was give her both.

Or at least make her *think* he was giving them to her.

Vin had never tried to pretend to be in love before, but how hard could it be? He'd been raised by a woman who was a master at it, who'd used the pretense of emotion as a means of manipulating others.

But could he pull it off? Scarlett was no fool. Would she buy it?

He'd have to move slowly…

Vin tilted his head as if in thought, then took a deep breath and looked up almost pleadingly.

"Maybe you can show me I'm wrong. Prove to me that love isn't an illusion for fools."

Her eyes widened in surprise, then faded. "Please. You'll never give your heart to anyone. You've made it clear that to you marriage is a business deal."

"Maybe I'm wrong. Because you're different from any woman I've met." That was certainly true. "I want you as I've never wanted anyone." Also true. "You're carrying my child. I respect your intelligence, your warm heart. I need you. Want you." Clawing his hand back through his dark hair, he gave her a crooked smile. "Maybe that's how it starts."

He held his breath, waiting for her response.

"You expect me to believe that... That you could someday love me?" She gave a harsh laugh. "Nice try. What kind of idiot do you think I am?"

"Just give me a chance," he said quietly. "To see where this could lead."

"How?"

He thought furiously. Then he knew.

His eyes pierced hers. "I'll marry you without a prenup."

"What?" she breathed. She shook her head in disbelief. "Like you said—you'd risk half your fortune! From the moment we spoke our vows!"

Vin watched her carefully, watched the play of conflicting emotions cross her pale, lovely face. The way her white teeth nibbled furiously at her full, pink bottom lip. "Maybe it's worth the risk."

Yes. He was taking a risk, gambling that he'd quickly make her fall in love with him, placing her securely under his thumb and willing to sign a postnuptial agreement before the ink on their marriage license was dry. Which, he thought arrogantly, was almost no risk at all.

He'd never tried to make a woman fall in love with him

before. Usually it was the opposite—getting women into bed and leaving them before any emotional attachment was formed. This would be interesting. He felt strangely excited by the challenge.

Or maybe it was just standing so close to Scarlett, beneath the golden sun, feeling the cool October breeze against his overheated skin, knowing that he would soon possess her. In this moment, he would have been almost willing to pay half his fortune just to get her in his bed.

"Will you?" he said softly, coming closer. "Will you take a chance on me, if I take one with you?"

She seemed to shudder, looking up into his eyes. Her expression was bewildered, vulnerable, as if she were fighting hope itself. "But why?" she whispered. "Why does marriage matter so much to you?"

He didn't want to answer, but the new role he was playing, that of a secretly vulnerable man who could possibly be open to love, forced him to at least partial honesty. "I know what it's like to grow up without a father. My son must have a better childhood. He must always know who his parents are."

She looked confused. "How could he not know that?"

Vin changed the subject. "Family starts with a name. With a home. Our baby must feel safe and loved. He must know where he belongs." He looked at her. "Marry me, Scarlett. Right now."

She bit her lip, visibly wavering.

He pressed his advantage. "My private plane is fueled up and waiting. We can be in Las Vegas in…"

"No!" He was surprised at the sudden vehemence of her tone. She licked her lips. "Um, Dr. Schauss said I could go into labor at any time—"

"She also said she saw no imminent signs." He looked at her pale face and added soothingly, "We can bring a doctor on board with us, just in case."

"Forget it." She swallowed. "I'm not getting on any plane."

"Why?"

She took a shuddering breath. "If I do, I'll die! We'll both die!"

"What are you talking about?"

Tears spilled over her lashes. "My father died in a plane crash…"

"Yes," he said, his voice gentle, "but that doesn't mean—"

"Two weeks ago, my own flight almost crashed." He vaguely recalled reading something about an emergency landing in Ireland for her London-bound flight. She continued, "After what happened to Dad, I should have known better than to get on a plane for any reason! I told myself I was being silly. I ignored my intuition, and it almost killed us!" Hugging her belly, she shook her head fiercely. "I'll never get on another plane—ever!"

"But, Scarlett," he said quietly, "there are, on average, a hundred thousand flights every single day. Almost every one takes off and lands safely, without incident. Statistically—"

"Shut up! Don't you quote statistics to me!"

Her voice sounded almost hysterical. He had the feeling if he pushed her, he'd lose even the small bridge of trust he'd created. So he changed tactics. "I own an airline and also have two private jets for my own use. I even have a pilot's license, should I ever need to fly a plane myself. So I can supervise the equipment check, Scarlett. I can personally guarantee you'll be safe."

Scarlett choked out a tearful laugh. "And I can personally guarantee that I'm never getting on another plane!"

He tried to think of a way to reason with her. But as he looked into her beautiful, anguished eyes, as he saw the tears streak down her cheeks, he suddenly didn't want to argue. He just wanted to make it better.

Without a word, he pulled her into his arms. She fell against him, and he wrapped her in his coat, stroking her hair and back, murmuring gentle words until her sobs quieted and she was no longer shaking.

"All right," Vin said softly. "We don't have to fly. I'll never make you do anything you don't want to do. I'll always look out for you, Scarlett. Always."

Nestled against his white button-up shirt, wrapped beneath the lapels of his long black coat, Scarlett lifted her head with a ragged breath. She looked so beautiful in the sunlight, he thought. Her tearful eyes shone like emeralds.

She was vulnerable. It was the moment Vin should have pressed his advantage, gotten her to acquiesce to his proposal, boxed her in.

Instead, he felt something twist in his heart. And instead of pouncing on her weakness, forcing her to agree to his demands, he did what he'd wanted to do since he'd first seen her standing in the New York cathedral, her red hair tumbling over her shoulders, her green eyes luminous and pleading beneath a beam of golden light.

Cupping her face in his hands, Vin lowered his head and kissed her.

CHAPTER FIVE

SHE HADN'T EXPECTED him to kiss her.

The world seemed to whirl around Scarlett, making her dizzy as Vin's lips moved against hers. The kiss deepened, his mouth becoming hard and demanding, as if she belonged to him, and he owned the right of possession. He held her tight, her rounded belly and overflowing breasts pressing against his taut stomach and the hard muscles of his chest. He wrapped her in his warmth, protecting her from the wind, and she shook as she felt a hot rough pulse of electricity course through her.

She'd forgotten what it was like to kiss him. She'd forced herself to forget. But now, as she felt the tip of his tongue flick inside her mouth, as she felt his hot mouth silky against hers, she clutched him closer, never wanting to let him go. She couldn't. Not when every night for eight and a half months, she'd ached for him, dreaming of the hot night he'd ruthlessly taken her virginity, given her mind-blowing pleasure and filled her with his child.

He'd made her feel wanted. Adored. Even...loved.

"I've wanted you so long," he whispered against her skin. Her heartbeat tripled in her chest. "Say you'll marry me, Scarlett. Say it..."

"I'll marry you."

His handsome face lit up with joy and hope, and she realized what she'd just said. With an intake of breath, she met his eyes.

"Do you mean it?"

She saw in his dark eyes that he wanted her to marry him. Desperately. And she…

She wanted to be in his arms. She wanted her baby to have a father. She wanted her child to be safe and loved and live in a comfortable home. Was she a fool? Of course she wanted those things!

But only if their marriage could be real. If she and Vin actually cared for each other, they might have a chance at happiness…

Will you take a chance on me, if I take one with you?

Vin was willing to marry her without a prenuptial agreement. He was taking the biggest risk. Was she willing to take a smaller one?

For the potential happiness—for all of them?

Yes.

"I'll marry you," she choked out and realized she was crying. She had no idea why, until he pulled her into his arms and held her tight, and she knew.

Vincenzo Borgia, so handsome and powerful, could have chosen any woman for his wife.

But he'd chosen her. Not only that, he was giving her incredible power over his life. If he could be brave enough to do that, so would she.

She'd be brave enough to make the choice based on her hopes, not her fears…

"I'd never take advantage of your trust," she whispered.

"I know," he said with a private smile, then kissed her tenderly. "You've made me so happy."

"Me, too," she said, smiling through her tears.

"Let's marry as quickly as possible." He caressed her cheek. "But the marriage laws are much stricter in Europe. My assistant says the quickest options include Gibraltar and Denmark, but at your state of pregnancy, I'm not sure you'd find a long car ride comfortable. I also have to be in Rome in five days to close a business deal."

"What deal?"

"A controlling interest in Mediterranean Airlines. After I lost the deal with Air Transatlantique so spectacularly a couple of weeks ago—" he gave a wry smile "—I'm determined to get it. It's a closely held company and the founder insisted on meeting with me before he'd sell his shares."

"So let's get married in Rome."

He hesitated, then nodded. "It'll take a little longer to get married there, with the required paperwork, but if we drive straight through, we could be in Rome by late tonight. I think I even own a house there."

She gave an incredulous laugh. "You *think* you own a house? You're not sure?"

A ghost of a smile traced the edges of his sensual lips. "I haven't been back to my birth country for twenty years. I grew up in Rome, but—" his lips twisted bitterly "—my memories aren't terribly happy there."

His voice was strained, and his jaw tightened in a way that suggested she shouldn't ask any more questions. But Scarlett was dying to ask them. It occurred to her that she knew very little about his past, or what had driven him to become a self-made billionaire who was cynical at the thought of love.

But before she could try to think of a way to formulate the question that he might actually answer, Vin took her hand and led her across the grass, back to the clinic's parking lot, where the bodyguards waited with the cars.

As they walked, Scarlett glanced down at Vin's hand holding her smaller one. Feeling the warmth of his rough palm against hers, skin on skin, his fingers wrapped so possessively around hers, made her tremble as she walked. Her lips still tingled from his kiss.

"Congratulate us." Vin brought her to the three hulking, scowling bodyguards. "Scarlett has agreed to be my bride. We'll be married in a few days."

The three bodyguards lifted up their mirrored sunglasses, and their scowls gave way to bright smiles. They looked almost human as Vin introduced each of them by name. Each man shook her hand, murmuring congratulations. It was amazing how much less scary they suddenly seemed. Scarlett couldn't help smiling back.

"You're on her protection detail now," Vin told them, "as much as mine."

The men snapped to attention. "We're on it, boss."

"Welcome to the family, Miss Ravenwood," the first bodyguard told her with a big smile. Then the sunglasses snapped back, along with the scowl. "We'll keep you safe."

"Thank you." She hid a smile. As if she needed protecting! What was she, some politician or celebrity or something? But she was willing to play along.

Vin opened the door of the red sports car for her, then spoke quietly to the bodyguards before he climbed into the driver's seat beside her. He started the engine with a low smooth roar.

To her surprise, he didn't drive back immediately to the expressway but went the other direction, with the bodyguards following them in the SUV, deeper into downtown Geneva. "Where are we going?"

Vin turned onto the exclusive Rue du Rhône. "You agreed to marry me."

"So?"

His eyes slanted sideways to her hand. "You need a ring."

An hour later, they'd left the elegant jewelry store and were crossing into the French Alps, near Chamonix and Mont Blanc, en route to Italy. The mountain scenery was breathtaking, but Scarlett couldn't take her eyes off the biggest rock she'd ever seen: the ten-carat, emerald-cut, platinum-set diamond now on her left hand.

As she moved her finger, the enormous diamond reflected sparkling prisms of sunlight against her body, against her face, against the luxurious interior of the car. Against the handsome, powerful man driving beside her.

"I didn't need such a big diamond," she said for the tenth time.

He changed gears. "Of course you need it. You're going to be my wife. You must always have the best."

The ring was spectacular, but she felt briefly troubled. She would have been fine with a plain gold band, but his desires had overridden hers. What if her original fears were proven true—that he would attempt to rule her life?

Calm down, it's just a ring, she told herself. And if she were truly honest with herself, part of her was dazzled by the huge diamond, over-the-top and impractical as it was. She tried not to think about how much it had cost. More than she'd ever earn in a lifetime, that was for sure.

The highway wound through mountains and tunnels as they headed south. As they traveled, Vin kept asking if she was comfortable, if she'd like to stop for a meal, for a break or just to stretch her legs and admire the view.

Anxious to arrive in Rome so she could be done traveling and settle in, she mostly refused, stopping only briefly at a truck stop near the Italian border.

As they crossed through Tuscany, the orange sun was lowering into the west horizon of lush autumn fields like a ball of fire, and Scarlett's stomach started to growl. "Could we stop for dinner?"

"Of course, *cara*." Vin glanced at the countryside around the highway. "There is an excellent restaurant not too far from here, in Borgierra. I often visited the town when I was young."

"Borgierra? Sounds like your last name."

"My family founded the village five hundred years ago." He paused, then mumbled, "My father still lives there."

Her jaw dropped. "Your *father*?"

"So?"

"You never mentioned him. I assumed he was…well…"

"He's not dead. I just…haven't seen him for a while. Since I left Italy."

"Wait—twenty years ago?"

"Contrary to popular opinion," he said irritably, "creating a billion-dollar airline doesn't just magically happen. I've had to work all day, every day, from the time I was fifteen and set foot in New York. Gambling every penny I had. Working until I bled."

"Don't try to distract me from the main point."

"Which is?"

"You haven't seen your father for twenty years. Why? Was he horrible? Abusive?"

Vin's hands tightened on the steering wheel. "No."

Then she didn't understand at all. "I want to meet him."

He stared stonily ahead. "We don't have time."

"We have time to stop for dinner."

"I'm not talking about this."

"Too bad, because I am." The interior of the sports car suddenly seemed very small. "Weren't you the one who insisted it would be morally wrong of me not to allow our child to be raised by a father, as well as a mother? Now you expect me to ignore his chance to have a grandfather?"

His jaw tightened.

She tried again. "You say your father is a good person, but after two decades, you seriously intend to drive right by his house without stopping?" She glared at him. "It makes me wonder…"

He glared back at her. "Wonder what?"

She looked down, twisting the enormous diamond engagement ring. "When you said family was so important, I actually believed you."

"You are my family now, Scarlett. You and our son."

"The more family, the better." She took a deep breath. "I never had any siblings or cousins. Since my parents died, I've been totally alone. Do you know how that feels?"

He didn't answer.

Their eyes locked, and Scarlett's heart twisted at something she saw hidden deep in his dark eyes. Some pain. She took a deep breath. "You should want our baby to have as much family—as much love—as he possibly can," she said quietly. "Two parents are great, but what if something happens to us? Your father is our baby's only grandparent. Why haven't you seen him in twenty years?"

"It's complicated." He stared grimly forward at the road. "My mother never married Giuseppe. She preferred more exciting men who treated her badly." He smiled grimly. "But she enjoyed keeping my father on a string, not letting him fall out of love with her, making him suffer. Most of all, she enjoyed him as a source of income to her jet-set lifestyle. Anytime he wished to see me, he had to pay her a small fortune."

Her lips parted with shock. His mother had made his father *pay* for the privilege of seeing his son? "Oh, Vin…"

"When I was ten, he finally was able to stop loving her. He married another woman, Joanne."

"A wicked stepmother?" Scarlett guessed.

He snorted, then sobered. "Not at all. She was kind to me. I spent Christmas with them when I was fifteen, when my mother was partying with her boyfriend in Ibiza. It was the best Christmas of my life, with them and my new half sister. Maria was barely more than a baby then. When I had to leave, Giuseppe and Joanne said they wanted me to come live with them full-time."

"So did you?"

Vin's gaze was unfocused as he stared ahead. Then he shook his head. "My mother refused to let me go."

Scarlett's heart broke a little at the thought of a young

boy, simultaneously ignored and used as a bargaining chip by his own mother, losing his chance to be in a stable home, safe and loved. No wonder he was so determined to be a good father to his own son.

"It doesn't matter." His voice changed. "My mother died shortly after that, and I moved to New York to live with an uncle."

"I'm sorry about your mother." She frowned. "But why didn't you go live with your father after she died? There was nothing to stop you then."

"It was all a long time ago," he said grimly.

"But—"

"Drop it, Scarlett."

She wanted to push, but something in his expression warned her. "Okay. For now." She took a deep breath. "But if we're driving by his house, can't we just stop by so I can meet him? Just for ten minutes?"

"We're on a tight schedule."

"Please…"

"They might not even be at home."

"I promise if we stop, and they're not home, then I'll quit talking about it the rest of the way to Rome."

Vin stared at her. Then, with a sigh, he picked up his phone and told the bodyguards in the SUV behind them they'd be taking a detour.

The night was growing dark as they drove through a wrought-iron gate in the Tuscan countryside. The moon was full over the trees and fragrant fields. Vin seemed to grow progressively more tense as they drove down the long, dusty road, edged on both sides by cypress trees.

At the end of the road, Scarlett gasped when she saw a gorgeous three-story villa with green shutters and yellow stucco lit up by warm golden lights in the dark night.

When they reached the top of the hill, they saw at least

forty cars parked around the circular drive and stone fountain.

"Looks like they're having a party," she said awkwardly.

Vin parked the car right by the front door and turned off the engine. For a moment he didn't move. His handsome face looked strangely bleak. She reached for his hand.

"Two minutes," he said, pulling his hand away.

"We agreed we'd stay for ten—"

At his look, she decided not to press her luck.

Moon laced through clouds, decorating the October night like bright pearlescent lace across black velvet. He walked toward the front door, looking like a man going to the guillotine. The bodyguards, after doing a quick eyeball check of the perimeter, hung back respectfully. So did Scarlett.

At the door, Vin glanced back at them, then set his jaw. He reached for the brass knocker and banged it heavily against the wood. For some moments, no one answered.

Then the door was thrown open, and light and music from inside the villa poured out around them. Scarlett saw a dignified gray-haired man standing silhouetted in the doorway.

"Buona sera," Vin began woodenly, then spoke words in Italian that she didn't understand.

But she didn't need to. He had barely spoken a sentence before the man in the doorway let out a gasp and, with a flood of Italian words, pulled Vin into his arms with a choked sob of joy.

Vin was furious.

He hadn't wanted to come here. He felt manipulated, backed into a corner. Exactly how he'd promised himself he'd never feel again: like someone else's puppet, under their control.

But Scarlett had made her threat clear, with her pointed insinuation, twisting her engagement ring, that she might change her mind about their marriage if he didn't do this. He'd barely contained his fury during their drive up the cypress-lined road. *This* was the thanks he received for striving to take good care of his pregnant soon-to-be wife, letting her have her way in everything? It still wasn't enough? Now Scarlett wanted to put her spoon into his heart and stir?

He hated her for this. Up till the very moment when he'd banged on the door.

Vin had been prepared for a servant to answer, or someone he didn't know, as there seemed to be a party. But he instantly recognized the man in the doorway.

Giuseppe Borgia had aged twenty years, with more lines on his skin and gray in his hair. But he'd known him. His father.

No. The man Vin had *believed* to be his father for his entire childhood. The man whose heart would be broken if he ever knew the truth.

The last time they'd seen each other, at his mother's funeral, Vin had been hostile and cold. Nothing like he'd been the week before, during the happy Christmas he'd stayed at this very villa, believing he'd found a place to call home and a real family who loved him.

But when he'd returned to Rome after Christmas and asked his mother if he could permanently live with his father, she'd barked out a cruel laugh.

"You're not even Giuseppe's son," Bianca Orsini had said. She'd taken a long drag off her cigarette. "It's time you knew. I got pregnant after a one-night stand with a musician I met in a bar in Rio." She smiled her brittle, hollow smile. "But I needed Giuseppe's money. So I lied."

"I have to tell him," Vin had choked out.

"Do it, and for reward, he'll just stop loving you." Her

fingers tightened around the shrinking cigarette. "Did you really think I'd let you go live with him and that British woman and give up my only source of income?"

Ironically, Bianca hadn't needed that income for long. She'd died a few days later, when, while distracting her current boyfriend with caresses of an intimate nature—at least that was what the police believed—she'd caused him to accidentally swerve his convertible off a cliff, killing them both.

Vin had barely been able to face Giuseppe and Joanna at the funeral a few days later. They'd tried to hug him, to console him, telling him to pack up and come home with them. But he'd known if they realized he wasn't really Giuseppe's child, how quickly they would have given him up. Especially since they had their own child, an adorable little girl of four, who actually deserved their love.

He couldn't wait around for them to reject him. Better that he do it first. So he'd gone to live with his mother's brother in New York, a lawyer who worked eighty-hour weeks and had little to offer his grieving, lonely nephew except his example as a workaholic.

Now Vin stared at Giuseppe in the doorway of the villa. The man he'd once believed to be his father, whose hair had since gone gray. They'd both changed so much over twenty years. Would Giuseppe even recognize him now?

"Good evening," Vin said haltingly in his native Italian. The language tasted rusty on his lips. "I apologize for the interruption. I'm not sure you'll recognize me—"

Giuseppe's lips parted. Then his eyes suddenly shone with tears.

"Vincenzo," he choked out. "My boy, my boy—you've come home at last!"

The old man's arms went around him, and he felt the force of his father's sobs. A stab went through Vin's frozen heart, as if it had painfully started beating again.

Giuseppe pulled back, wiping his eyes, and called out loudly in Italian. Suddenly there were more people at the door, including two dark-haired women, one young, the other older, both pretty and smiling.

His stepmother, Joanne, and...could that be his sister, Maria, now a young woman of twenty-four? They both hugged him with cries of joy, and Giuseppe, weeping openly, hugged all three of them in his vast arms.

Vin blinked fast, feeling like his soul was peeling.

His father. His *family*. He longed to love them again. But he didn't have the right. And if they ever knew the truth, their love would evaporate.

"But who's this?" Giuseppe said in Italian, looking past Vin's ear. He saw Scarlett fidgeting shyly behind him in the gravel driveway. Heavily pregnant and still in the same casual khakis and jacket she'd worn in Gstaad, she looked incredibly beautiful, with her red hair, chewing her pink lower lip, her green eyes uncertain.

Vin took her hand.

"This is Scarlett, Papà," he said quietly in the same language. "She's carrying my child and we're going to be wed."

His father gasped, and all the new people now flooding around them—only a few of whom he confusedly recognized—immediately began crying out their welcome and approbation.

"You brought her home to meet us?" Reaching out, Giuseppe patted her cheek.

Vin said drily, "She insisted."

"Then she is already beloved by me," the old man said.

"Scarlett doesn't speak Italian."

He smiled. "She understands." And indeed, she had a bright, joyful smile as she looked between him and Giuseppe. She thought she'd brought Vin and his father back together.

If only it was the truth. If only it were even possible.

But in this moment, surrounded on all sides by love, Vin could not fight it. He pushed away his shame about the lie. As the Borgias whisked them into the villa, it was easier to just pretend, for just a short while, that he really was their long-lost son, their long-lost brother. Easier to pretend he was actually deserving of their love and care.

"You came to my engagement party!" His dark-haired young sister said happily, slipping her arm around his as she led him through the grand hall toward the courtyard outside. "You have made this a party to remember!"

"You are engaged, Maria?" he said incredulously. "You were a toddler last time I saw you! Do you even remember me?"

Her smile broadened. "I confess my memory is not perfect, but I know you from your picture." Her smile faded. "Our father often cried over it."

"Maria…"

"But all is forgiven now you are here." Brightening, she motioned across the decorated courtyard, her eyes sparkling. "That is my fiancé, Luca."

Luca barely looked old enough to be out of college, Vin thought. Or maybe he himself was just old. Outside of Manhattan most people did not wait until they were thirty-five to be wed. And even in New York, no one waited that long to fall in love.

"Forgive me for interrupting your party. If I'd known—"

"Vincenzo, having you here is the best engagement present in the world! Did you see Papà's face? He's prayed for this. When we sent you the invitation, we never dreamed you would accept."

Vin hadn't gotten the invitation, because he'd instructed his assistant to toss anything from the Borgia family straight into the trash. "Um…"

"And now you are engaged as well, and expecting a child," Maria said, her eyes shining. "Our family is growing!"

Beneath the fairy lights of the large courtyard, guests were dancing to the music of a small band. It didn't even feel cold, with the heat lamps. A beautiful evening party, with a panoramic view of the moon-swept Tuscan countryside.

He looked back at Scarlett, already sitting at a table near the dinner buffet, a plate of food in front of her as she talked to Giuseppe and Joanne. Amid all the elegant suits and gowns, she was still wearing the same casual clothes she'd worn on her morning walk in Gstaad. But it didn't matter. Just looking at her, Vin felt a flash of heat that blocked out all other thoughts and feelings. A welcome distraction.

As if she felt his stare, Scarlett turned. Their eyes locked across the crowd, and electricity thrummed through him, as if they were the only two people in the world.

Then his stepmother rose from the table, gesturing her to follow. Finishing a last bite of dinner, Scarlett rose. Lifting her eyebrow at him with a mysterious smile, she turned and disappeared inside the villa.

It was as if clouds suddenly covered the moonlight. Clearing his throat, Vin turned back to Maria, trying to remember what they'd been saying. "Ah… I hope you'll both be very happy."

"You, too, brother." Her smile broadened. "But since you're in love, getting married and having a baby, something tells me you're about to be happier than you can even imagine."

Ten minutes later, Scarlett was staring at herself in the full-length mirror.

"Thank you," she breathed, looking at herself in the

borrowed floaty knee-length dress with charming bell sleeves. "Oh, thank you so much!"

Vin's stepmother, Joanne, beamed back at her. "It's vintage, darling. Haven't worn it in years. I'm just glad I had a dress with an empire waist!" She glanced fondly at Scarlett's belly. "How wonderful it will be—" she sighed happily "—to have a new baby in the family. Now I don't even have to pressure Maria about children for a while, because you're making me a grandmother!"

From the moment Scarlett had met Vin's parents, they'd treated her like family. While talking with them in the courtyard, Scarlett had shyly mentioned she felt woefully underdressed for the party, in wrinkled khakis.

"Your bodyguards just brought in your suitcase," Joanne had said helpfully, but Scarlett shook her head, looking down at her casual clothes with regret.

"All my clothes look like this."

"Don't worry!" Joanne had said suddenly. "I know just the thing!"

Scarlett had immediately liked the dark-haired British woman, with her obviously kind heart. Now, blinking back tears, she reached out and impulsively hugged her. "I'm so glad we're going to be family."

"Me, too, darling." Joanne smiled as she drew back, her eyes glistening with tears. "I can't remember the last time I saw Giuseppe so happy. You've put our family back together and added years to my husband's life. Now—" she shook her head briskly, wiping her eyes "—we just need to find you better shoes. I think Maria has some sparkly sandals about your size…"

After Scarlett was dressed, she brushed out her red hair and put on a bit of lipstick. Feeling nervous as Cinderella, Scarlett went back out to the noisy courtyard to join the party.

She'd hoped for a family reconciliation, but she'd never

imagined a family like Vin's—so loving, so warm, so ready to welcome Scarlett and their coming baby with open arms!

Vin's father, Giuseppe, smiled at her as she returned to the festive tables on the edge of the courtyard. He said in accented English, "I'm glad you're here. I can see the love between you and my son."

Scarlett blushed and let the remark pass. She could hardly tell Giuseppe that she and Vin had gotten pregnant by accident. They didn't love each other.

But she wanted to love him.

Yes, Vin was ruthless. But he was also honorable, determined to do the best he could—as he saw it—for their baby, and for Scarlett, too. He'd repeatedly put her needs in front of his. Agreeing to drive, instead of fly. Agreeing to introduce her to his family. Most of all, agreeing to marry her without a pre-nup! She could only imagine how his shark lawyers would have their heads blown off at that one.

"When is your wedding?" Giuseppe asked.

"I'm not exactly sure. Sometime soon in Rome. We haven't really planned it yet. But I do hope you'll all be able to come..."

Her voice trailed off as Vin saw her across the courtyard. He started pushing through the crowd toward her.

Her body felt the rhythm of the music, the beat of the dancers' pounding feet against the flagstones. But she was unable to move, unable to even breathe, captured in his dark hungry gaze.

He was breathtakingly handsome. His muscled legs were barely contained by well-tailored black trousers and his broad shoulders seemed to expand the sharp white shirt with the top button undone. But it wasn't the broadness of his shoulders or sharp line of his jaw or even the intensity of his black eyes that shook her. His sex appeal was obvious to anyone with eyes.

This was more.

Scarlett felt like she knew a secret. Something no other woman had been privileged to see. Something he hid from the world and would deny to the death if ever accused of it.

Beneath the layers of slick designer suits and hard brutal muscle, Vin secretly had a good heart.

"Scusi," he said now to his father, who smiled indulgently.

"But of course, you want to be with your future bride."

Reaching out, Vin pulled Scarlett away. Beneath his touch, her body flashed hot, then cold. As they stood together on the crowded dance floor of the villa's courtyard, as the fairy lights swayed above them in the moonlit night, her heart was pounding.

She suddenly couldn't meet his eyes. She focused on the curve of his neck. On the hair-dusted forearms casually revealed by his rolled-up sleeves. The hard edge of his unshaven jawline. The upturn of his cruelly sensual lips.

Blood was suddenly rushing in her ears. Her knees felt weak. What was happening to her?

"Cara," he said softly. "You look so beautiful in that dress." He pulled her into his arms. "Dance with me."

The slow dance was pure torture for Scarlett as she felt his hard, powerful body brush against hers. His muscles moved against her breasts and belly, and his hands slowly traced down her back.

Her full breasts felt heavy, her nipples tightening, aching to be touched. Even the barest brush of him against her was almost too much—and yet not nearly enough. Agonized desire flowed through her, twisting deep, deep inside her. She ached for him to kiss her, to stroke her naked skin, to thrust inside her, fill her fully, stretch her wide—

Her breaths came in gasps. She tried to hide her desire. She couldn't let him know that such an innocent slow dance, while surrounded by his family and friends at an engagement party, was making her insane with need. How could she be so wanton? What was wrong with her?

The song finished, and she exhaled. "Um, thanks…"

But as she tried to leave the dance floor, he held her tight, murmuring, "Don't go."

His large hands moved slowly from her hips to her lower back. He pulled her back against his body, crushing her breasts against his hard chest. Dizzy with need, she looked up at him.

He smiled down at her. Powerful. Sure of himself.

There was a lull in the music. His expression changed, became dark. Hot. His lips slowly lowered toward hers—

"Vincenzo!"

They turned as Giuseppe's voice called across the courtyard. Vin's father beamed at them, his arm around his wife's shoulders, with Maria smiling beside them.

"My son," he announced, "there is no sense in you getting married in Rome, with strangers." He gesticulated wildly. "We have decided you and Scarlett should be married right here."

"Say yes," Maria begged.

"It would make us so happy," Joanne added warmly. "What do you say?"

Having her wedding at this beautiful Tuscan villa, surrounded by Vin's family? Scarlett wanted it instantly. Holding her breath, she looked hopefully at Vin.

But his expression was strangely shut down. Scarlett didn't understand why he seemed so tense at the idea. But whatever the reason, she knew he didn't want to do it. She sensed he'd been pushed as far as he'd be pushed. But he remained stubbornly silent, forcing Scarlett to be the one to give his family the bad news.

Biting her lip, she forced herself to say apologetically, "Thank you, but we want to be wed as quickly as possible—"

"All the more reason to do it here," Joanne pointed out. "What is the point of getting married in Rome? It will just take longer to get all the paperwork done. Here, it will be quicker because Giuseppe is mayor—"

"*Sì*, mayor," he repeated proudly.

"And he'll make sure all the necessary documentation is completed as fast as humanly possible. You're both American citizens now—" Joanne glanced humorously at her stepson, as if to say *What a fool you were to trade away this beautiful country* "—so no banns are necessary."

"Please!" Maria clutched Scarlett's hands. "I'll arrange a beautiful wedding for you. It'll be good practice for planning my own. Why shouldn't you get married here? It's your home now, too, Scarlett!"

Put that way, it was impossible to refuse. Scarlett looked desperately at Vin.

He scowled. "I have connections in Rome. It can be done quickly enough."

Giuseppe snorted. "Amid strangers! What about your family? What about your bride?"

Vin's jaw tightened. "I don't—"

"Please," Scarlett whispered.

He stared at her for a long moment, then sighed.

"Va bene." His shoulders looked tense. "We will have our wedding here, since my bride wishes it." As Maria clapped her hands together with joy, he added fiercely, "But I must be in Rome within five days."

"No problem!" Joanne said.

"Easy!" Giuseppe said.

"You will see," Maria chortled. "I bet we can do it in three!"

Vin's expression said he feared three days would last an eternity. Why? Scarlett wondered. What could possibly be making him so tense? Was it cold feet? Had he changed his mind about wanting to marry her? The thought caused a shiver of nervousness to go through her. Because she was starting to not hate the idea of marrying him.

"Perhaps it's not an entirely bad idea," Vin murmured, looking down at her. His arms tightened. "If we're staying, that means no more driving tonight. Which means," he whispered, "I can take you to bed now."

Fire flashed through her, and she almost tottered on her borrowed strappy sandals. Her heart was pounding so hard and fast she felt light-headed.

Her whole world shrank down to the sensation of his body near hers, his hand supporting her arm. Did he intend to seduce her? No, surely not. She was eight and a half months pregnant. Not exactly a sexpot. She wanted him. Definitely. But she was surely imagining the dark fierce smolder in his eyes.

And part of her was afraid of what would happen if he made love to her. How much of her soul he might take, along with her body...

"My fiancée is tired," he said abruptly. "I am sorry, but we must cut our night short."

"Of course, of course," came the chorus around them in English and Italian. Everyone looked at her belly and smiled. Everyone loved a pregnant woman.

"Where can I take her to rest?"

"Follow me," his father said, waving them along. He took them through the beautiful villa, up the sweeping stairs to the quieter second floor, then triumphantly through double doors to a huge, luxurious bedroom.

"But there's only one bed," Scarlett whispered to Vin in consternation. His father heard her and chuckled.

"There is no reason for you to pretend you do not share a bedroom," he said with a laugh, eyeing her belly. "We are not so old-fashioned as to need that deception. Or so stupid as to believe it! Do not be embarrassed. We wish you only to be comfortable."

Refusing to meet Vin's eyes, Scarlett said stiltedly, "Perhaps other rooms could be found—"

"Yes, of course." His father nodded, but before she could sigh with relief, he finished, "The villa is full of party guests, but we did find rooms for your bodyguards. I appreciate your concern for them," he said approvingly. "You've chosen the right woman, Vincenzo. So thoughtful and kind. Look." He nodded toward her duffel bag and his sleek designer suitcase, stacked neatly on the closet floor. "Our staff already unpacked your clothes for you. We were hoping to convince you to stay. So now there is nothing—" his eyebrows wiggled suggestively "—to prevent you both from having a good night's sleep."

Giuseppe left, shutting the double doors behind him.

Alone in the shadowy bedroom, standing next to the enormous bed, Scarlett and Vin looked at each other.

"What now?" she whispered, shivering. "What should we—"

Before she could finish her sentence, before she could even finish her thought, Vin pulled her roughly into his arms. Claiming her lips as his own, he twined his hands in her long red hair, kissing her with deep, ferocious hunger that could not be denied.

CHAPTER SIX

VIN HADN'T FELT so emotionally out of control for a long, long time.

All night, he'd been forced to endure feelings he'd ignored for twenty years, since he'd left Italy and closed the door marked "love and family" forever in his mind.

But that door had been wrenched open. He was out of practice dealing with any feeling but anger, so staggered by conflicting emotions.

Right now, there was only one thing he wanted to feel.

This. Kissing Scarlett, Vin stroked his hands up her arms, feeling the silky fabric of her empire-waist dress slide beneath his fingertips. Feeling the warmth of her body beneath. He could be sure of this.

And this. He deepened the kiss, teasing her with his tongue.

Her sigh was soft in his mouth, like a whimper, but he felt the way she moved, her belly hard against his, her breasts swollen and soft.

This was all he wanted to feel. What he could physically grasp. What he could hold.

Scarlett.

Distantly, he heard the raucous noise of the party downstairs in the courtyard. But here in the hush of the darkened bedroom it felt strangely private, even holy. This was a place out of time, belonging to them alone.

Vin felt her tremble against him. Her lips parted beneath his, open and ripe for the taking. The rational part of his brain disappeared. It was like he'd never kissed anyone before.

He caressed her cheek, running his hand down the back of her neck, through her long hair tumbling down her shoulders. He drew back, looking at her. She was so sexy. So impossibly desirable. Beneath the silk bodice of her dress, he could see the hard nipples of her swollen breasts.

His body was screaming to take her now, take her hard and fast.

He exhaled, forcing himself to stay in control. She was heavily pregnant with his child, so he'd have to be gentle. She would need to be on top. To set the rhythm.

Plus, she was nervous. He felt that in her hesitation, in the way she'd shyly asked for separate rooms. She was afraid of what their lovemaking would start between them.

She was right to be afraid.

He intended to use every weapon he had to make her fall in love with him. To make her acquiesce to his every desire, and give him total command.

He needed to lure her slowly. Until she wanted him so badly that she was the one pushing him back roughly against the bed, and climbing on top of his naked body, easing her soft, wet core around him, driving him hard until they both screamed, clutching each other—

He shuddered with need. Patience, though a virtue, wasn't his strong point.

But he was starting to suspect that the torture of wanting her, and waiting for her, would make this conquest the single most spectacular sexual event of his life. For that, it was worth a little self-control.

If he could keep himself from losing it...

He gentled his kiss, making his lips seductive and soft. She leaned her body against him, reaching up to twine her hands in his short dark hair, pulling his head down harder against hers. Her rough, savage kiss made him feel so, so good, his body taut, his blood rushing and pounding and spiraling with need—

With a silent curse, Vin pulled away. She wouldn't be able to resist now if he drew her to the bed. He saw that in her sweetly mesmerized face. She wasn't the problem.

He was.

He couldn't lose control. Not now. Not ever. He needed a new strategy to force himself to slow down.

Scarlett's big eyes gleamed in the shadowy room as she looked up at him, dazed with desire. Cupping her cheek, he said in a low voice, "You have had a long day, *cara*. You need some comfort. Let me take care of you." Her forehead furrowed, then smoothed as he ran his hand gently along her shoulder. "I saw a marble tub in the en suite. Shall I start you a bath?"

"A bath?" she said, sounding bewildered, and he couldn't blame her.

"A deliciously sensual bath." He smiled. "One you'll want to linger in."

"That would be lovely—if you're sure you don't mind?"

She was already sighing in anticipation. She *had* had a stressful day, he thought. Considering she'd woken up that morning a single mother, a cook working in a Swiss chalet, and now was in Italy, Vin's fiancée, the proven mother of his child, with a ten-carat diamond on her finger. She'd met his family and was about to share his bed. That was a lot of change for anyone. And more was soon to come.

He smiled down at her. "It will be my pleasure."

And it would be.

Going into the luxurious en suite bathroom, Vin turned on the water, then looked around quickly. How to make it even more romantic? Pulling fresh roses from a nearby crystal vase, he crumpled rose petals into the warm running water. But he wanted more. Digging through the bathroom cabinet, he found expensively perfumed bubble bath and triumphantly discovered four candles and a box of matches in the bottom drawer.

"Can I come in?" she called.

"Not yet." He carefully placed the candles around the white marble bathroom with its elegant silver fixtures. He checked the water temperature—not too hot—and added a few more rose petals over the bubbles for good measure. He lit the candles, then turned out the lights. "Now."

Scarlett came into the bathroom, then stopped, her mouth agape. She looked at him, her own beautiful face suddenly nervous. As well she should be, he thought smugly.

"For you, *cara*," he said innocently. "I'll leave you to it."

He did leave the bathroom. He was that much of a gentleman. In the bedroom closet, he found his clothes unpacked in a drawer and pulled off his formal white shirt and tailored black trousers, exchanging them for just one article of clothing that would be easy to take off—low-slung sweatpants. When he heard the water slosh in the bathtub, heard her sigh as she descended into the warm, fragrant water, he gave a single knock on the bathroom door and pushed it open.

The white bubbles covered Scarlett's naked body modestly in the flickering candlelight. Only the tops of her breasts and a small bit of belly protruded as she looked back at him in surprise.

Her long red hair was piled high in a topknot, but tendrils of hair fell down her neck. Her cheeks were flushed pink, her full lips red and parted.

Vin had braced himself for seeing her naked, but the image still hit him low in the gut. Very low. It wasn't like he could hide his desire, either, in the low-slung sweatpants. His chest was bare, showing his shape from hours burning off energy and rage in the boxing gym and martial arts dojo. His hard flat belly was dusted with dark hair, like an arrow pointing down to the center of his desire.

So be it. Let her look.

Let his intentions be clear.

"What are you—" Her voice came out a croak. She swallowed, then looking up at his face, she said in a steadier voice, "What do you want?"

"I told you." He came closer, giving her a sensual, heavy-lidded smile. "I want to make you feel good."

"You made me this bath."

"I can do even better," he said silkily. "If you'll let me."

For a moment, she seemed to hold her breath.

"What did you have in mind?"

Vin sat behind her, on the tiled edge of the enormous marble tub.

He knew he could reach down, turn her face to his and claim her lips. Claim all of her. But he forced himself to take it slow. To seduce her, bit by bit.

"Let me show you," he said softly.

With agonizing slowness, he lowered his hands to her naked shoulders peeking out above the bubbles. Amid the flickering shadows, he sucked in his breath at the sensual shock of feeling her warm, slippery skin beneath his fingers, and knowing that she was naked beneath the rose petals and bubbles, there for his pleasure, just waiting for him to claim her.

Closing his eyes so he wouldn't be tempted by the soft sway of the water visibly caressing her round breasts, he began to rub her shoulders. His massage was light at first, then gradually he increased the pressure.

Scarlett exhaled, as though the stress of months or years was melting beneath his touch. Using his fingertips, his thumbs, he rubbed the knots away from her shoulders and neck. She closed her eyes, her rosy face the picture of pleasure as she leaned against his hands, like a cat meeting his stroke.

After a few minutes, when her face was blissfully peaceful, his hands began to move differently. Slowly, he moved past her shoulders to her upper arms, then her neck. He brushed the tender flesh of her earlobes with the flicker of a caress.

By now, the bubbles had mostly disappeared, and he could see the curves of her naked body beneath the water. He had himself under control now—for the moment—but he was also only a man. Too much of this and he might dive headlong into the enormous bathtub with her, to make love to her against the hard marble, amid the slosh of the cooling water.

Lowering his head to the nape of her neck, Vin brushed the red tendrils of her hair aside and kissed her, his lips lingering sensually on her skin.

Scarlett felt the brush of Vin's lips against the sensitive skin of her neck, and it was like lightning sizzling through her. All peace disappeared.

The water's temperature had cooled, and more alarmingly, the bubbles had diminished, no longer providing camouflage. Her breasts were entirely visible now, gleaming wet and flicked with only a few tiny bubbles like decorative pearls. Her hard nipples were rosy beneath the water.

"Scarlett, look at me," Vin said in a low, savage voice.

She had no choice but to obey. Tilting her head, she looked at his handsome face. Her eyes unwillingly traced his half-naked body, his thickly muscled chest, the trail of dark hair that led downward from his belly to the low waistline of his dark gray sweatpants, and below that...!

Even in the soft candlelight, she could see the outline

of him, huge and hard for her. Involuntarily, she sucked in her breath with a whimper.

"I want you," he growled.

She swallowed. She wanted him, too, desperately. But she was afraid of what would happen if she surrendered to him completely. Would it be the start of a wonderful, loving, lifelong marriage? Or would it be the beginning of a lifetime of misery?

He was physically perfect. While she… She glanced back at her own body and her cheeks burned self-consciously. "But I'm so big…"

"Yes. You are." His hand reached down to cup a pregnancy-swollen breast, as if feeling the weight. It overflowed his hand as he tightened his fingers around an aching nipple. "And I want you as I've never wanted any woman."

The pleasure of his touch was so sharp and raw it made her gasp.

Lowering his head, he kissed her, his lips hot and smooth as silk. Fire flooded through her. She kissed him back, water sloshing around her as she placed her hand against his cheek.

"Oh, Vin," she breathed. "I want you, too…"

And she kissed him recklessly.

Abruptly, his arms plunged into the bathtub. Reaching around her, he lifted her naked, wet body from the cool water, carrying her against his hard bare chest as if she weighed nothing at all. He slowly set her down to stand in front of him, her naked body sliding against his, before her feet reluctantly touched the white fluffy rug.

She was eight and a half months pregnant, and standing naked in front of him. She was so heavy. How could he want her? How could any man find her sexy, let alone Vin Borgia, who was so handsome and powerful he could have had any woman on earth?

But he didn't love her. She shivered. If she surrendered now, would she regret it for the rest of her life?

"You're cold," he murmured. Grabbing an enormous white cotton towel, he gently wrapped her in it.

But she wasn't shivering from cold. Swallowing, she looked up at him, her heart in her throat.

"I'm not exactly your usual supermodel," she said, trying for levity, but her voice trembled around the edges.

"No. You're not." He ran his hands gently through her hair, loosening the topknot so the damp waves tumbled down her shoulders. "There is nothing *usual* about you, Scarlett. You are special. The most beautiful, resourceful, kindhearted woman I've ever known." Holding the towel, he pulled her closer. "But that's not why I want you in my bed."

"It's not?"

He shook his head. "My need for you is far more primitive than that." His fingertips traced the bare skin lightly from her collarbone to the hollow between her breasts. "You're in my blood, Scarlett." His voice lowered almost to a growl. "You belong to me, and I intend to have you."

The moment stretched out between them, threatening to snap.

Belong to him?

She couldn't belong to him.

Not when he didn't belong to her. He didn't love her, and she didn't know if he ever would.

Panic rose from her heart to her throat. "No—"

Ripping the towel from his grasp, she turned and fled, practically slamming the door behind her.

In the bedroom, she beat the world record for finding her oversize T-shirt and cotton panties in a drawer. Within thirty seconds, she was tucked into the enormous bed, the heavy bedcovers pulled tightly to her neck.

The bedroom was dark. Her heartbeat drummed in her

throat as she waited for Vin to come out of the bathroom. What did she hope to achieve by hiding in this bed? They were sharing the room. He'd just have to sleep on the sofa by the window, she thought.

But Vin Borgia didn't seem like the kind of man who would politely take himself off to sleep on the sofa. Not when he'd made such a ruthless declaration.

You've in my blood, Scarlett. You belong to me, and I intend to have you.

She jolted when she heard the door abruptly open, causing a trickle of light across the bed. She squeezed her eyes shut as she heard him blow out the candles in the bathroom, one by one. Then silence.

"Go sleep on the sofa!" she tried to say, but her voice wouldn't work. She heard the echo of heavy footsteps coming toward her. They stopped.

The mattress beneath her swayed. She felt his warmth, breathed in the scent of sandalwood. Nervously, she scooted to the other side of the enormous king-size bed. Her heart was pounding. Part of her yearned desperately for him to reach out and pull her into his arms—but she was oh, so afraid of giving him complete power over her!

He reached for her in the darkness, and without a word, slowly, he turned her to face him. She felt his fingertips tantalizingly trail the edge of her hair, her shoulder, her hip.

His hand cupped her full breast, his palm moving against her aching nipple through her thin white cotton T-shirt. His other hand moved lingeringly over the curve of her belly, moving lower, and lower still. She felt something pressing hard against her and realized he was naked.

Tension coiled deep inside her, a sweet ache of need that was starting to build beyond her control.

She'd thought she knew desire from their first night together, their night of escape and exploration and discovery. But this was something else. Something else entirely.

Pregnancy hormones had given a fierce edge to her sexual need that she'd never experienced before. Or maybe it was because she now wore his ring on her finger, she was sleeping in his bed, she was pregnant with his child and soon would be his wife.

She wanted him. She wanted *this*. All of it. A home with warmth and comfort. A family. But most of all she wanted something impossible: she wanted him to love her...

She pulled back, struggling to see his face in the darkness. Her eyes adjusted, and the scattered moonlight from behind the window blinds silhouetted the hard edges of his cheekbones and jawline with silver.

Could he ever love her? Or was he just seducing her into marriage, for the sake of their baby?

She yearned to ask but didn't have the courage. Instead, she whispered, "Kiss me."

She heard his intake of breath, then felt the hard, sweet taste of his mouth on hers.

He kissed her for minutes—or hours—until her cheeks felt abraded from the roughness of the dark bristles on his jawline. His mouth was hungry and hard, pushing her lips apart as he teased her with his tongue. She clutched his shoulders, electrified by the heat of his hard naked body, the strength and size of him against her. She gripped him tight as his hands roamed possessively over the curves of her breasts and thighs.

Breaking the kiss, he pushed her back against the bed and slowly kissed down her body, stroking her full breasts and the mound of her belly and her voluptuous hips through her thin cotton T-shirt until he knelt at the foot of the bed. Spreading her feet apart, he caressed the hollows of her feet, the tender skin of her ankle.

Then he started moving upward. He kissed and caressed her calves. He kissed her knees, and the hollows beneath them, with a sensual flick of his tongue. Moving inexorably toward her thighs, he pushed her T-shirt up to her hips, leaving her cotton panties exposed.

Stroking the outside of her thighs, he positioned his head between them, and she started to shake.

Using his large hands to spread her legs wide, he kissed and nibbled her inner thighs. His breath warmed her skin, causing prickles of heat and furious desire to spread like wildfire through her body.

He teased her, kissing her softly with little flicks of his tongue along the edge of her panties. He cupped her mound over the thin cotton, rubbing the most sensitive part of her with his palm, leaving her gasping with need.

Her hands gripped the bedsheet as her hips moved of their own accord, swaying beneath his touch.

He slowly pulled her cotton panties down the length of her legs, in a whisper of sensation. She held her breath, squeezing her eyes shut as he moved back to her.

Placing his large hands on her inner thighs, he lowered his head. She felt his hot breath full against her, teasing her, and she quivered beneath him.

Spreading her wide, he took a long, languorous taste.

She gave a soft cry at the immediate wave of pleasure. It was almost too much. She tried to twist her hips away, but he held her more firmly against the bed.

He flicked the tip of his wet tongue lightly against her, swirling around her hard, aching nub in a circular motion. Then he spread her wide, lapping her hungrily with the full width of his tongue. She felt wet, so wet. She gasped as he eased a finger inside her.

Sweet agony built inside her, higher and higher. Her hips started to lift off the bed. A low cry came unbidden from her lips as he worked her roughly with his tongue, and his expert fingers teased her. Gripping his shoulders, she screamed, blinded by the bright explosion of pleasure.

He did not wait. With a low growl, he pulled her upright and yanked off her flimsy T-shirt, leaving her completely naked beneath him.

Her body was still boneless and satiated as he fell beside her on the mattress, rolling her over him, so she straddled his hard, naked body, her belly huge between them. With her knees over the hard planes of his hips, she felt the intimate press of his rock-hard body. He was enormous.

Her swollen breasts were angled toward his mouth. Lifting his head, he suckled each one greedily in turn, causing her to gasp and arch her back with the new sweet sensation of his lips and tongue and teeth. With her legs spread wide over his hips, she slid against him on instinct, her body tightening as she felt him press against her slick core, demanding entry.

He lifted her, positioned himself, then slowly thrust inside her, filling her inch by inch, filling her to the hilt.

She moaned as she felt him push deep inside her. Her hips moved, swaying, quivering around him. He was so thick, so hard. So deep—

Hearing his intake of breath, she looked down at his face. His eyes were closed, his expression rapt, and she suddenly realized that if he had power over her, she had power over him.

Slowly, she began to ride him. As his lips parted in a soundless gasp, she rode him harder and faster, her breasts swaying with the rough movement.

Tension coiled and built inside her, even higher than before. She leaned forward, gripping his muscled shoulders with her fingertips. She felt him tense beneath her, heard his gasp. She felt him try to draw back, to slow down—

But she wouldn't let him withdraw. She rode him hard, pushing him until his body started to shake beneath her.

She heard his rising growl and felt him explode inside her. Only then did she let herself go, and as she heard him cry out, her own world exploded into a million sparkling colors, before going black with the savage intensity of their joy.

CHAPTER SEVEN

AWARENESS CAME SLOWLY to Vin. It seemed like hours later when he opened his eyes.

Blinking in the darkness, he remembered they were in the guest room of the villa. Scarlett moved in his arms, warm and soft. His woman. His hands tightened on her as she slept.

He'd deliberately teased her, intending to make her insane with desire, to make her love him. But she wasn't the only one who'd lost control.

Setting his jaw, Vin stared up grimly at the ceiling.

What if his lie about the possibility of falling for her hadn't been a lie?

Could he really be starting to care?

No, he told himself fiercely. No way. He enjoyed having Scarlett in his bed. It was sexual pleasure. That was all it could possibly be.

But this place was messing with his brain. All of it. Italy. This villa. Being around family again. It all reminded him of who he'd once been, when all he'd wanted was to have a real home, to be loved.

But Vin had toughened up since then. Smartened up. Home could be anywhere. He owned more houses than he could keep track of, mostly as investments but also for his convenience. They were all decorated the same, modern and Spartan in stark black and gray, devoid of many personal details or clutter. That was always how he liked his relationships, too. In his opinion, "love" was a fancy decoration, as tacky and inappropriate as pink flounces or Victorian chintz.

He put his hand to his forehead, feeling a sense of vertigo. He couldn't let himself return to the vulnerable, tenderhearted boy he'd been. The boy who'd actually cared. The boy who'd felt things. Who'd hungered for things that had nothing to do with money—

It was this *place*, he thought angrily.

No. He looked at Scarlett sleeping so trustingly in his arms. It was *her*.

He couldn't let himself lose his head. He had to keep it together. Stay cool. Stick to the plan.

They would be married soon, he told himself. All he had to do was make her love him enough to sign the postnup. That was all.

But it was hard for Vin to keep his vow.

It took four more days, not three, before they were able to wed. The Borgias had been wrong. Even with the town mayor expediting paperwork, even with copies of their birth certificates—Vin's listed paternity a glaring lie that set his teeth on edge—there were certain formalities that had to be completed, and not even political connections or deep pockets could completely circumvent them.

Four days.

Four days of spending every moment with beautiful, intuitive, keen-eyed Scarlett and the wonderful people who believed themselves to be his family. Four days of listening to Maria prate on excitedly about her plans for their wedding. A required visit to the American Consulate in Florence turned into a pleasurable day of sightseeing with Scarlett, gawking at the Duomo followed by lunch at a charming café in the Piazza della Signoria. Four days of taking long walks in the Tuscan sunshine, eating glorious food.

Four days of talking to Scarlett, of learning about her, of finding new things to admire. One rainy afternoon by the fire, she'd suddenly set down her book and on impulse offered to show him the intricacies of picking a pocket.

He appreciated the lesson and, in return, offered to teach her how to fight. "My dad already showed me," she said primly. "I tried my punch out on Blaise in New York."

"I bet you did," he said, grinning at her. "All right. Here's how to use your own body weight against an attacker who grabs you from behind. Bet your dad didn't teach that."

Vin still smiled, remembering how pleasurably those lessons had ended—in bed together.

Such a strange way to live, Vin thought. He wasn't accustomed to such a luxurious squandering of time. He usually spent eighteen-hour days in the office, and that was what he should have been doing now, nailing down the details of the upcoming Mediterranean Airlines deal.

Instead, he sent his assistant on to Rome without him. He told his staff to handle everything, promising only that he'd arrive in Rome for the face-to-face meeting required by the other company's CEO, Salvatore Calabrese.

He'd spent the last twenty years focused on work. He told himself he'd be justified to take a few days off, but this was no mere vacation. He had a clear goal: making Scarlett love him so she'd sign the postnuptial agreement giving him the permanent control he needed to protect his son.

At least that was what Vin told himself as he spent hours walking with Scarlett through brilliantly colored autumn fields, on footpaths laced with cypress trees, holding her hand as they talked about everything and nothing. Hours of lingering together over meals, midday picnics beneath the golden sunlight, evening dinners inside by the fire. Vin found out why Scarlett was such a bad cook. "The day after my mother died, I tried to cook a can of soup over an open stove and nearly burned the house down." She smiled. "My father declared he'd be in charge of meals for safety reasons. My job was to keep the house clean and focus on school, when I was able to go."

She smiled about it now, but when Vin broke down the many sources of pain in that sentence—her mother died, they had to cook over an open stove, she wasn't always able to go to school—he marveled at her resiliency. He admired her strength.

That didn't stop him from arguing about what they'd name their son. He wanted a simple name like John or Michael. She wanted an Italian name from his family. "Like Giuseppe," she'd suggested hopefully. Vin had shut that idea down fast.

But he was afraid his emotions were starting to be compromised after four solid days of getting to know her mind and heart. Four nights of utterly exploring her body.

He'd spent hours kissing Scarlett, running his hands over her lush curves and overheated skin, as they'd set their bedroom on fire. They'd made love in every possible way as he'd explored every possibility of giving her pregnant body the deepest pleasure.

All in all, they'd been days and nights he would never forget. He was almost regretful to see them end.

But his plan was working. He could see it in Scarlett's green eyes when she looked at him now.

Against her will, she was starting to love him.

Perhaps Scarlett would have fallen in love with him anyway, without him trying so hard. Most women did. It was not something he was vain about; it was simply a fact. They could not resist his sex appeal, his raw power and the underlying attraction of his billions in the bank. He didn't have to *try* with women. It was usually the opposite. He would be cold to them, and they stunningly and stupidly loved him for it.

Scarlett was different.

For one thing, she didn't lust for money. In fact, she was suspicious of it as a manipulative tool. That just proved her intelligence, which made her even more desirable.

Seducing her in bed had been easy. Winning her heart was a little more tricky.

He'd had to share his *feelings*.

His *regrets*.

He still shuddered a little, remembering their conversation as they'd walked beneath the cypress trees last night, in the cool October air.

"Why did you move to New York after your mother died?" She'd looked up at the villa, the windows gleaming with warm light in the darkness. "You were only fifteen. Why didn't you come live here?"

His body had tensed. He should have known she wouldn't let that go. He'd wanted to say something sarcastic, or tell her to mind her own business. But looking at her hopeful, vulnerable expression, he'd known he had to do better than that, at least until they were safely married and he had the signed post-nup. And as intuitive as she was, he couldn't tell her a lie, either. So he'd shaped his mouth into something he hoped looked like a smile and told her part of the truth.

"Even at fifteen, I dreamed of starting my own company. Building my own fortune. My uncle was a hard-driving corporate lawyer. I knew if I moved to New York he'd be able to help me."

And Iacopo Orsini had. When Vin was eighteen, he'd taken all the money he'd saved from constant work, and the untouched payout from his mother's life insurance, and asked his uncle to help him draw up the necessary papers to set up his first company. Iacopo had also led by example, showing Vin it was possible to work every waking hour, and avoid inconsequential things, like spending time with family and loved ones. Or even *having* loved ones.

"Oh," Scarlett had said, and the light in her eyes had faded as she bit her lip. "That makes sense, I guess."

"Flying makes me feel alive," he'd heard himself add. "It gives me a sense of control. I can go anywhere. Do anything. Be whoever I want to be."

"It's your idea of freedom."

"Yes."

"That's funny. My idea of freedom is being able to stay in one place, as long as I want, surrounded by family and friends. Freedom," she said quietly, "would be a real home, filled with love, that no one would ever be able to take from me."

Their eyes locked in the moonlight, and for one crazy moment he'd wanted to tell her everything. He'd been tempted to offer up not just his body, not just his name, but his past, his pain, his heart. His future.

But it was a risk he couldn't take.

"Come on," he'd said abruptly. "Let's go inside."

The memory of how he'd felt last night still left Vin feeling uncomfortable. Vulnerable. Exposed. He didn't like it. It was a situation he didn't intend to repeat.

He had to get the papers signed as soon as possible so he could get back to a life he recognized, a life under his control.

But first things first.

Today was their wedding day.

Vin looked at his bride now, as she stood across from him in the villa's courtyard with the view of the wide Tuscan fields, as Giuseppe, as mayor of Borgierra, spoke the words that would bind the two of them in marriage.

In the distance, Vin could hear the plaintive cry of birds as they soared across the bright blue sky, as they were watched by Joanne and Maria and the other friends and Borgia relatives who'd packed in around them.

Vin couldn't look away from Scarlett's beautiful face. Her warm green eyes sparkled in the sun, shining with joyful tears as she smiled up at him. She was wearing a simple sheath dress in creamy duchesse satin, purchased in Milan, altered for Scarlett's advanced state of pregnancy. Her red hair tumbled down her shoulders, and she had a tiny fascinator with a single cream-colored feather and a bit of netting that his sister had selected. Large diamond studs to match her ring now sparkled in her ears, a gift from Vin. Marla had wanted her to hold a bouquet of white lilies, but on this one detail, Scarlett was firm: no lilies. "They're not just stinky, they're appallingly overpriced."

Vin smiled at the thought of Scarlett being worried about the price of flowers, when the diamonds she was wearing cost hundreds of thousands of euros.

Instead, she held a bouquet of autumn wildflowers. It was just like her, he thought. The vivid blooms were as bright as her hair, and the scent as sweet as her soul. But the wild roses still had thorns—little flashes of temper and fire.

Solemnly, Vin, then Scarlett, spoke the words that would bind them together as husband and wife. He didn't exhale until it was done and they were actually married. After everything it had taken to get her to the altar, it was surprisingly easy.

No man could now tear them asunder.

"You may kiss the bride," Giuseppe said happily.

Scarlett Ravenwood—Mrs. Scarlett Borgia now— looked up at him with joy suffusing her beautiful face.

Looking into her eyes, Vin felt dizzy with happiness. She was wearing his ring. Carrying his baby. Bearing his name. He hadn't felt like this since—

A cold chill went down his spine.

The last time he'd felt this happy had been in this very same villa, that Christmas when Giuseppe and Joanne had asked him to live with them. At fifteen, for the first time in his life, he'd felt wanted and loved. But within a week, he'd lost everything.

Looking at his wife's beautiful, joyful face, Vin felt a sharp twist in the gut, a darkness curling around his heart like a poisonous mist.

Letting himself be happy, letting himself care, was like asking for abandonment. For loneliness. *For pain.*

He couldn't let her change him. He couldn't let himself be vulnerable. He had to be tough. Strong. He had to keep his fists up.

"You can kiss her, son," Giuseppe repeated in English, smiling.

Lowering his head, Vin kissed her. The touch of her lips electrified him like a blessing—or a curse.

He heard applause and teasing catcalls from the loving, kind people around him. He wrenched away from the kiss. Staring at Scarlett, he suddenly couldn't breathe.

Giuseppe, Joanne, Maria and even, *especially*, Scarlett were so wrong to love him. If they only knew the truth—

As beaming family and friends came forward to offer their congratulations, Vin loosened the black tie of his tuxedo, feeling attacked by all the overwhelming, suffocating, terrifying love around him.

CHAPTER EIGHT

As SCARLETT SPOKE her wedding vows, looking up at Vin's dark eyes, she felt like every dream she'd ever had was coming true today.

Every day had been a new dream, from afternoons spent together in the cool autumn countryside, walking hand in hand as they talked about everything and nothing, to the deliciously hot nights they'd explored each other in bed, doing things that had nothing to do with talking. He made her feel…joyful. Sexy. Exhilarated.

He'd made her feel free. Like he accepted her just as she was. Like he…cared for her.

And she'd come to care for him, to respect and admire him. She'd started to even… But the thought scared her.

After all the romantic days and nights together, gazing into each other's eyes beneath the loggia and teasing each other with hot kisses behind the thick hedges of the garden maze, today's beautiful courtyard wedding, presided over by Vin's father, was the perfect end to such perfect days.

As she and Vin spoke their vows in the courtyard, surrounded by his family and friends, Scarlett looked up at him. She'd never seen such stark emotion in his dark eyes.

Was it possible Vin might be falling for an ordinary girl like her?

Scarlett's voice trembled as she spoke her vows, but Vin's voice was calm and steady and deep. She felt his lips brush softly against hers as a pledge of forever, and she thought she might die of happiness.

Then everything changed. The tenderness in Vin's

expression hardened, turned cold. As their family and friends came forward in the villa's courtyard to congratulate them, her brand-new husband dropped her hand as if it burned him and backed away, loosening his tie, as if he could barely stand to look at her.

What had happened? Scarlett didn't understand. She felt confused and hurt as she followed him into their wedding reception lunch, held immediately afterward in the great hall inside the villa. She tried to tell herself she was being too sensitive. They'd just gotten married, with a lifelong vow. That was what mattered. Not that he'd dropped her hand after he kissed her, and his eyes suddenly looked cold.

But it troubled her as she sat beside Vin at the head table through the elegant wedding lunch.

She looked around the great hall. Maria had outdone herself. The enormous room was filled with flowers and people and music. It was so warm with love, it barely needed the fire in the enormous stone fireplace. When the staff served a lunch of pasta and salad, Vin ate silently beside her. Scarlett smiled at him shyly.

He glowered back.

Scarlett's cheeks turned hot with embarrassment as she looked away. Maybe it was the sudden tension between them, but her lower back and belly started to ache strangely. She sipped sparkling juice instead of champagne, one hand rubbing her belly over the knee-length, cream-colored satin dress.

She told herself to relax. Whatever was bothering Vin, they had hours to work it out before they left for Rome tonight. He would close the deal with Mediterranean Airlines tomorrow morning. Vin wanted to check them into a suite at the best hotel in Rome tonight, their wedding night. While he was signing the papers, she could meet her new doctor and prepare for their baby's imminent birth.

She was trying to convince him that they should skip the hotel and go directly to live in the home he'd grown up in, but he resisted.

"It's a mess," he'd said shortly.

Now, sitting at the wedding luncheon, Scarlett sighed. Pasting a smile on her face, she turned away from Vin, who was still glowering silently at nothing, and turned to chat with Giuseppe and Joanne and Maria and her fiancé, Luca. She laughed and applauded as their friends and neighbors offered champagne toasts, half of which she couldn't understand, as they were in Italian, but they were lovely all the same. She just wished her parents could have been here to see her wedding day.

Tears rose to her eyes as her new father-in-law and mother-in-law and sister-in-law all hugged her and teased her and constantly asked if they could get her anything.

She had a family again. After all her years alone, she hated to leave them.

Rome was only three hours away, she comforted herself. She glanced at her handsome new husband. Maybe Rome would be even more amazing. The city where their baby would be born. Their first real home. It would be where their life together would begin.

Tears filled her eyes as she listened to Giuseppe's emotional toast, as he praised his son and expressed his gratitude that he'd returned to the Borgia family after so many years apart. She was still wiping her eyes and applauding at the end of his speech when Vin suddenly growled in her ear, "We need to go."

"Go?" Scarlett blinked. "But you said we could stay the entire day—"

"I changed my mind." He tossed his napkin over his empty plate. "I want to be in Rome before dark. I still have a lot of work to do. We've wasted enough time here."

Wasted? The best days of her life?

Scarlett took a deep breath, struggling not to take it personally. "All right. I understand." She was trying to understand, but her heart felt mutinous. She bit her lip, looking around. "We'll need a little time to say goodbye—"

"You have two minutes." Rising to his feet, he stalked toward the table where his bodyguards were busily flirting with two of the local girls.

Scarlett stared after him, shocked and hurt. The muscles around her pregnant belly clenched and she felt a sharp tinge in her lower back that made her leap to her feet.

"What is it?" Giuseppe said.

"I'm afraid we have to go," Scarlett said. "Vin is anxious to get to Rome. You know he has the big business deal in the morning…"

"That is a pity," Giuseppe said, rising to his feet. "You can't stay the rest of the day?"

"Thank you." Vin was suddenly beside her. He held out his hand to Giuseppe and said coldly, "It was a very nice wedding."

"You're welcome?" His father looked bemused as Vin shook his hand, then Joanne's in turn.

"You can't leave, Vin!" cried his sister. "You haven't even cut the wedding cake! I've planned activities for the rest of the day. There's a dance floor, and…"

"I'm sorry. As I told you from the beginning, I have an unbreakable appointment in Rome."

"Oh. Right." Maria looked crestfallen. Her fiancé, Luca, put his arm around her encouragingly. She bit her lip, tried to smile. "Of course, I… I understand."

Scarlett didn't understand. Why did they have to leave so soon, cutting off their wedding celebration? It seemed not just rude, but nonsensical. But she forced herself to hold her tongue.

Vin held out his hand to his sister, but the young brunette just brushed his hand aside and threw her arms around him in a hug. He stiffened, but she drew back with a smile. "We will see you soon, brother. Luca's family lives in Rome. He's trying to convince me to have our wedding there!"

"Oh?" His voice was cool.

"But we will see you sooner than that, I hope." Looking at Scarlett, she said, "Call us when the baby comes."

"Of course," she replied warmly, trying to make up for her husband's rudeness. "We will never forget all your kindness."

"Not kindness," Giuseppe insisted, patting Scarlett's shoulder. *"Family."*

She swallowed, blinking fast. "You've all been so wonderful…"

"Ciao." Vin grabbed Scarlett's wrist and pulled her away. She waved back at them, and they waved in return, until Vin and Scarlett were out of the villa and in the fresh air outside. The bodyguards were packing their luggage into the SUV.

"That was rude," Scarlett said to Vin as he helped her into the passenger side of the two-seater.

Vin's face was chilly as he climbed in beside her, starting up the engine. "You asked me to stop here for ten minutes, and we stayed for five days. What did you want, *cara*—to live here permanently?"

Without looking back, Vin pressed on the gas, driving around the stone fountain with a squeal of tires.

Twisting her head, Scarlett saw a crowd had poured out of the villa's front door to wave goodbye and cry out their good wishes. "Vin, wait!"

He ignored her, pressing down harder on the gas pedal until they were on the cypress-lined road, out of the villa's view, and all she could see were the bodyguards following in the big SUV behind them.

"What is wrong with you?" Scarlett demanded as she faced forward in her seat, folding her arms over her belly. "Why are you acting like this?"

"I'm not acting like anything. We stayed for the wedding. I thanked them for their kindness. It's time to go."

"We were rude! After everything they did for us—"

"Send them a thank-you card," he said harshly.

Gripping the wheel of the car, he made record time down the tree-lined road across the wide Tuscan fields, and they soon returned to the main road.

Scarlett was fuming. Arms folded tightly, she glared out her window, lips pressed tightly together. The interior of the car was silent for a long time, until they were back on the heavily trafficked *autostrada* headed south toward Rome.

"Stop pouting," he said coldly.

"I'm not." She continued to glare out the window at the passing Italian countryside. "I'm mad, which is something else entirely."

"Stop being mad, then." He paused. "I meant to tell you. I got you a wedding present."

Her jaw tightened, but she still refused to look at him.

"It isn't a gift that I could wrap," he continued, obviously counting on her curiosity to overcome her fury. "It's something I did for you."

"Well?" Wiping her eyes, Scarlett turned her glare on him. "What is it?"

Dodging through the increasing traffic of the highway, he said, "Blaise Falkner."

She frowned. "What about Blaise?"

Vin gave her a triumphant sideways glance. "I've ruined him." His lips spread into a grin. "He'll never be able to threaten you again. Or anyone."

Scarlett stared at Vin, feeling hollow. "What do you mean, you ruined him?"

"He's penniless, disgraced, destroyed. Abandoned by his friends. Even the Falkner mansion is getting repossessed in New York. So he's also homeless." Vin turned dark eyes on her. "I did it for you."

"I never asked for that!"

His jaw was hard as he focused on the road. "I protect what is mine."

Scarlett shivered, hearing an echo of memory.

What century do you think we're living in?

The century a rich man can do whatever he wants. To whomever he wants.

As the red car sped down the highway, she felt her belly again tighten painfully. It had been doing that with increasing frequency. Stress would do that, she told herself. It was stress. Not the early signs of labor.

She breathed, "What did you do?"

"Falkner wasn't as rich as people thought." Vin changed lanes rapidly, rather than slow down with the traffic. He gave a smug, masculine smile. "His inheritance barely covered half his debt. He refused to work and was spending thousands of dollars every night for bottle service in clubs. And women. I merely made sure his lines of credit were not extended and allowed his true financial situation to become public."

"You used your influence with the banks?"

"I'm a very good customer."

"And dropped hints to some aggressive reporter?"

He tilted his head thoughtfully. "I believe in freedom of the press."

"But how did you get his friends to abandon him?"

"Ah, that was the easiest part. Half of them only endured his company because he always footed the bill. He owed the other half money. Once he was broke—no more friends."

Scarlett might have felt bad for Blaise Falkner, if she

didn't still remember the terror she'd felt when he'd threatened to take her baby away and force her into marriage.

But still…

"Revenge is wrong," she said in a low voice.

"You're angry?" Now Vin was the one to look shocked. His expression turned hard. "He deserved it. He deserved worse."

Vin's expression scared her. He didn't look like the good-hearted man she'd come to know in Tuscany. He looked like the ruthless billionaire she'd fled in New York.

She felt tension building in her body. She put her hands on her baby bump and felt the muscles of her belly harden. Like a contraction. She took a quick breath. "You could have…just left him alone."

"I have the right to protect my family."

"We aren't in danger! We're thousands of miles away!" She took another deep breath, trying to will her body to calm down, to relax. If she could, then maybe these contractions would stop. "It was revenge, pure and simple."

"What do you want, Scarlett?" His black eyes flashed. "Should I have bought the man a pony, tucked him in with milk and cookies, thanked him for the way he threatened my wife and child? Is that what you think?"

"I think—" Her breathing was becoming increasingly difficult. She was beginning to feel shooting pains radiating from her lower spine with increasing frequency. Then—

She sucked in her breath as she felt a sudden rush, a sticky mess. She looked down at her cream satin wedding dress in dismay. At the expensive black leather seat below it.

She whispered, "I think I'm in labor."

"You—" His hard voice abruptly changed in tone. "What?"

"My water just broke."

Scarlett felt scared. Really scared. She looked at her husband. Vin stared at her, his dark eyes shocked.

Then his jaw tightened. "Don't worry, Scarlett." He grimly changed the gears of the Ferrari. "I'll get you to the hospital."

He stomped on the gas, and they thrust forward on the highway as if shot by a cannon. If she'd thought the car was going a little too fast before, now it went on wings, flying past the other cars like a bullet.

She braced herself, gripping her seat belt with one hand and her tightening belly with the other. Yet strangely, in this moment, her fear was gone.

Scarlett looked at her husband's silhouette. Through the opposite window, she saw the darkening shadows of the Italian countryside flying past in smears of purple and red. And though she had been so terrified a moment before, she suddenly knew Vin, so capable and strong, would never let anything bad happen to her or their baby. He would protect them from any harm. Even death itself...

She glanced behind them. "We lost the bodyguards."

"They'll catch up."

Scarlett held her belly as she gasped out with the pain of a bigger contraction. She felt Vin automatically tense beside her. Then she made the mistake of looking behind them again. "Oh, no—"

Vin glanced in the rearview mirror and saw flashing police lights. Scarlett saw him hesitate. She knew he was tempted to keep driving, even if every single policeman in Italy chased them.

But with a rough curse, he pulled abruptly off the *autostrada*.

The police car parked behind them. As Vin rolled down his window, the young policeman came forward, speaking in good-natured Italian. Vin interrupted, pointing at Scarlett in a desperate gesture. The man's eyes widened when he saw her sticky wedding dress, as she gripped her belly and nearly sobbed with the pain.

Five minutes later, a police car was clearing their path with siren and flashing lights as their car roared south to the nearest hospital.

Standing in the bright morning light of their private room in the new, modern hospital, Vin cradled his newborn son in his arms, staring down at him in wonder.

"I'll keep you safe," he whispered to the baby, who was gently swaddled in a soft blue baby blanket. "You'll always know I'm watching out for you."

Vin looked up tenderly at his wife, who was also sleeping. Labor hadn't been easy. She'd been too far along in her contractions to get any kind of epidural.

So her only option had been to just get through it, to breathe through each wave of agony that brought her closer to their baby being born. With each contraction, Scarlett had held Vin's hand tight enough to bruise, looking up at him pleadingly from the bed. He'd tried to stay strong for her, to hide his own anguish at seeing her pain. All he could do was hold her hand and uselessly repeat, "Breathe!"

Now Vin looked at Scarlett in wonder. She'd been so strong. He'd never seen that kind of courage. As she slept, he saw the smudged hollows beneath her eyes, dark eyelashes resting against her pale cheeks, subdued red hair spilling on the pillow around her.

He looked back down at their baby's tiny hand wrapped around his finger, and another wave of gratitude and love washed over him.

"Happy birthday," he said to his son, smiling as he touched his small cheek with his fingertips. "I'm your *papà*."

The baby kept sleeping.

Outside the hospital room window, Vin saw a beautiful October morning, a bright blue sky. He blinked, then yawned, stretching his shoulders as much as he could without disturbing the baby. What a night it had been.

Sitting down in a chair beside the hospital bed where his wife slept, Vin held the baby for an hour, watching over them. He brushed back his baby's dark, downy hair, marveling at the tiny size of his head, his fragility. Vin could never let anything happen to his wife. Or his child.

His son would have a different childhood than he'd had. Vin's own earliest memory in life was of crying himself to sleep after his nanny locked him in his bedroom when he started crying loudly for his mother. His mother hired servants based on their cheapness, not their reliability or kindness, and he was often left to their care for weeks while she enjoyed time with her latest boyfriend in St. Barts or Bora Bora.

Except on those rare nights Vin's grandfather came to stay, no one ever comforted him when he heard a scary noise in the darkness or was frightened there was a monster under his bed. Vin had learned that the only way to survive was to be meaner than any monster. The only way to survive was to pretend not to be afraid.

But now, holding his son, Vin felt real fear. Because he knew that if this tiny baby was ever hurt, it would destroy him. It made him wonder how his own mother could have cared so much more for her momentary pleasures than her own son.

Vin took a deep breath. He'd be nothing like her. His son would always be his priority. From now on, that was his only duty. His only obligation. To keep his wife and child safe. He'd have to build an even bigger fortune, to protect them from worry or care. Vin's heart squeezed. He had a family to protect now. And he would. With his dying breath.

"Vin."

He looked up to see Scarlett's tired eyes smiling up at him. She held out her hand, and he immediately took it.

"Look at our son," he said softly. "The most beautiful baby in the world."

"You're not biased," she teased.

He shook his head solemnly. "It's not opinion. It's fact—" he smoothed back the soft edge of the baby blanket "—as anyone with eyes could see. He'll be a fighter, too."

"Just like his father."

It didn't sound like criticism, but praise; and hearing that from her made him catch his breath. The golden light of morning flooded the bed and the white tile floor, casting it in a haze as their eyes locked for a long moment. Then, leaning forward, he gently kissed her.

When he pulled away, her green eyes were luminous. Then they turned anxious. "But, Vin, what about your meeting? The deal with Mediterranean Airlines?"

Vin's jaw dropped. He'd *forgotten*. He'd totally forgotten about the meeting that was so important it had been circled in red on the calendar of his mind. He looked at the clock on the wall. He'd been so determined to get to Rome, and here he was, in a hospital just north of the city. The time was nine fifteen. The meeting had started at nine.

"Maybe you can still make it," Scarlett said. "Give me the baby. We can have Larson or Beppe meet you outside. You still—"

"No." His voice was quiet, but firm.

"Are you sure?" He could see the desperate hope in her eyes that he would stay, even as she said, "I know what this deal means to you. You should go."

He wondered what it cost her to say that. Being abandoned in an Italian hospital outside Rome, exhausted and still recovering from her physical ordeal, with an hours-old baby, couldn't be what she wanted. But she encouraged him because she wanted him to have what he desired most.

But for the first time, something compelled Vin more than his business, or money, or even power.

He couldn't leave his wife and their newborn son. Not now. Not after everything he'd just seen Scarlett endure. Not when his baby was still so tiny and fragile and new.

His place wasn't in a boardroom in Rome. His place was right here, keeping watch over the ones who depended on him far more than any employees or stockholders. The ones who really mattered. His family.

And if part of him was incredulous he was making this choice, even mocking him for it, he pushed that aside. "I'm staying." He looked back at the baby. "What shall we call him?"

She looked at him with barely concealed relief, then smiled. "A name that has meaning in your family. If not Giuseppe, what about Vincenzo?"

"After me?" Vin shuddered, then shook his head. "Our baby deserves better. He must have a name of his own." He thought for a moment, then said haltingly, "My *nonno*— my mother's father— was very kind to me. He died when I was eight, but I never forgot him. He made Christmas special." His lips quirked at the edges. "He said it was his job, because of his name. Nicolò."

She considered. "Nicolas?"

Vin looked at his baby son's face and nodded. "Nico," he said softly. "I like it."

For long moments, they held hands without speaking, Scarlett propped against pillows in the hospital bed and Vin cradling their baby in the chair beside her. He thought he'd maybe never been happier, or so at peace.

But it ended too soon as Ernest, his executive assistant, burst into the hospital room. "Sir, did you turn off your phone? I have been calling."

"Obviously," Vin said tightly, "I did not wish to be disturbed. Whatever the problem, you can handle it."

"The deal just fell apart and the other CEO stormed out when you didn't appear this morning. Everything is a shambles in the Rome office…"

As he spoke, a nurse bustled in and wanted to check over Scarlett and the baby. Nico himself began to complain that he was hungry and wanted his mother.

As Scarlett eagerly took her baby into her arms, the chaos increased as Vin heard an argument in the hallway. Ernest went to check it out, closing the room's door behind him. But the arguments only got louder through the door.

"Handle your guests, please," the nurse told Vin crisply in Italian. "This is a hospital, not a nightclub."

Vin ground his teeth, then turned to his wife with a bright smile. Kissing her forehead, he excused himself and went out into the hall.

One of his bodyguards was physically blocking a slender man in glasses who was yelling and trying to push into the private room. Ernest was trying to mollify him in a low voice.

"What is going on?" Vin demanded.

"Ah. Signor Borgia." The slight man immediately relaxed and turned to him politely. "Salvatore Calabrese sent me. He wished to convey his displeasure at your disrespect today."

"No disrespect to Signor Calabrese was meant. As you can see, I was unable to personally meet him this morning to close the deal with Mediterranean Airlines because I was called away on urgent family business."

"Signor Calabrese found your lack of commitment to the business deal very disappointing. He wished me to inform you that he is father to four children and was not present at a single one of their births."

Vin wondered that any man would brag about something like that, but he said merely, "I would be pleased to reschedule—"

"That is sadly now impossible." The man pushed up his wire-rimmed glasses. "Signor Calabrese will be exploring options with your Japanese and German competitors, many of whom have larger, more established airlines than yours. He hopes you enjoy family time," the man continued politely, "as you'll soon have much more of it. Without the expansion your airline needs, you'll soon be ripe for takeover yourself." The man gave a little bow. "Good day."

As he departed, Vin stared after him in shock.

The Japanese and German airlines who also hoped to take over Mediterranean Airlines were indeed formidable and powerful. It hadn't been easy to convince Salvatore Calabrese that SkyWorld Airways was the right choice. Vin had been forced to personally meet with him in New York and London.

"All right. I'll take a gamble with you, kid," Salvatore Calabrese had told him finally. "You remind me of myself when I was young. A shark who'll win at any cost." He'd given Vin a hard smile. "Just meet me in Rome to sign the papers. I need that mark of respect. Plus, I need to know I'm selling my baby to a man who'll always put his company first."

Now Vin clawed his hand through his dark hair, thinking of the hours, money and effort that he and his team had spent, costing millions of dollars and thousands of hours, to put the deal together. This on top of the public debacle in New York of losing the Air Transatlantique deal. The snotty little assistant had been right. Vin's rivals would start to smell blood in the water.

A stab went through him as he felt the cost of making his family the priority today. Twice now, his relationship with Scarlett had wrecked badly needed business deals. And now, just when he most needed his airline to succeed, for the sake of his family, for the sake of his son's future legacy, he was facing another failure.

"It'll be all right, boss." Ernest looked at him nervously. "Plenty of other fish in the sea. Lots of ways to expand our airline. Right, Mr. Borgia?"

His executive assistant clearly expected reassurance, but Vin stared at him blankly.

For the first time ever, he didn't know his next move.

Maybe this was what happened, Vin thought numbly. When you started choosing with your heart, instead of your head.

CHAPTER NINE

"CAN'T YOU GO SLOWER?" Scarlett pleaded.

"No." Her husband sounded annoyed.

"Just a little—"

"Scarlett, this is Rome. If we go any slower, we'll be run over."

Sitting in the backseat of their brand-new Bentley SUV, she looked anxiously at their three-day-old baby quietly tucked in his baby seat beside her, looking up at her so trustingly, with those big dark eyes like Vin's.

At least, she comforted herself, he hadn't insisted on using the sports car. The two-seater had been professionally cleaned, and Vin had donated it to the highway police. "A little gift to say thanks," he told her.

Scarlett was glad it had gone to a good home, and grateful to the kindhearted policeman who'd helped them get to the hospital so quickly.

She still remembered how terrified she'd been that day, and how awful labor had been. Her body had felt ripped apart. But already, that memory of pain was starting to fade every time she looked at her baby.

Scarlett was happy to be leaving the hospital. The hospital staff had been lovely, but she was ready to go home. Ready but also terrified. Because that meant there would no longer be medical professionals hovering to give quick advice if Nico couldn't sleep at night or didn't seem to be eating enough.

But at least Scarlett knew she had one person she could rely on. One person she could trust. The person who'd never left her side, not once, even though that choice had cost him dearly. And she loved him for it.

She loved Vin for that, and so much more.

She was totally, completely in love with him. There could no longer be any question. She'd known it when, after holding her hand uncomplainingly through long hours of labor, he'd tenderly placed their newborn baby in her arms.

"Look what you've created, Mrs. Borgia," he'd said, looking down at her with a suspicious gleam in his black eyes. "You should be proud."

"*We* created," she'd corrected, looking up at him.

"We," he'd whispered tenderly.

And that was that.

She loved Vin.

Another thing that thrilled her—and terrified her.

Heart in her throat, she looked at him, in the front seat beside their driver. Bodyguards were following in the black SUV. Vin had told her he wished to remain in Rome for the foreseeable future, in hopes of patching up the deal with Mediterranean Airlines. Scarlett had been delighted. She already adored this country, this city. How could she not?

But at the moment, her husband was looking back at her, his handsome face the picture of disbelief. "Are you sure you really want to do this?"

His tone implied she was crazy. He'd asked her the same question at least six times since their driver had picked them up from the hospital.

"I'm sure," Scarlett said calmly.

"I have reservations at the best hotel in Rome. The royal suite. We'd have an entire floor to ourselves, in total luxury with an amazing view. Room service," he added almost desperately.

Smiling, she shook her head. "That's not what I want."

Vin folded his arms, his expression disgruntled. "It's a mistake."

"It's not a mistake to want our baby to have a real home, instead of living in some hotel. I don't care how fancy it is."

"You'll care tonight, when there's no hot water and the beds are lumpy. The roof probably leaks."

"You'd really rather stay at a hotel than your own childhood home?"

"It wasn't particularly great then, and I'm sure it's worse now." He turned away as the driver drove them deeper into the city. "I've rented it out for the last twenty years, and from what my staff has told me, the tenant didn't exactly improve the situation."

"Oh, come on," Scarlett said with a laugh, rolling her eyes. "It's a villa in Rome. How bad could it be?"

The answer to that question came soon, as she gingerly entered the faded, dilapidated eighteenth-century villa, set behind a tall gate with a guardhouse and a private cobblestoned drive.

Holding the baby carrier carefully in her arms—she'd refused all offers from bodyguards and her husband to carry it, as her baby's eight pounds was precious cargo to her—Scarlett went through the enormous front door into the foyer. Stepping over the crumpled trash on the floor, she went farther into the villa.

On the high ceiling of the great room, a disco ball gleamed dully in the shadows. She stopped.

Black leather furniture, zebra and leopard print pillows, strobe lights and multiple bowls of overflowing cigarette butts decorated the room. In front of the enormous marble fireplace was a bearskin rug stained with red wine... at least she hoped it was wine. Empty liquor bottles littered every corner.

Wide-eyed, Scarlett turned to her husband, who was watching her with amusement. "I told you."

"Was your tenant a playboy?" she said faintly. "From the early seventies?"

"Styles change. People don't always change with them." Vin's lips quirked. "Luigi did live here a long time. He was quite the ladies' man, for eighty-five."

"Eighty-five! So did he move, or…?" She paused delicately.

Vin shook his head with a grin. "Decided he was finally ready to settle down. Moved to Verona and married his childhood sweetheart."

"Wow," Scarlett breathed. "Getting married. At eighty-five."

"Just goes to show it's never too late to change your life." His sensual lips lifted to a grin. "He only moved out last week. So this place hasn't been remodeled yet." He tilted his head. "The suite at the hotel is still available…"

Scarlett shook her head. "No hotels. When I was young, we didn't live in any house long enough to make memories, good or bad. Don't worry," she said brightly. "We'll make this the home of our dreams!"

He snorted. "Dream—or nightmare?"

"This house has good bones," she said with desperate hope. "Wait and see."

Later, Scarlett looked back and thought the next two months of remodeling the Villa Orsini were some of the happiest of her life.

Their first night was admittedly a little rough. The bodyguards brought in the necessary supplies, then hastily decamped to a neighboring three-star hotel. Only the bodyguard who'd lost the coin toss was forced to remain, and he chose to sleep on a cot in the foyer rather than face the rats' nests of bedrooms upstairs.

So it was just Vin and Scarlett and their baby sleeping

in the great room, where the black leather sectional sofas were in decent repair, that first night.

She and Vin heated water themselves on the old stove for the baby's first sponge bath. It was almost like camping. There were no servants hovering. No phones ringing incessantly. No television or computers, even. They just shared a takeaway picnic dinner on a blanket on the floor, then played an old board game that Vin found in a closet upstairs, before they both crashed on the sofa, with Nico tucked warmly into his portable baby car seat next to her.

Her husband was protective, insisting that Scarlett take the most comfortable spot on the sofa, offering to get her anything she needed at any moment. When the baby woke her up at two in the morning to nurse, Vin woke up as well and tucked a pillow under her aching arm that held the baby's head.

"Thank you," she whispered.

"It is nothing, *cara*." His eyes glowed in the darkness. "You are the hero."

Just the two of them, she thought drowsily, regular first-time parents, a married couple in love, with each other and with their newborn baby.

The next morning, the hiring began, of designers and architects and a construction crew to start the remodel. No expense would be spared. "If you're determined to live here," Vin told her firmly, "we'll get it done as soon as possible."

As the villa was cleared out, cleaned, and slowly began to take shape, Vin suggested that they bring in permanent house staff. He wanted two full-time nannies—one for day, one for night—and a butler, housekeeper, gardeners. After their blissful night alone together, Scarlett had been crestfallen. She'd tried to convince Vin that she could take care of the villa herself. He'd laughed.

"You want to spend your every waking hour scrubbing

floors? No. Leave that to others." He kissed her. "You have a far more important job."

"Taking care of Nico?" she guessed.

His dark eyes became tender. "Being the heart of our home." She melted a little inside. Then his smile lifted to an ironic grin. "You've got your work cut out for you, married to a ruthless bastard like me."

He was joking, of course, she thought loyally. Vin wasn't a ruthless bastard. He was a good man, and in spite of his tyrannical instincts, she knew he saw her as an equal partner. After all, he'd let her make the decisions about driving instead of flying, about remodeling the villa rather than enjoying the comfort of a hotel. And most of all, he had married her without a pre-nup. As partners, they had a chance to be happy in this marriage, she thought, really happy, for the rest of their lives.

The days passed, turned to weeks. November became December. Scarlett had pictured the Eternal City as a place of eternal sunshine, but to her surprise, winter descended on Rome.

The villa had become livable. Tacky old furnishings were removed, and the walls and floors of ten bedrooms were redone. The kitchen was expanded and modernized. Bathrooms were scrapped and remodeled, and one of the extra rooms was turned into a master en suite bathroom with walk-in closet. Vin had wanted to fly in the interior designer who'd decorated his New York penthouse, but remembering the stark black-and-gray décor from the single night she'd spent there, Scarlett had refused. She wanted to make the villa warm and bright and, above all, comfortable. She'd do the decorating herself.

She loved every minute. Each morning when the baby woke her up to be fed, Scarlett woke up with a smile on her face, stretching happily in the enormous bed. She didn't get much sleep, with the baby waking her through the night, but in spite of feeling tired, Scarlett had never been so happy. Joy washed over her like sunshine.

She had the home she'd always dreamed of. The family she'd always dreamed of. The husband she'd always dreamed of. She had everything she'd ever wanted, except one thing.

Vin hadn't told her he loved her.

But soon. Soon, she told herself hopefully. In the meantime, the villa was larger than she'd imagined her home could be, so she brought it down to size. Made it homey and inviting for family and friends.

She carefully began to add household staff. Wilhelmina Stone was the first person she hired, luring her away from Switzerland as housekeeper by doubling her salary.

"You don't need to pay me so much," Wilhelmina had grumbled. "We're practically family."

"Which is why I insist," Scarlett replied happily.

Then a few other employees were added, two maids and a gardener, but Scarlett flatly refused the idea of a butler and two full-time nannies. Instead, the kind, fiercely loyal housekeeper soon became a second grandmother to Nico.

When the guest rooms became habitable, the baby's actual grandparents, Giuseppe and Joanne, came down from Tuscany for a visit in December, bringing Maria and Luca with them. They all enjoyed a weekend of sightseeing, which was ostensibly to "show the baby the sights of Rome"—as if a five-week-old in a stroller who couldn't yet sit upright would appreciate the Colosseum, the Pantheon and the Trevi Fountain.

"Of course he appreciates them," Giuseppe said expressively, using his hands. "He is my grandson! It is in his blood!"

"He can't even taste gelato yet," Vin pointed out, rather peevishly, she thought.

It was the only discordant note to the joyful melody of Scarlett's life. Vin seemed strangely uncomfortable around his family, and the more loving they were, the more he seemed to flee. Thirty minutes into their sightseeing tour, he abruptly announced an emergency at the Rome office that seemed like an excuse to leave. But Scarlett must be mistaken, because why would he want to flee his family, who loved him so?

In spite of that small flaw, Scarlett was happy and proud to share their newly beautiful home with the family that had been so kind to her. The best moment was when Maria and Luca announced they'd picked a wedding date: the second week of January, in Rome.

"A winter wedding, in Rome," Maria had beamed, holding her fiancé's hand. "It'll be so romantic."

"*You* are romantic," Luca had said rapturously and kissed her.

Scarlett had looked at Vin, but he'd avoided her gaze.

Since his parents' visit, he'd seemed even more strangely distant, spending all his time at the office, where his company was trying to devise a new offer to interest Mediterranean Airlines' CEO, Salvatore Calabrese. But the man flatly refused to have anything to do with Vin now. It made Scarlett indignant, but she knew her husband would wear him down. No one could resist Vin for long. Scarlett knew this personally.

Except she hadn't had to resist him at all lately. At least not *personally*.

He hadn't touched Scarlett in bed since their baby was born. It had been two months now since they'd last made love. At first, healing from the birth and exhausted from waking up with their baby, sex had been the last thing on Scarlett's mind. But now her body was starting to feel normal again, though she hadn't quite lost all the baby weight, and her breasts were still very full. Did he not find her attractive anymore?

She tried to ignore the feelings of rejection. She focused on the baby, who was growing chubby and starting to babble and coo. She made friends with her neighbors and started private Italian lessons with Mrs. Spinoza, a kindly widow who lived down the street. But it hurt.

Then one day while she was despondently surfing the internet, she had an idea about how to bring them close again.

According to what she read, men's needs were simple. Food. Home. Sex.

All she had to do was turn herself into the perfect wife.

Step one. Food. A man's heart was through his stomach, according to what she read online. So Scarlett learned how to cook. She started with boiling water, but within a week, she'd graduated to simple, fresh pasta dishes, which Wilhelmina tasted and pronounced, with some surprise, to be "delicious."

Vin didn't notice, of course. He generally got home late at night and would eat whatever wrapped dinner plate he found in the fridge, by the light of his computer at the dining table at midnight, usually long after Scarlett had gone to bed. But she learned new skills when he wasn't looking.

Step two. Home. A man's house was his castle. Make it warm and comfortable, and he'd never want to leave it. She looked around their newly remodeled, redecorated home. Check.

Step three. Sex.

For Scarlett, this was the hardest thing of all.

But on Christmas Eve morning, she woke up knowing that it was now or never. Today was the day.

She felt like Vin had barely talked to her in weeks. He always made an effort to play with the baby right before work, but all Scarlett seemed to get from him were cold

lectures when she evaded her security detail or told her
assigned bodyguard, Larson, he didn't need to follow her.
Which was exactly what she was getting this morning, too.

"Stop it." Vin glowered at her, coldly handsome in his
suit and tie. "I specifically assigned Larson to keep you
safe. Don't make it so hard for him to do his job."

Still wearing her nightshirt and white fluffy robe, Scarlett rolled her eyes. "You seriously think I'm going to be
attacked on the streets of Rome in broad daylight while
I'm pushing the stroller to Mrs. Spinoza's apartment? It's
silly! How am I supposed to practice my Italian with Larson glaring at her through his sunglasses? He makes her
so nervous she stutters!"

"I mean it, Scarlett," Vin replied. "Either do what I tell
you and let him do his job, or…"

"Or what?"

His jaw was tight. "I can't answer for the consequences."

Then he coldly left the villa, briefcase in hand. Without so much as a goodbye kiss!

She prayed her outrageous plan would solve everything.
Otherwise, she was about to make a horrible fool of herself. But she had to take the chance. As her father had always said, if you want things to change, change yourself.

The moment Vin left the villa for work, Scarlett got to
work, too. The enormous tree was delivered to the great
hall, along with boxes of beautiful decorations. She sent
the last members of the household staff on surprise vacation, leaving Scarlett and the baby alone in the villa, with
her bodyguard, Larson, at the tiny gatehouse across their
private cobblestoned drive.

Holding Nico on her hip, Scarlett decorated the tree
herself, talking happily to her baby, singing him Christmas songs, including one in Italian. Later, she started a
roaring fire in the enormous fireplace and prepared a din-

ner she thought Vin would love. Leaving the sauce simmering on the stove as evening started to fall, she gave her sleepy baby his dinner and bath, changed him into his footsie pajamas and tucked him into the nursery.

After Nico was safely asleep, she went into her luxurious master bathroom and started a bath. She groomed herself as carefully as a bride on her wedding night—the wedding night they'd never actually had, since she'd gone into labor on her wedding day—and moisturized her body with lotion to make her skin soft as silk. She brushed out her long red hair until it gleamed.

She didn't get dressed. Following the advice she'd read online, she left off her clothes entirely, for maximum visual impact. Not even lingerie. Not even panties. She just covered her naked body with only an old-fashioned pinafore apron.

Then Scarlett waited, terrified and breathless, for Vin to come home from work.

Tonight, she would tell him she loved him.

And then he'd tell her he loved her, too, and their lifetime of happiness would begin.

Either that, or…

She shuddered, caught between longing and terror as she waited for the door to open.

As Vin stepped out of his chauffeured Bentley into the frosted darkness of his street, he felt bone-weary.

It was late on Christmas Eve night, almost ten o'clock. He gave a low curse as he looked at his expensive watch. "I'm sorry, Leonardo," he told his driver in Italian. "I've kept you from your family. Thank you for staying."

"No problem, Mr. Borgia." His driver beamed at him. "The Christmas bonus you sent is sending our whole family on vacation to the Caribbean next month. My wife also appreciated the delicious homemade *panettone* from Mrs. Borgia." He kissed his fingertips expressively. *"Delizioso."*

Vin stared at him blankly.

"I need to thank you, too, boss," Beppe, his bodyguard on duty, interrupted. The hulking man actually blushed. "I used the bonus to buy an engagement ring for my girl-friend. I'm giving it to her tomorrow morning. And Mrs. Borgia's *panettone* was delicious. I ate the whole cake watching last night's game."

Vin was shocked. Scarlett had learned how to bake? She'd arranged Christmas gifts for his staff? And not just the practical gift of money, but a personal gift of home-made Christmas cake? "Oh. Yes." He cleared his throat. "I'm glad you liked it."

He hadn't even known. Hadn't realized.

But then, he'd been distracted lately. As his bodyguard raced ahead to enter the security code, Vin trudged to the door. He'd really thought he'd be able to convince Salva-tore Calabrese to sell him Mediterranean Airlines. But the man still wouldn't talk to him. Through his skinny assis-tant, he'd sent Vin a single cold message: "I'm interested in selling to sharks, not minnows." And no amount of corpo-rate diplomacy could now convince him Vin was a shark. Not since he'd put his family's needs over a business deal.

Vin felt like he was failing. At his company. At home. Working such long hours, he barely saw his baby son an hour a day. As for his wife...

Vin shivered.

He wanted to see more of her.

Much more.

They hadn't made love since Nico's birth, and at this point, all Vin could think about when he was around her was that he wanted to throw her against the wall and take her.

But he couldn't.

After what he'd seen Scarlett go through in the hospital, he didn't know when—or even if—she'd ever want him to touch her again. He didn't even know how to broach the subject. He'd never had to struggle with this before. So rather than constantly feel sexually on edge around her, like a mindless beast with only the barest thread of self-control, it was almost easier to avoid her entirely.

Looking up at the four-story elegant villa that had become a palace beneath her magical touch, and his wife the untouchable princess living inside it, Vin felt weary.

"Go home," he told his bodyguard. "We'll be fine tonight."

Beppe looked doubtful. "That's not protocol. Especially when there's the danger of—"

"It's Christmas Eve," Vin cut him off. He didn't want to think about Blaise Falkner tonight, or the fact that the man had disappeared from New York two weeks ago and couldn't be found. Another arena in which things hadn't gone to plan. "Go home. We have the security alarm. I saw Larson in the gatehouse. He'll call you if he needs you."

"If you're sure…"

"Go home to your girlfriend."

Beppe's eyes lit up. "Thank you, Signor Borgia. *Buon Natale!*"

"Merry Christmas," Vin replied dully. Alone, he pushed open the tall oak door of the villa. He went into the foyer.

Yawning, he closed the door securely behind him, turning on the security alarm. Tossing his briefcase on a table, he hung up his long black coat. Wondering if Scarlett had already gone to bed, he walked into the great room.

And he stopped.

An enormous Christmas tree, twenty feet tall, now stood in the great room by the blazing fireplace, lit up with thousands of brilliant lights like stars beneath the wood beams of the high ceiling.

Beneath the tree, he saw something even more dazzling.

"Welcome home," his wife murmured, smiling as she
held out a martini on a silver tray.

She was wearing a pretty, ruffled pinafore apron tied
around her waist. And beneath that...

Vin suddenly couldn't breathe.

She wasn't wearing anything under the apron.

Nothing at all.

Eyes wide, he stared at her as all the blood rushed south
from his head. He couldn't think. He gaped at her.

Scarlett tilted her head, looking up at him mischievously beneath her dark eyelashes. "Don't you want the
martini? It's eggnog-flavored."

He stared at her, frozen, drinking in the vision of Scarlett's long red hair tumbling down her shoulders, to the
tops of her full breasts, just visible above the ruffled top
of the apron. He could see the pale curve of her naked hips
around the edge of the fabric.

"No? Pity." Turning, she set the silver tray down on a
nearby table. He almost fell to his knees as he got the first
view of her naked backside, her lush flesh swaying, each
mound perfectly shaped for his palms to cup roughly in
his hands. He licked his lips.

"Where's—where's Nico?" he said hoarsely.

"Sleeping upstairs."

"And Mrs. Stone?"

"It's Christmas Eve, darling. I told her to take some
time off. Gave her a first-class ticket back to see her family in Atlanta."

Vin stood in the great room, surrounded by shadows
and light, dumbfounded by the vision of his wife, half-
naked below the enormous, brilliantly lit Christmas tree,
like the gift he'd waited for all his life.

A wicked smile traced her lips as she started to walk

toward him, slowly, deliberately, her hips swaying. She stopped directly in front of him, without touching him. He could smell the faint cherry blossom of her hair, the soft floral of her perfume.

His heart was pounding. He was afraid if he touched her, he would explode.

He was afraid he would explode if he *didn't* touch her.

"I made dinner," she murmured. "Pasta. I'm keeping it warm for you." She looked at him demurely, beneath the sweep of her black eyelashes, and tilted her hip, putting a hand on her bare, creamy skin thrusting out from the edge of her apron.

Vin didn't speak. Looking down at her, he deliberately started pulling off his tie.

Scarlett's expression, which had been flirtatious and saucy, turned wide like a deer's. She took a nervous step back.

But Vin had no intention of letting her flee. It was too late for that.

Sweeping her into his arms, he pushed her roughly against the wall, gripping her wrists and holding them firmly against the cool stone. "What else have you been keeping warm?"

"Vin," she breathed, searching his gaze. "There's something I've wanted to tell you…"

But more talking was the last thing he wanted. Cutting her off, he lowered his head, plundering her mouth in a ruthless kiss. He felt her soft, plump lips part beneath his own. Releasing her wrists, he tangled his hands in her hair, tilting her head backward to deepen the kiss.

She gave a sound like a sigh as her arms wrapped around his shoulders, pulling him closer. He stroked the sides of her body, her bare skin that wasn't covered by the prim apron. He shuddered as his fingertips and palms touched the warm, silky flesh of her hips, her tiny waist beneath the apron tie, the side curve of her voluptuous breasts. She stood on her tiptoes, straining to match the hunger in the kiss. He cupped his hands over the fleshy globes of her naked backside, feeling her sensuality, her heat—

With a low growl, he lifted her up, pushing her back against the wall, wrapping her bare legs around his hips. His rock-hard erection strained between them, with only his trousers and her thin apron separating them.

Bracing her against the wall, he held her sweet backside with one spread hand—nearly gasping with the pleasure of holding her there—and yanked open the tie of the apron. Pulling the fabric off her, he tossed it to the flagstones.

And just like that, he was holding his beautiful wife, in his arms, naked against the wall of their villa in Rome.

The flicker of warm red firelight glowed against her creamy skin, against her huge breasts with taut red nipples, her long red hair. Her red lips, swollen from the force of his kiss. Red, so red. Scarlet, like her name.

As he kissed her, Vin's body shook with need. He struggled to hold himself back. It was the first time they'd made love as man and wife, the first time since the baby was born. He should go slow. Carry her upstairs to their elegant bedroom, to the perfectly appointed king-size bed. Take his time. Be gentle. Make it last...

She pulled away from his kiss. With her naked legs wrapped around his trouser-clad hips, she leaned forward. He felt the warmth of her breath, the faint brush of her lips against the sensitive flesh of his earlobe as she whispered three little words.

He realized what she'd just said. With an intake of breath, he looked down at her.

They were alone in the great room, beneath the lights of the enormous Christmas tree that stretched toward the forty-foot ceiling. But even brighter than the lights of the tree, brighter than the orange and red flames of the fire, was the blazing glory of Scarlett's eyes.

"I love you," she repeated, as if the words had been building up so long that she could no longer keep them inside. Reaching out, she cupped his jawline, the rough bristles of his five-o'clock shadow. His whole body was shaking.

I love you.

He lost his last tendril of self-control, yanking his tailored trousers so violently that a button popped to the floor. He ripped his zipper roughly apart, tearing the fabric to shove his trousers down his taut hips.

Holding her backside with both hands, he spread her wide, and with one thrust, he pushed his thick, rock-hard length inside her, filling her hard and deep.

She gasped, clinging to him. He thrust into her again, holding her roughly against the wall, stretching her to the hilt. She gripped his shoulders, head tilted back, eyes closed in fervent need.

He watched her face as he pushed inside her a third time, slowly now, his own pleasure building as he saw the ecstasy on her face. A whimper escaped his own lips. Going slow was agony, sheer masochism, when he ached to rut into her, to explode. Her fingertips gripped deeper into his tailored white shirt, into the flesh of his shoulders. Her nails cut wickedly into his skin.

I love you. The soft hush of her words still rang through his ears. Through his heart. *I love you.*

He forced himself to be still inside her. He was so close to exploding, hard and thick and aching with need. Drawing back, he filled her again, inch by rock-hard inch. He felt her hips move against him, sucking him deeper inside her, as her full, heavy breasts swayed forward. She held her breath, her muscles tense. She suddenly threw back her head, crying out his name—

As he heard her scream her pleasure, he could no longer hold himself back. He rammed into her, fast and rough, crushing her soft breasts against his hard chest. His growl rose to a shout as he exploded inside her in pleasure so violent that, as he poured into her, for a single second his vision went black.

When he regained consciousness, emotion rose in his heart, emotion stronger than he'd ever felt, emotion that would not be repressed or denied.

"I love you."

The whisper was low, guttural, achingly vulnerable. For a moment, he didn't recognize the voice. Then Scarlett, still gripping his shoulders, looked at him with the most pure joy he'd ever seen on any human face.

And Vin realized with equal parts joy and horror that the voice had been his own.

CHAPTER TEN

HE LOVED HER.

The rhythm of those words was like the beat of Scarlett's heart, the rush of her blood.

He loved her.

She'd been terrified, waiting for him to come home. More than once, she'd changed her mind and started to get dressed. What if he rejected her? What if he laughed? What if one of the bodyguards walked in first?

But that hadn't even been her biggest fear.

What if her blatant gamble to seduce her husband back into her bed, and more important, to confess her love to him, was a total humiliating failure?

Growing up as she had, Scarlett had needed to be invisible for most of her life. But somehow, loving Vin gave her the courage to be outrageous enough to reach for her dreams.

Now they'd all come true.

Christmas morning, Scarlett woke with a smile on her face, hearing her baby's soft hungry whimper from the nursery next door. She looked at her husband sleeping beside her, and her smile became a beam of pure joy.

She loved him. And he loved her.

She blessed the internet. The crazy advice had worked better than she'd ever dreamed. After he'd taken her body so roughly against the wall, after he'd told her he loved her, Vin had wrapped her shivering body tenderly in his black jacket, and they'd gone into the enormous new kitchen to eat the dinner she'd prepared, homemade bread and *fettuccine alla carbonara.* Sitting together in the shadowy kitchen, he'd smoothed a bit of sauce off her cheek, looking at her with dark unreadable eyes, and all she could think was that she'd never been so happy.

He loved her.

Vin actually loved her.

After dinner, he'd held out his hand and led her upstairs. In their dark bedroom, he'd silently taken off his clothes and pulled her into the big bed, where he made love to her again, this time with aching gentleness. This time, as he pushed into her, their eyes locked, soul to soul. No separation. No secrets.

He loved her.

Now Scarlett shaped her lips silently into the words, tasting their sweetness again and again.

Creeping out of bed quietly, so as not to wake him, she wrapped her body in a white robe and went to the en suite nursery, where she lovingly swept their two-month-old baby into her arms. Cuddling him in the nearby glider, she fed him and rocked him back to sleep in the darkness. Once he was full and drowsy, she tucked him back in his crib.

Straightening, she looked out the window at the dark frosty dawn breaking over Rome.

She'd never been so happy. She didn't know what she'd done to deserve such happiness. Her heart was almost breaking with joy. Padding back on the soft rugs over the hardwood floor, she returned to the master bedroom, into the enormous bed that she shared with her husband. Closing her eyes, she pressed her cheek against his naked back and fell asleep.

A noise woke her.

Opening her eyes, Scarlett saw by the golden light filtering through the shades that it was midmorning. She blinked dreamily, smiling. "Merry Christmas." Then she blinked. Her eyes focused on Vin across the bedroom. "What are you doing?"

"Packing," he said tersely, tossing more clothes into the open suitcase. He was already dressed, in black tailored trousers, white shirt, a black vest and red tie. His dark hair was wet from the shower.

"Yes, I see that, but packing for what?"

Vin stopped, looking at her. His dark eyes were cold, and the gorgeous mouth that had kissed her into such uncontrollable spirals of pleasure just hours before was now pressed into a severe line. "I'm leaving on a business trip."

"When?"

"Immediately."

"What?" She sat up straight in bed. "But your parents are expecting us to drive up to Tuscany with the baby—"

"Impossible," he said flatly. "I just learned Salvatore Calabrese is in Tokyo to make a deal with another company. It's my last chance to make him sell to me instead."

"But you can't leave!" Scarlett struggled to calm her voice. She sounded like a whiny child, even to her own ears. "It's Christmas Day!"

He turned on her fiercely. "What do you expect me to do, Scarlett?" His tone was scathing. "Sacrifice my company, our son's future, just to stay here and play happy family with you over the holidays?"

Yes, that was exactly what she expected. She drew back, hurt and bewildered.

Vin stared at her for a long moment. Then he turned away to pack. "I'm not sure how long negotiations might last. It could be days. Even weeks."

"You might be gone through New Year's?"

"You'll be busy anyway. Packing for you and the baby."

"Packing for what?"

"We're moving to New York."

Scarlett's jaw dropped. Was she dreaming? She stared

at her husband in the bedroom she'd personally decorated, in the villa that, after all her devoted work, felt like home. "What are you talking about? We live here! In Rome!"

"And once we're back in New York," he continued relentlessly, "I want the baby to have another paternity test."

Scarlett sucked in her breath, feeling like he'd just punched the air out of her, falling back against the pillows. "Why would you ask that?"

He shrugged. "I want to be sure."

"Why?" Scarlett, who was not a violent woman, barely contained the impulse to leap out of bed and slap his face. "How many tests do you need? How many men do you think I've slept with? How big of a liar do you think I am?"

"It is a reasonable request. I've been lied to before."

"Not by me!"

"By others," he conceded, then glared at her. "I do not appreciate you taking this hostile tone."

"Hostile! You haven't begun to see me hostile!" Rising from the bed, she stomped across the bedroom and snatched up her white fluffy robe. Tying the belt around her, she ground out, "Nico is two months old, we've been married since October and you're suddenly wondering if he's your son?"

"Scarlett—"

"Go to hell!"

He grabbed her hands. "Stop it."

"I won't." Her breath came in angry gasps as she looked up at him with flashing eyes. "Last night you said you loved me, but now it's like you're suddenly *trying* to make me hate you. Why, Vin? Why?"

His hands tightened. His gaze fell to her lips, to the quick rise and fall of her breasts. For a moment, she thought he might kiss her. That he'd tell her what was really going on. That everything would be all right.

Instead, he abruptly let her go. "I expect you to be settled in my penthouse in New York by the time I'm done in Tokyo."

"Do you?" she retorted. "Let me guess. You already have a Manhattan doctor on standby to give Nico a few more paternity tests." She was shaking with emotion. "I'd almost think you want proof you're not his father!"

"That's not true, and you know it," he bit out. "I chased around the world to find you and my son. My intentions should be clear. I want you both in New York. We are a family." His voice was impersonal, chilly. "Furthermore, you will make sure Larson is always with you and the baby when you leave this house. I mean it, Scarlett."

"I told you, I'm fed up with having a stupid bodyguard! This is Rome! Who do you think will attack us?"

"I was attacked once in midtown Manhattan. In the middle of the day."

She exhaled. "What?"

"I was seventeen, an easy target, and the guy wanted my wallet. For twenty bucks, he sent me to the hospital." He looked at her. "When I got out, I learned how to fight. When I became a millionaire, I also hired bodyguards." His jaw was tight. "I protect what is mine, Scarlett. That now includes you and my son."

"I'm sorry about what happened to you, but that was a long time ago, and Rome is very safe…"

"I'm leaving one of the private jets for you," he continued implacably. "I expect you and Nico to be en route to New York by the end of the week."

"We're not flying anywhere!"

"Scarlett." He ground his teeth. "I own an *airline*. You need to get over it!"

Get over it?! She was quivering with rage but kept her voice calm. "No, thank you. Neither I nor my child will be getting on one of those flying death traps again."

"So let me get this straight," he ground out. "You believe the airline I've built into a multibillion-dollar business to be made entirely of *flying death traps*. You refuse to live in New York. And you intend to flout my wishes by evading the bodyguard I've hired for you, leaving both you and Nico continually at risk."

"That's pretty much it, yes."

"You have so little respect for my judgment? For my leadership?"

"Why should I listen to you, when you've made it clear you aren't listening to me?" Her arms, which had been folded angrily, fell to her sides. "I don't want to leave Rome," she whispered. "I'm learning Italian. I've made friends. Your parents live just a few hours away. Your sister's getting married here next month!"

"We can order flowers sent from New York."

"You can't be serious. She's your sister!"

"What did you think, Scarlett? That we'd live here forever?"

That was exactly what she'd thought. She'd been happy and she'd thought it would last forever. She whispered over the lump in her throat, "It's our home."

"Home?" Looking around the luxurious, comfortable bedroom, he gave an incredulous laugh. "This place isn't my home. It *was* my home, when I was a miserable child at the mercy of adults. But now, thank God, it's not." He closed his suitcase firmly. "My company is based in New York."

"I have no good memories there. None."

"You must have friends in the city."

"Blaise Falkner?"

"He's no longer in New York." His lips pressed together. "My head of security recently informed me that without money or a place to live, he's fled like the rat he is." He paused, and she got the feeling there was more he wasn't telling her. He finished, "So you have nothing to worry about."

"I know I don't. Because I'm not living there."

A knock on the bedroom door interrupted them. An unhappy-looking bodyguard appeared to collect Vin's suitcase. Scarlett whirled angrily on her husband.

"You're making Beppe work today? He was going to propose to his girlfriend!" She looked at the man miserably. "I'm sorry."

"Va bene, signora," he muttered.

Ignoring him, Vin glared at her. "I grow weary of your constant criticism."

"Oh, I see. I should just tremble and obey?"

"You're twisting my words."

"What am I, if not your partner? Am I your housekeeper? Your nanny?" Her cheeks burned. "Or just your whore?"

She had the satisfaction of seeing his eyes widen. Then they narrowed. "You're my wife. The mother of my child."

"Then how can you be so unfeeling? You said you loved me!"

Vin glanced grimly toward Beppe, now walking out with his suitcase, pretending to be deaf and blind to the whole conversation. "I am simply educating you in how it's going to be. You and the baby will fly to New York within the week. You'll be ready and willing to take the paternity test!"

Vin stalked out of the bedroom in his turn, slamming the door behind him.

Woken by the noise, their baby started crying in the nursery next door. Scarlett flashed hot, then cold. In a fury, she ran to the top of the staircase.

"We're not going anywhere!" she screamed down at him. "You can't force us!"

Vin's face was startled at the bottom of the stairs. But

he didn't answer. He didn't even pause. Just kept walking, straight out the door.

Hearing the roar of the engine as his car drove away,
Scarlett slumped on the top stair, tears running down her
cheeks.

How had it all gone so wrong, so fast?

Just that morning, she'd been so happy. So sure he
loved her.

But he couldn't. Otherwise, how could he act like this?

He didn't love her. All her dreams came crashing down
around her. Covering her face with her hands, Scarlett
choked out a sob.

Then, hearing her baby's wails, she took a deep breath.
Wiping her eyes, she rose from the top stair, hoping, as
she went to comfort her crying child, that she could somehow comfort herself.

From the penthouse bar of his ultramodern, luxurious
Tokyo hotel, Vin stared out unseeingly through floor-to-
ceiling windows displaying a panorama of the city, from
Hamarikyu Gardens to the illuminated Rainbow Bridge
stretching across Tokyo Bay. The night sky was dazzling
from the bar on the thirtieth floor.

Beautiful.

Bright.

Cold.

Vin took another gulp of his scotch on the rocks, then
set it back on the gleaming bar. He leaned his forehead
against his palm, feeling inexpressibly weary.

It had been two weeks since he'd last spoken to Scarlett. Two weeks since their argument. For two weeks, he
hadn't seen his baby, who in his short life might already
be forgetting he had a father. Vin's heart felt twisted, raw,
hollow.

He tried to tell himself it was worth it. Because Mediterranean Airlines was his.

It had been a hard fight, against a worthy rival, a far larger company. But Salvatore Calabrese had been duly impressed by Vin abandoning his wife and baby on Christmas Day to spend the week through New Year's and beyond focusing only on negotiations. Vin had spent the last two weeks holed up in this hotel with lawyers.

It was fortunate the view was so nice, because other than the ride from the airport, this was all he'd seen of Tokyo.

But the deal was done. They'd signed the papers an hour ago. Mediterranean Airlines was now part of Sky-World Airways.

Vin had won.

So why didn't he feel happier?

Sitting up straight on his bar stool, he tried to shake the feeling off. Scarlett was still in Rome, stubbornly defying him. She hadn't packed a thing, according to the bodyguards, whom she also continued to evade at will. She just continued her life as before, taking care of the baby and their home, helping his family arrange the last-minute details for his sister's upcoming wedding.

His so-called *sister*.

His so-called *family*.

Vin ground his teeth. It was physically painful for him to be around the Borgias, in spite of—actually, *because of*—their love for him. If they knew the truth, that he wasn't really Giuseppe's son, that Bianca had lied to him and used him for all of Vin's childhood, they would stop loving him.

It would be subtle, of course. They'd probably claim they were "still a family." But soon they'd be making excuses not to visit. Christmas cards would grow rare. Finally, there would be no contact at all, to the unexpressed relief of both sides.

Vin was done with Rome. It was the place where he'd been forced to feel emotions he didn't want to feel.

Especially for Scarlett.

His hands tightened on his glass of scotch.

But it would all soon be over. He glanced at his black leather briefcase on the bar stool beside him.

Ten minutes after he'd left Rome, with Scarlett's hurled accusations still ringing in his ears, he'd coldly called his lawyers and had the post-nup drawn up.

He should have done it weeks ago. But after their marriage, after the birth of their son, part of his soul had recoiled from betraying Scarlett. He'd known after he tricked her into signing a post-nup, she would hate him, too. So he'd put it off, telling himself there was plenty of time.

He'd been weak. He never should have allowed himself to delay his original plan. Of course he had to make Scarlett sign the post-nup. It was the only way Vin could make sure he could always keep them safe. He had to be in control.

Without it, Scarlett would continue to blithely ignore his demands that she keep the bodyguards close.

She didn't know that when Blaise Falkner disappeared from New York, he'd left a threat behind: "You'll lose even more, Borgia."

But that was just the point. Vin shouldn't have to explain such dangers to his wife. He didn't want to scare her. He just wanted to keep her safe.

Why did she have to fight him?

He'd felt so stupidly happy in her arms on Christmas Eve, making love to her. *Stupid* being the key word.

Waking up in the cold light of Christmas morning, he'd looked down at his wife in his arms, at the sweetly trusting smile on her beautiful face as she slept. For a split second, he'd been filled with joy. Then he'd felt a suffocating panic, even worse than the day they'd wed.

Happiness led to loss. It led to pain. And the joy of love could only end two ways: abandonment or death.

He'd decided long ago that he would never love anyone. He'd never give anyone that power over him.

But had he?

I love you.

He still remembered how he'd trembled when he'd heard Scarlett say those words. When he'd heard himself say them.

I love you.

He angrily shook the memory away.

He wouldn't think of it. Wouldn't feel it. And Scarlett's love for him would evaporate, along with her trust, after he tricked her into signing the post-nup. She would hate him then.

Good.

Vin's expression hardened as he took another sip of eighteen-year-old scotch. Taking love out of the equation would make things easier all around. Safer. Because he didn't like the things Scarlett made him feel.

Desire, when he thought of her.

Frustration, when she defied him.

Fear, when he thought of a life without her.

Without even trying, his wife made him feel vulnerable, all the time, in every way. This had to end.

Staring blankly out at the Tokyo night, Vin leaned his head against his hand. He'd return to Rome, ostensibly to attend Maria's wedding, with the post-nup in his pocket. He'd get Scarlett to sign it. And then—

He'd get his life back. Well-ordered. Controlled. With Vin completely in charge, and no risk of love or being vulnerable ever again.

"Borgia. Didn't expect to find you here."

Vin was jolted by a hearty clap on his shoulder. Looking back, he saw Salvatore Calabrese, still wearing the same designer suit and bright silk tie as when he'd signed the papers selling Mediterranean Airlines.

Vin already felt like he'd spent more than enough time around the self-involved, arrogant man, but he stifled his dislike and bared his teeth into a smile. "Hello, Calabrese."

The older man slid onto a nearby stool at the glossy wooden bar and gestured to the bartender as he continued, "Glad you finally pulled yourself together to convince me you were the right man to take my airline global."

"Me, too." Wishing the man would leave, Vin looked idly down at the ice cubes in his glass, so precise and modern, as was everything about this bar, this hotel, this beautiful city.

Calabrese ordered a drink from the bartender, then sat back on the sleek leather bar stool. "You learned a valuable lesson. Never put your family ahead of yourself, kid. Take it from a man who knows."

That was true enough, Vin thought. Calabrese was supposedly estranged from all three ex-wives and his four grown children, and he'd never even met his only grandchild. He definitely didn't put his family ahead of himself.

The gray-haired man tossed some bills on the glossy wooden bar, leaving a huge tip, then glanced at Vin indulgently. "I know you'll take Mediterranean Airlines to the top."

"That's the plan." Vin wondered how to get rid of him so he could order the second scotch he wanted in peace.

"As for me, I'm going to enjoy the big payout. Take life easy for a while." He picked up his martini and looked across the room. "Maybe I'll get married again. One of those girls could talk me into it."

Following his gaze, Vin saw a trio of beautiful young

models—Asian, pale blonde, dark-skinned brunette—sitting cozily on a white leather sofa by the floor-to-ceiling windows, with Tokyo as their backdrop.

Smiling, Calabrese raised his martini glass in their direction. They giggled, rolling their eyes and whispering to each other.

"You want to get married again?" Vin said, astonished.

"Why not? A wife's cheaper than a mistress. As long as she signs a pre-nup. Always make them sign. Take my advice." He winked. "If not for your current marriage, for the next one."

Vin watched Calabrese rise from the stool, then sashay toward the young women, his martini glass held high. Vin's stomach churned as his gaze fell back on his briefcase.

He was nothing like Calabrese, he told himself fiercely. *Nothing.* Their situations were completely different.

But when Vin left Tokyo that night on his private jet, he couldn't sleep, tossing and turning on the long flight.

When he finally arrived in Rome, the January light was gray. The holidays were over, leaving only the cold comfort of winter.

His driver was waiting to drive him from the airport. When he arrived at the villa, Vin set his jaw, wondering what he'd find.

He didn't have to wait long.

"Vin!" Scarlett appeared at the top of the stairs. Her skin looked pale against her vibrant red hair, her eyes flashing emerald green. She was simply dressed in a pale silk blouse and simple trousers, but he was newly overwhelmed by her beauty. He waited, expecting her anger.

To his surprise, she rushed down the stairs and threw her arms around him.

"I'm so glad you're home," she whispered.

The feel of Scarlett's body against his, the warmth of

her, was like fresh oxygen when he hadn't realized he'd been suffocating. Vin breathed her in, inhaling the scent of cherry blossoms and soft spring flowers.

She was the one to finally pull away. Her eyes were luminous in the shadowy foyer. "I haven't been able to stop thinking about our fight. I was…I was so—" he braced himself "—wrong," she finished quietly. "I was wrong."

Her admission shocked him. Vin would never have admitted he was wrong about anything. If he ever was. Which he wasn't. "About?"

"New York." She gave him a wobbly smile. "You're right. It's your company headquarters. What am I going to do—" she gave an awkward laugh "—demand that hundreds of employees uproot their families and move to Rome, just because I love it here?" She took a deep breath, then tried to smile. "I was being selfish. I'm the one who said we should be partners. So…we should at least talk about it. I still won't take a plane, but maybe I could take a ship. Isn't marriage about compromise?"

"Yes," he lied.

"But—" Scarlett gave him a shy smile "—I'm sure you want to see the baby…"

"Yes." And he meant it.

Taking his hand, she led him upstairs. Entering the shadowy nursery, Vin looked down at his sleeping son. He heard the soft snuffle of his breath, saw the rise and fall of his chest. Nico. His precious boy. He was here. He was safe. The baby already looked different. He'd grown in two weeks. Vin hated that he'd been away so long.

Never again.

He looked at Scarlett. There could only be one person in control of his life. His home. His child. And that was Vin.

The ends justified the means, he told himself. Scarlett might hate him at first, but eventually she would thank him.

Or she wouldn't. But either way, he would get his life back. Without the chaos and messy emotion she brought.

All Vin had to do was lull her back into her previous happiness and trust in him, then once she'd lowered her guard, trick her into signing the postnuptial agreement, written in Italian, giving him every right and power over every decision.

Her love for him was her weakness.

As for his own feelings—he would not feel them. They did not exist.

The one who cared least was the one who'd win.

"I missed you, Scarlett." Vin gave her a smile so sensual that she blushed to her ears. Excellent. "I swear to you on my life," he said softly, "I'll never let us be apart so long again."

She smiled happily, not knowing his dark intentions. Taking her hand, he rubbed his thumb lightly against her palm, then kissed it, feeling her shiver.

Soon, she would be unable to defy him. His decisions would automatically prevail. She would be forced to get over her ridiculous fear of flying and travel with him when he wished. It would be good for their family. And their marriage. A flash of heat went through him as he looked down at her, at the curve of her white throat, the shape of her full breasts beneath her silk blouse.

From now on, she would have no choice but to obey. In his home. In his bed. She'd be at his command. Exactly where she belonged.

CHAPTER ELEVEN

SOMETHING HAD CHANGED in Vin. As Scarlett welcomed him back from Tokyo, she couldn't quite figure out what it was.

Their last time in bed together, on Christmas Eve, had been rough and sensual and explosive. Even when he'd been tender, as he pushed inside her, his emotion had been raw on his face.

But today, since he'd returned, she felt a distance. Even as he smiled at her, even as he held her in his arms, even as he leaned down to kiss her, his dark eyes hinting at untold delights to come later—even then, there was something hidden behind his expression.

What was he hiding?

Was she imagining it?

She puzzled over it all day as they played with the baby, then got ready to go out for the evening. When she broached the subject of moving to New York, he told her he didn't want to discuss it. "Tonight, I just want to enjoy your company, *cara*."

They went out that night to his sister's wedding rehearsal dinner at a charming restaurant not too far from the Piazza Navona. Giuseppe, Joanne and Maria were delighted when he'd arrived. They'd all missed him, too. Halfway through the dinner, when Scarlett rose to her feet and publicly toasted his success with the Mediterranean Airlines deal, everyone at the table clapped and cheered.

Vin ducked his head, looking embarrassed. After all the work he'd put into the deal, his boyish humility made her more proud of him than ever. And love him more than ever.

Finally, after they returned home, after he tucked their sleeping baby into his crib, he took Scarlett to bed, too. She relished the warmth of him, the strength of him, the feel of him beside her.

She'd missed him for those two weeks.

It scared her how much she needed him now.

This time, as Vin made love to her, he held her gently, tenderly, looking deeply into her eyes. But his own eyes were carefully blank.

He touched her as if his fingertips wished to tell her everything he could not put into words. She tried to guess. He was sorry? He regretted their fight—which had been so awful, so brutal to her heart? That he hadn't lied when he said he loved her?

He made her body explode with ecstasy as he poured into her with a groan, then afterward he held her all night, snugly against his chest, in a way he'd never done before.

Cradled against him, with his strong arms around her, Scarlett felt protected. She decided she was imagining things, creating problems where they didn't exist. They were husband and wife. They were partners in life. They were in love.

She woke up smiling for the first time in two weeks. She heard a morning bird singing outside and stretched, yawning, every bit of her body feeling deliciously satisfied. How could she be anything other than happy? Vin was home at last. And today was Maria's wedding day.

Whatever conflicts arose between her and Vin, they'd work through them. Maybe they'd live in Rome for half the year, New York the other half.

She looked over at his side of the bed, but it was empty.

Scarlett started to get out of bed in her negligee, when she heard the bedroom door kick open. Startled, she saw

Vin, wearing only a towel wrapped around his trim waist, holding a breakfast tray with a rose in a small bud vase.

"You brought me breakfast?" Scarlett said in surprise. "But you must be exhausted. You traveled so long yesterday…"

"Exactly. I left you here alone to take care of Nico and my sister's wedding and all the rest. It's time I took care of you for a change." His dark eyes crinkled as he smiled, setting the tray on her lap, over the white comforter.

"By the way," he said casually as he turned away, "I've left some papers on the tray for you to sign. They're under the rose."

Frowning, Scarlett looked down. "What kind of papers?"

"No big deal." He shrugged. "Just to officially mark that you are my wife. For the Italian authorities."

She glanced at the top sheet. It was written in Italian and did seem to say something about being his wife. But her Italian language skills, in spite of her recent study, weren't strong enough to sort through the indecipherable legalese. She hesitated. "My dad always said only a fool signs something he doesn't understand. I should get it translated before I sign it."

"Sure, whatever you want," he said carelessly as he left the room. A minute later, he returned with a carafe. Coming back to the bed, he poured steaming coffee into a china cup, adding liberal amounts of cream and sugar, then put it on her tray, smiling down at her tenderly. "From now on, I'm going to take better care of you. Treat you like you deserve. Like a princess. Like a queen."

Looking up at him, Scarlett's heart twisted with love.

"Enjoy your breakfast, *cara*." He cracked a sudden grin. "I'm going to take a shower. Feel free to join me if you're feeling—" he lifted a teasing eyebrow *"—dirty."*

With a whistle, he turned away, dropping his towel to

the floor. Scarlett's lips parted at the delicious view of her husband's muscular backside before he disappeared into the bathroom. It took several seconds before she was able to focus again.

She looked down at the papers, thinking of everything she had to do today before the evening wedding. After weeks of procrastination, she still hadn't figured out what to wear. She desperately wanted to look good at the formal event, to show her respect to Maria and the rest of Vin's family. But the dreaded the pressure of scouring the chic designer shops of Rome. She always felt like a chubby bumpkin. The thought of also going to look for an English-speaking lawyer to translate and advise her felt like one unpleasant task too many.

Besides, she was Vin's wife, the mother of his child. For better or worse. If she truly believed she was his partner, why treat him like an enemy? She didn't want to be suspicious. She wanted to trust him.

So she would. End of story.

Smiling to herself in relief, Scarlett signed the papers with a flourish, then enjoyed the delicious breakfast. She polished off the almond croissant at the exact moment she heard her baby starting to fuss in the nursery. She brought the baby back to their bedroom and was cuddling and nursing him in bed when Vin came back, wrapped in a white terry cloth robe, his dark hair wet, his black eyes smoldering.

"Did you enjoy your breakfast, *cara*?"

"It was amazing. Thank you so much." She held up the signed papers. "I have these for you."

His eyes lit up with something dark and deep. He came forward. He gently took the papers from her. Seeing her signature, he kissed her on the temple and said in a low voice, "Thank you, Scarlett."

"No problem," she said, smiling up at him. Then she

sighed. "If only I could solve the problem of what to wear tonight so easily."

His own smile widened. "*Cara*, that is one problem I can solve for you."

With a single phone call, Vin solved everything. He arranged for a team of stylists to come to the villa. Beauty specialists appeared that afternoon to do her nails, hair and makeup. As Nico rolled around on the soft pad of his baby gym nearby, cooing and batting at soft dangling toys, Scarlett sipped sparkling mineral water while clothing stylists presented thirty different gowns to choose from, each more exquisite than the last.

Then she saw one that took her breath away, long and sapphire blue. When she tried it on, it made her figure look like an hourglass, especially with the lingerie underneath, a push-up bra more outrageous than she would have ever selected for herself. It made her breasts high and huge with sharp cleavage beneath the gown's low-cut bodice. The hairdresser twisted her red hair in an elegant chignon, and the makeup artist made her lips deep red, darkening her eyes with kohl. When Scarlett finally saw herself in the mirror, she gasped. She almost didn't recognize herself.

"*Bellissima,*" her hairstylist said, kissing his fingertips expressively. Scarlett blushed.

Vin had said she'd be treated like a princess, and she felt like one. She turned anxiously to Wilhelmina, who was now holding the baby. She'd become Scarlett's trusted friend. "What do you think?"

The housekeeper looked her over critically, then smiled. "Sugar, I think that husband of yours is likely to die of pride."

Scarlett prayed she was right, and that Vin didn't think she looked like an ordinary girl playing dress-up, pretending to play the role of a glamorous, sexy, sophisticated woman.

Kissing her baby's cheeks, which were getting chubbier every day, Scarlett floated out of the master bedroom, into the hall, still trembling, wondering what Vin would say when he saw her. She paused at the top of the staircase as she heard low words from below.

"Blaise Falkner..."

The voices cut off sharply as Vin and his assistant saw her. But why would they be talking about that awful man?

Her husband's eyes widened as she came down the stairs, holding the handrail carefully so she didn't trip on her four-inch, crystal-studded high heels. He met her at the bottom of the staircase.

"You dazzle me," he murmured too softly for his assistant to hear. Taking her hand, he whispered, "Forget the wedding. Let's go back upstairs..."

Her cheeks burned pleasantly, but she bit her lip. "Were you talking about Blaise Falkner?"

Vin started to shake his head, but Ernest, his assistant, interjected, "We haven't been able to track him since he left New York."

"Track him? What do you mean?"

Vin glared at his assistant, then kissed the back of her hand. Scarlett shivered as she felt the hot press of his sensual lips against her skin. "It's nothing to worry about. He's probably just too embarrassed to show his face. Drowning his sorrows in a gutter." He looked at her. "Scarlett. You are so beautiful."

Her blush deepened. "Thanks. Um. You look nice, too."

Her praise felt woefully inadequate. His black tuxedo jacket was tailored perfectly, showing off his amazing physique from his muscular shoulders to his taut waist. His dark eyes were intense in his handsome face with a jawline and cheekbones that would cut glass. But he wasn't just superficially handsome. It was more than that. Some might think he was arrogant, but Scarlett alone knew his heart, his goodness, his love for his family. That was what she loved.

Frowning, Vin tilted his head. "You just need one thing."

"What?"

Reaching to a nearby table for a flat black velvet box, he drew out a large, dazzling diamond necklace. She gasped as she felt the cold weight of the diamonds clasped gently around her throat. Then he kissed her at the crook of her neck, and she felt a rush of heat. She whispered, "Thank you."

"Now we can go," he said softly.

They kissed their baby son good-night, leaving him happily cuddled in Wilhelmina's arms, and went out into the cold night. Vin gently draped her white stole over her shoulders as they crossed their cobblestoned driveway to the waiting limousine. The gate opened on the street, and the driver, with two bodyguards traveling behind them, whisked them off to the grand *palazzo*.

Maria and Luca's evening winter wedding was sublimely beautiful, lit with candles and white flowers in the gilded receiving room of the *palazzo*. Giuseppe walked her down the aisle, tears shining on his face. Sitting nearby, Joanne cried, as well. Scarlett watched the young couple speak their vows and her heart felt overwhelmed with joy as she looked at her husband beside her and felt all the love around them.

Afterward, they adjourned to the ballroom for a formal dinner. The young bride and groom sat at a table on a dais, with their immediate families on each side of them. That included Vin and Scarlett. She hugged the bride and groom, and then Giuseppe and Joanne. She listened to the speeches toasting the bride and groom, mostly in Italian, and tried to understand. She enjoyed the freedom to drink champagne.

But the whole time, Scarlett was aware of her husband beside her, looking down at her with his darkly sensual gaze. He kept giving quick stolen kisses on her bare shoulder above the sweetheart neckline of her strapless blue gown. He kissed her on her cheek. On the lips. She leaned against him, reveling in his nearness. It was a beautiful wedding, but she could hardly wait to get home…

"We're going to miss you," the bridegroom's father, a wealthy businessman who owned this grand *palazzo*, called across the table to Vin halfway through the third course. "My son was secretly hoping your wife would give Maria some cooking lessons."

"Papà!" the groom protested.

"Luca!" The bride tossed her head in her elegant white veil, pretending to pout. "But if I learn to cook, how would we support the restaurants? One must think of helping the economy!"

But Scarlett frowned at Luca's father. "What do you mean, you'll miss us?" She looked at her husband with dismay. "Are you going on another business trip?"

"I heard you're moving to New York," Luca's father said. "In fact, I heard you've already rented out your villa here on long lease to some Hollywood actor and bought a brand-new duplex in New York for some obscene amount. I read it in the paper—was it fifty million dollars?"

Scarlett relaxed, laughed. "I'm afraid you've heard incorrectly, Signor Farro. We are talking about New York, but we haven't decided anything. We certainly haven't rented out our…"

Her voice trailed off as she saw Vin's face. Ice entered her heart.

"You wouldn't do that," she said in a small voice. "Not without talking to me. After everything I put into our home, you wouldn't rent it out from underneath me…"

Vin's expression was closed. "The decision has already been made."

"By who?" Scarlett pulled away. "By you?"

The smiles had fallen from the faces of the bride and groom. Their parents started to look anxious. Chic guests at nearby dinner tables turned to look as their voices rose.

Vin set his jaw. "Yes, by me. You were being unreasonable."

Her lips parted in disbelief. "Unreasonable?"

"I allowed you to stay in Rome—"

"Allowed!" she cried.

"—until Maria's wedding. But I already made it clear. My headquarters is in New York. Tomorrow, we will pack a few suitcases and fly there. The rest of our things can be forwarded. It's true. I have bought a brand-new penthouse close to my office, near good private schools for Nico."

Vin sat back, looking pleased with himself, as if he expected praise. Scarlett felt numb.

"We already have a home, here in Rome," she whispered.

"You'll like New York even better when we arrive tomorrow night."

"I'm not getting on a plane."

Vin's expression changed to a glower. "You have to face your fears."

She hated his patronizing tone. "No, I don't."

"You have no choice now. You—"

"Children, children…" Vin's father broke in, his weathered face anguished. "Scarlett, my dear one, I am sure my son only meant the best. But if you do not want to leave Rome, he will not force you. He is a good man. Vincenzo, my son, you must tell her that…"

Vin stood up so fast his chair fell to the floor of the dais. The noise of the crash echoed in the suddenly silent ballroom. His voice was cold as he looked at Giuseppe.

"Stop calling me your son. I am not."

Giuseppe goggled at him. Joanne and Maria both drew back in shock.

Vin's lip curled. "You wondered why I ignored you for twenty years?" he said in a low voice. "Right before my mother died, when I asked her if I could live with you in Tuscany, she laughed in my face. She told me I was the result of a one-night stand with some musician in Rio. She lied to you, Giuseppe," he said deliberately, almost cruelly, "so you'd give her money. And you paid her. Blindly. Just as you blindly loved me all those years." He slowly looked to Joanne and Maria. "So do not presume to lecture me. You are not my family." He turned to Scarlett, his eyes like ice. "And you will do what I say. You have no choice. You signed the agreement."

"Agreement?" She was still reeling from his revelation that Giuseppe was not his father. Then she realized what he was talking about, and a sick feeling rose inside her. "Those papers this morning—"

He glanced at all the people in the ballroom, then spoke too quietly for them to hear. "I always intended to make you sign, Scarlett. Either before marriage or after."

The pre-nup he'd once threatened her with. The agreement that gave him the right to make all decisions about their baby's life, and hers. The agreement that gave Vin full custody of Nico if he ever decided to divorce her. *And she'd signed it.*

Scarlett's world was spinning, crashing, on fire. Standing up from her chair, she stared at him in horror. Then, snatching her crystal-encrusted minaudière from the table, she turned away in her four-inch heels, ducking around the waiters who'd just come pouring into the ballroom with the next course. By the time she fled the ballroom, she was crying.

How could she have been so stupid?

She should have listened to her fears, not her hopes.

Don't tell him about the baby.

Don't get a DNA test.

Don't marry him.

Don't love him.

And most of all:

Always read before you sign.

Furiously, she wiped her eyes, but tears clouded her vision as she stumbled into the empty, high-ceilinged hallway. She saw Beppe leave his post outside the ballroom door and start to follow her.

"Don't even think about it!" she barked. She'd never spoken sharply to him before. She had the unhappy satisfaction of seeing him stop, his expression hurt.

Turning away, Scarlett ran past a security guard sleeping in a chair inside the foyer. She went out the front door of the *palazzo*, through the same door where she'd arrived with such happiness on Vin's arm just hours before.

Then, the exclusive Roman street had been jammed with arriving cars, gleaming and luxurious, many driven by chauffeurs. Now, the street was dark and cold and empty.

It was so cold, the drizzle of rain had turned to soft, silent snowflakes. A small dog trotted down the street sniffing at doorways. She saw a shadow of a homeless man leaning against the corner. She shivered as snowflakes melted like ice on her bare skin. She'd been in too much of a hurry to grab her white stole. But who cared about being cold?

She'd been so happy. She swallowed against the ache in her throat. With her baby. Her home. The man she loved. So completely happy.

But it had all been an illusion. Vin baiting his trap.

She had to get out of here.

Scarlett's heart pounded as she stood alone in the darkness in front of the *palazzo*. Down the street, she saw a taxi coming her direction. She could flag it down. She could rush to the villa, grab Nico and disappear. She knew how. She'd done it before.

Her heart pounded as she watched the taxi draw closer. The thought of leaving Vin, even now, and also separating him from the baby he loved, filled her with anguish.

She tried to steel herself. She told herself she had no choice. She raised her hand to flag down the taxi.

Freedom. For her entire childhood, freedom had been her rallying cry. She had to follow her dream—

Scarlett remembered the look on her father's face the day she turned eighteen and told him she'd given up her dreams of college and ever settling down. With tears in his eyes, he told her that after all their years on the run, he was turning himself in.

"What about freedom?" she'd cried.

"We were never free," he'd said quietly. "Not once. I made a horrible mistake, Scarlett. I was a coward. Running away all these years, I ruined your life, and your mother's. But no more. You will be free now." He'd taken a deep breath. "I'm doing this so you'll be free."

"Signorina?"

The taxi driver was looking at her impatiently through his open window.

Scarlett stared at him. Then, lowering her arm, she slowly shook her head. Numbly, she watched the taxi drive off.

She'd run from Vin before. If she ran now, kidnapping her innocent baby from his father, starting life as a fugitive, she wouldn't be following a dream of freedom. Not when her only idea of real freedom was to have family, stability and a real home.

"Scarlett!"

Her shoulders tightened at Vin's angry voice behind her. With a deep breath, she turned to face him.

He stopped in front of her as gentle snowflakes flurried softly to the sidewalk in the dark, cold night. "There's no point in running away," he said quietly. "The postnuptial agreement gives total control of our baby's future to me. And since I know you'll never be parted from him—" he reached out to caress her cheek "—that gives me total control over you."

For a second, she shook with fear, with regret, with rage. Then she remembered the one thing she still had.

Love.

With a deep breath, she lifted her chin, looking straight into his eyes.

"I'm not going anywhere. I'm staying right here."

Vin looked surprised. Then he caught himself and glared at her. "Good—"

"But I'm not going to let you push me around." She put her hand over his. "I love you, Vin. And you love me. That was the whole reason for this, wasn't it?"

"What are you talking about?"

"You're afraid to love me."

He dropped his hand with a snort. *"Afraid."*

"Yes, afraid. So you tried to create a wall between us." She stepped closer, until she could see the white of her breath mingle with his in the faint light. She could see the snowflakes that had fallen in his dark hair and eyelashes. "But I'm not going to let you do it. We love each other. We belong together."

"You signed it. There's nothing you can do now."

"You're wrong." Reaching up, she gently caressed his rough cheek and whispered, "I can call your bluff."

His eyes widened, and he staggered back.

"You won't hurt me," she said. "You can't. Because you love me. And I love you."

"Stop saying that—" he said hoarsely. He clenched his hands at his sides, then turned on his heel, stalking back into the *palazzo*, leaving Scarlett standing alone on the sidewalk on the dark, quiet street.

She turned her face toward the snowflakes, relishing the feel of them, soft and cold, against her overheated skin.

She had to be right. She had to be.

If she was wrong…

Scarlett heard heavy footsteps behind her. Had Vin already returned to tell her he'd changed his mind about the postnuptial agreement? Filled with hope, she turned.

But it wasn't her husband. The scruffy-looking homeless man from the corner now stood before her.

Confused, she drew back. "Can I help you?"

The man was dressed badly, his face lumpy. But when he smiled, she suddenly choked out a gasp as she recognized his face beneath the dirt.

"Yes, Scarlett." Blaise Falkner's eyes looked crazy above his evil smile. "You can."

As Vin entered the *palazzo*, his whole body felt tight, his hands clenched at his sides. He didn't even know where he was going. He just felt sick inside. Panicked. Like he had to either fight or run.

He couldn't fight Scarlett, so he'd run. He'd never run from anything in his life.

Vin ran an unsteady hand over his forehead.

When he'd told Scarlett about the post-nup, he'd expected to feel triumph, or at least a sense of calm control.

Instead, watching the happiness in his wife's eyes melt into horror, Vin had experienced a physical reaction he'd never expected. His hands had tightened into fists. He'd instantly wanted to destroy whomever had hurt her.

Except he had no one to blame—but himself.

"Vincenzo."

Vin abruptly stopped in the gilded, high-ceilinged hall-way when he saw Giuseppe waiting for him.

Just what he needed. He gave a silent curse. Another person to heap scorn on him, when he was doing a fine enough job heaping it on himself. He bit out, "What do you want?"

Giuseppe came forward, solemn in his formal tuxedo. "We have to talk."

"Make it quick."

"I always knew you weren't my biological son." He gave Vin a small smile. "Is that quick enough for you?"

He gaped at him, dumbfounded. "What?"

The older man shook his head. "Vincenzo, your moth-er's eyes were blue. So are mine. What are the chances we could conceive a child with eyes as dark as yours?"

After twenty years of keeping the secret, Vin was stag-gered. "But my mother used you for money. For years. Why didn't you tell her to go to hell, tell her I wasn't yours?"

"Because you *are* mine," he said, coming forward. "From the moment I held you as a tiny baby, Vincenzo, I was your father."

Vin thought of the first moment he'd held his own son in his arms. He knew what that felt like.

Giuseppe put his hands on Vin's shoulders. "I didn't give a damn what some DNA test might say. I loved you. You were—you *are*—my son. And you will always be."

Vin felt dizzy, like he'd gotten drunk on that one glass of champagne. The floor was trembling under him.

He'd been so wrong. He, who'd believed he could never be wrong about anything, had been wrong about every-thing.

He thought he'd never run away from a fight?

He'd been running for twenty years.

All these years he'd avoided Giuseppe and Joanne,

avoided emotion, avoided life. For what? For the sake of a secret that didn't matter?

His whole adult life, he'd tried to control everything, to make sure he never felt tied to anyone, so he'd never feel pain when they left. When, against his will, he'd come to care for Scarlett, it had terrified him so much he'd thought he needed to bring her to heel. To make her his slave.

Had he really thought he could rule her with a piece of paper? He was powerless where she was concerned. No pre-nup or post-nup in the world could change that.

I love you, Vin. And you love me. That was the whole reason for this, wasn't it? You're afraid to love me.

Giuseppe sighed ruefully in the hallway. "I just wish I'd known that was the reason you stayed away from us." He glanced at his wife, who'd come up behind him, followed by Maria. "We were foolish to keep silent, but we didn't want to give you more reasons to stay away."

"You knew, too?" Vin said to Joanne. She smiled, even as she wiped tears away.

"Of course I knew, darling. Giuseppe and I have been married a long time. We have no secrets."

"Well, I didn't know!" Maria cried sulkily behind her, tossing her long white veil. "No one tells me anything!"

Vin glanced at his young sister in her white wedding gown, and in that instant, his whole life came sharply into focus.

Scarlett was right. About everything.

Part of him had thought if he pushed her, she would flee, which would prove his worst beliefs and justify his actions in making her sign the post-nup.

He'd *wanted* to push her away.

You're afraid to love me. Yes, afraid. You tried to create a wall between us. But I'm not going to let you do it. We love each other. We belong together.

From the first moment he'd met Scarlett, so silly and

free in the New York dive bar, choking at her first taste of vodka, he'd been enchanted. He'd never met anyone like her, so feisty and sexy and warm.

He'd wanted her from the start, and he'd been willing to make deals to possess her—like his ridiculous fantasy that he could protect his own heart, and stay in control, by making her sign a form, or by trying to love her less, because he, the one who cared less, was the one who had the power.

But that was wrong. He saw that now.

It wasn't the one who loved less who had the power, but the one who loved more. Not because you could control the outcome, or keep from getting hurt, but because it meant you were brave enough to live without fear, hurtling yourself headlong into both joy and pain.

Being a fully alive human being, with the courage to love completely—what could be more powerful than that?

And as much as he loved his son, it wasn't the baby who'd first cracked open his heart.

It was Scarlett.

He looked at his father. "I need to go talk to my wife."

"Go, son," Giuseppe said fiercely. "Show her who you really are!"

Vin nodded, turned back down the hall.

He never should have rented their home out from under her. Another way he'd tried to push Scarlett into hating him. It had never felt like his home—until now. Scarlett had taken the sad, faded, tumbledown prison of his childhood and brought it to joyous life.

She'd done the same for him. Before they'd met, Vin had been focused on money and power, to the detriment of his own happiness. He'd been so afraid of being vulnerable that, if Scarlett hadn't shown up in the New York cathedral that day, he would have married a woman he didn't give a damn about.

If not for Scarlett, he would have turned into a man like Salvatore Calabrese: selfish, shallow and cold, too insecure to risk the only thing that mattered. His heart.

So many things Scarlett had done for him, and all she'd asked in return was for him to love her. For him to be the man he'd been born to be. The man she deserved.

Vin's walk turned into a run. Nodding at the sleepy security guard sitting inside the foyer, he pushed open the front door.

Outside the *palazzo*, the street was dark and quiet. Silent white snow fell softly to the ground. But where was Scarlett?

Then he saw her.

Still in her diamond necklace and sapphire-colored gown, her red hair looked tangled and twisted, and she had terror in her eyes.

A man was holding her. A man with a gun. A man with all kinds of darkness in his eyes.

"Vin!" she cried, struggling.

"Borgia." Blaise Falkner gave him a cold, evil smile. "I should have known you wouldn't keep away for long. You've wrecked my plan, but I'm almost glad. Now you'll see what I'm going to do to her, right in front of your eyes."

Terror ripped through Vin's heart as he looked from Falkner's face to the revolver, black as a deadly snake, held against Scarlett's forehead. For a split second, Vin's world started to go dark with fear.

Then he took a deep breath. He didn't *do* fear. Ever. And he wasn't going to start now, when his wife needed him to be strong. There was only one emotion he could let himself feel right now. He let the waves of it roll over him, like an ocean in a storm.

Rage.

CHAPTER TWELVE

WHEN BLAISE HAD pulled a gun on her in the quiet, snowy street, Scarlett had thought bitterly of how Vin had ordered her to keep a bodyguard nearby. Why hadn't she listened?

Because she'd never imagined she might need a bodyguard in the center of Rome. She'd never imagined that anyone might want to attack her...

"I've been watching your house for a week," Blaise had said, keeping his black revolver trained on her. "Hoping to get you alone."

"Why?" Her teeth chattered. "You can't still want to... to marry me?"

"Marry?" His lip had twisted scornfully as he came closer, until she could smell the sickening stench of old sweat half masked with musky cologne. "I'm way past that now. Your husband made this personal. He ruined my life. Now I will do the same to him."

Snowflakes fell softly against her skin. But that wasn't what froze her to the bone. "How?"

"He loves you."

"You heard us argue—"

"Yeah, I heard it all. It's perfect." His smile became venomous. "Now when you disappear, he'll blame himself for the rest of his life and think he drove you away. He'll always wonder. He'll never know."

"You can't!"

"Watch me." With his gun still trained on her, he snatched her crystal-encrusted clutch bag from her hand. "My car is around the corner..."

"I'm not going anywhere with you." She straightened. "Shoot me here."

"You'll go. Or my next stop will be at your house. Your baby is there, with no one but the housekeeper to protect him. Shame if they had a little accident. If the doors were blocked and the place went up in flames."

"No!" she cried, whimpering at the thought. "I'll go with you. Just leave them alone…"

"That's more like it." Blaise motioned with the revolver. "Over there, in the alley…"

But as she started to move, the front door of the *palazzo* banged open. Quick as a flash, Blaise grabbed her, placing her in front of him, holding the gun to her forehead.

Scarlett nearly cried when she saw Vin had come out of the *palazzo*. His black eyes went wide when he saw them. Then his hands clenched into fists.

"Let her go, Falkner." Vin's dark gaze focused on Blaise. "We both know I'm the one you want to hurt."

"Not just hurt. I want to destroy you. And hurting her— " he gripped into her shoulder painfully, causing Scarlett to gasp aloud "—is the best way to do that."

Vin took a step toward them. "We can talk about this. Negotiate…"

"There's nothing to negotiate, and if you take one more step, she's dead."

Vin stopped. His voice was low. "You'll die the second after she does."

Blaise gave a cackle. "You think I care? You took everything from me, Borgia. My whole life. I can never go back. And now neither can you…"

Blaise pressed the cold barrel of the revolver sharply into her skin.

Vin threw Scarlett a brief glance full of meaning. "You'd attack her from behind?"

And she remembered that rainy afternoon in October.

Here's how to use your own body weight against an attacker who grabs you from behind... She gave him a single trembling nod, and then everything happened at once.

The door of the *palazzo* banged open as Beppe and two other bodyguards rushed out. As Blaise whirled to look, Vin planted his feet, lowering his body into an instinctive crouch.

With an exaggerated sigh, Scarlett sagged as if she'd fainted. It wasn't hard at all. She was so terrified she was perilously close to fainting anyway.

Her unexpected weight broke his hold, and she fell hard to the cold, wet sidewalk.

With a loud curse, Blaise pointed the gun at her. He cocked it. She saw the deadly intention in his face.

As snowflakes whirled around her, Scarlett's life flashed before her eyes. Her mother. Her father. Her baby. All the love she'd had. And Vin. Always Vin...

As she closed her eyes, bracing herself for death, she saw a shadow fly across her field of vision. But there was no mercy. The gun went off with a jarring bang, and she flinched, gasping.

But she felt nothing.

Was this what it felt like to be dead? Scarlett's eyes opened, then she quickly ran her hands over her body. Somehow, though he'd shot her from four feet away, he'd missed her!

But Vin and Blaise were still struggling for the gun. The revolver fired once more, echoing loudly in the night.

"Die, you Italian bastard!" Blaise panted.

Vin! Scarlett scrambled to her feet, desperate to save him, terrified he'd been shot. But even as the bodyguards descended from all sides, Vin flung Blaise over his back like a sack of potatoes. For half a second, Blaise was suspended in midair with a shocked, stupid look on his face. Then he crashed hard to the concrete, where he lay still.

"The police are on the way, Mr. Borgia," Beppe said.

Scarlett heard the distant whine of a siren. She knew the steps in front of the *palazzo* would soon be covered with medical and police personnel.

Blaise lay faceup, flat on his back. Unmoving, he wheezed, "You… You…"

Vin looked down at him coldly. "You are going to prison, Falkner. For a very long time. You should pray you never get out." As bodyguards surrounded him, Vin turned to Scarlett. His expression changed. He reached for her. "Scarlett—"

"You saved me," Scarlett choked out, pressing her cheek against him. Then she drew back, frowning. "But you're wet. You…" There was a darkening patch on his right shoulder, and another on his left thigh. With a gasp, she lifted the lapel of his tuxedo jacket and saw red blooming across his white shirt, like a flower. And it was in that moment she realized why she was still alive. Vin had taken two bullets for her.

When Vin saw Falkner put his finger on the trigger, everything had become crystal clear.

He would either save his wife or die with her.

Their son would know that his father had loved his mother enough to sacrifice his own life to try to save her.

That was the best legacy any father could leave his son. The only real legacy. It had nothing to do with leaving a fortune, or a billion-dollar company. A man's true legacy was his example, of how a man should live—and how he should die. *For the ones he loved.*

"*Cara.*" Vin pulled Scarlett into his arms, holding her like the precious treasure she was. He felt a sharp pain in his shoulder, and another in his thigh. He gritted his teeth against the pain. "He was right about one thing. If anything ever happened to you, it would utterly destroy me."

"Vin, we need to try to stop the bleeding until the paramedics…"

"Not yet," he breathed. He curved his hands around her, needing the feel of her body against his. "Everything you said was true. That's what I came to say. I was afraid to love you." He searched her gaze. "Now the only thing I'm afraid of is not having the chance to love you for the rest of my life."

She looked closely at the holes in his jacket. "It looks like this bullet went straight through your shoulder and out the back. But your leg…"

He was barely listening. "I was a coward."

"Coward? Vin, you took two bullets for me!"

"It's true," he insisted roughly. He was still shaking. It was only now that he held her, now she was safe in his arms, that he could admit how terrified he'd been. "I promised myself long ago that I'd never love anyone— never give anyone that kind of power over me. Then on Christmas Eve, after I told you I loved you, I was afraid. I was desperate to regain control."

"Control over what?"

"You, me, everything. Life."

"Oh, Vin," she whispered through cracked lips. "No one can control all that."

"I realized that today." His lips twisted as he leaned on her. He could no longer put any weight on his left leg. He wondered how much blood he'd lost. But he couldn't let her go. Not yet. "I've made so many mistakes. I just found out Giuseppe has always known he's not my biological father. He just didn't care."

"No!"

He gave a low laugh, swaying on his feet. He was starting to feel dizzy. "Control is an illusion. I understand that now. All I can control in life are the choices I make. The man I choose to be." He took her hand in his own, pressing it against his chest. "You have my heart, Scarlett. No matter if you hurt me. No matter if you leave me." Her beautiful face blurred in his vision as he whispered, "After the way I tricked you into signing those papers, I wouldn't blame you."

Paramedics and firemen and policemen were swarming the street, and inquisitive wedding guests were pouring out of the *palazzo*. But all Vin could see was Scarlett's pale, determined face.

"You listen to me, Vin Borgia," she said hoarsely "This is something I want you to remember for the rest of your life." She took both his hands in hers. Her green eyes looked enormous. "You're safe with me, Vin. As long as I live, I'll watch out for you."

It was a strange thing to hear from a woman so much smaller than he. But as he swayed, feeling weak from loss of blood, she was beneath his arm, supporting him, the source of his strength. As he was the source of hers.

"And I know I'm safe with you," she whispered, her eyes filling with tears. "I will never leave you. I'm yours for life."

Her love washed over him like an enveloping embrace. Vin exhaled. He hadn't realized he'd been holding his breath for so long, waiting to hear those words. Years. Decades.

He breathed, "Scarlett…"

Snow fell softly in the dark January night, frosting the streets of Rome. As people swarmed all around them, Vin pulled her close. He felt new, reborn. She'd made him the man he'd been born to be.

Then he staggered back as his vision got a little hazy.

"You're losing too much blood!" She waved wildly to the paramedics. "Over here! Quick!"

The paramedics swiftly assessed Vin's injuries and worked to control the bleeding, applying pressure and bandages before leaning him into a backboard, to carry him into the ambulance. "We need to get him to the hospital, *signora*."

"Yes," she said anxiously.

"Wait." Feeling woozy, Vin looked at his wife. "We'll live in Rome."

She tried to smile. "What about the long-term lease to Mr. Hollywood?"

"Canceled. We'll stay."

She looked down at him, her tangled red hair streaked with snow and blood. "No."

"No?"

She shook her head. "That's not how marriage works. It's not my decision." Taking his hand in hers, she kissed it. "It's ours. I love you, Vin."

He looked at her, now holding nothing back, letting her see his whole heart and soul. "I love you more."

"Are you ready?"

No, Scarlett thought, biting her lip hard. She shivered, then nodded.

"Good." Vin held out his hand.

She took it and stepped onto a plane for the first time in almost a year.

"You can do this," he said.

She took a deep breath. She looked at his hand in hers, then squared her shoulders. "I know."

He smiled. "That's my girl."

The plane was tiny, a four-seater Cessna. There would be no flight attendants. Only one pilot. And only one passenger.

But it was going to be all right, Scarlett suddenly knew. Because she trusted this pilot with her life.

She sat beside him now as he pushed knobs and flicked

on switches. He moved the throttle, then glanced at her. "Maybe someday you'll get your own pilot's license."

"Ha-ha," she said, then realized he was serious.

Vin looked at her. "The best way to live is to do what scares you most. You taught me that, *cara*."

Maybe he was right, Scarlett thought suddenly. Maybe. But...

"I'll just survive being a passenger first," she said, gripping her headphones tightly.

He reached over and put his hand on her knee. "Look at my face."

She did and relaxed.

"There's no way we can crash." He sat back in the pilot's seat with an encouraging grin. "I'm safe with you, remember? You'll watch out for me."

"I meant it." She knew he wouldn't let anything happen to her, either. If anyone could keep Vin safe, it was Scarlett. If anyone could keep Scarlett safe, it was Vin.

She took a deep breath, clutching her armrests.

So much had changed in the last eight months, since the night of Maria's wedding, when he'd been shot by Blaise Falkner. Vin had spent days recovering in the hospital, where he'd also been interviewed by the police. But he'd been lucky.

"If he'd shot you a little lower in the shoulder," the doctor had told him, "the bullet would have hit you in the heart. If he'd shot you a little higher in the thigh..." He hesitated.

"I'd be done fathering children?" Vin had grinned up at Scarlett, standing by his hospital bed. "Remind me to visit Falkner in prison and thank him for his poor aim."

She didn't find it funny at all. "This is no laughing matter."

"Oh, *cara*, but it is." Vin had kissed the back of her

hand, then looked at her seriously. "One should always be joyful in the presence of a miracle."

When he finally was able to return home, he'd embraced his baby son happily swinging in his bouncy chair, who had no idea of the tragedy that had nearly taken his parents' lives. Vin had kissed his son's downy head, kissed his wife's lips, then gone straight to the study and thrown the signed postnuptial agreement into the fire.

He'd also ripped up the villa's lease to the movie star. The man had immediately threatened to sue, but Vin had solved the problem by paying for him to stay three months at a fancy hotel, and the actor quit complaining.

"Room service," Vin explained succinctly.

Vin had also insisted on paying for his sister to have a second honeymoon. It was the least he could do, he said, after ruining her wedding reception. After the young couple had returned from Tahiti, while Giuseppe and Joanne were visiting their grandson for a week, they had the whole family together for dinners and game nights.

Eventually, when Vin's wounds had healed and Scarlett felt ready, they had a farewell party to say *ciao* to Rome. They packed up what they needed most and took the train to London and, from there, a luxurious ocean liner to New York.

Scarlett had felt guilty about the six-day voyage—so much longer than a transatlantic flight—but her husband hadn't grumbled once. In fact, he'd claimed he enjoyed the vacation, and the chance to dance with his wife every night on the dance floor while Mrs. Stone kept a close eye on Nico in their lavish suite.

"In fact, I might consider a fleet of ships for my next SkyWorld expansion," he'd told Scarlett, waggling his eyebrows. She still wasn't sure if he'd been serious.

The two of them had agreed to compromise, and split their time between Rome and New York. But since they'd

moved to Manhattan, Scarlett had found to her surprise
that she'd come to love this rough-and-tumble city, too.
Next week, when they returned to Rome, she might even
miss New York. Living in their delightful two-story penthouse with a view of Central Park—which she'd decorated
to be homey and comfortable—meant she often passed
St. Swithun's Cathedral on Fifth Avenue.

"The place you decided to marry me," she liked to tease
Vin, "in the middle of your wedding to someone else."

He grinned. "*Bella*, I know a good thing when I see
her."

"I love you," she said.

"I love you more," he said seriously.

Which of them loved the other one more was, of course,
not their only quarrel. They were human, after all. Sometimes Vin worked too much, or Scarlett fretted about their
perfectly happy baby, who could now sit on his own and
loved to giggle and was starting to talk. But even during
their rare arguments, Vin would claim that Scarlett was
perfect, the most wonderful woman in the world. It irritated her to no end. How could she properly fight with a
man who continually insisted she was perfect?

So when Vin suggested one tiny, tiny thing she might
do for his birthday, she had to listen. He asked her to take
a plane ride. "I have a little Cessna parked at Teterboro.
I'd be the pilot. We'd fly for fifteen minutes, tops. Short
circle, totally uneventful, then we'd land." He looked at
her hopefully. "What do you say?"

She hadn't wanted to disappoint him, so she'd agreed.
But now…

"I can't believe you talked me into this," she breathed,
as the engine noise started to build, shaking the small
plane.

He grinned. "You'll love it. Trust me."

And the funny thing was, she did trust him. So maybe

he was right. Maybe she would love this. Maybe the fear that had been holding her back all this time from flying was the same one that had made him afraid to love her.

It was normal to be afraid of taking a risk. But wasn't it the point of life to find courage—even if it took a little while—and be bold enough to fly?

"Are you ready, Scarlett?" her husband asked quietly.

She felt green with fear. But she knew that if anyone could keep her safe, if anyone truly loved her, it was Vin. She took a deep breath. "Hit it."

"I love you," he said, pushing the throttle forward.

She looked at him, her heart full. "I love you more."

The Cessna started to increase speed down the runway, going faster and faster. And as the nose lifted off the ground, and their little plane soared off the runway into the bright blue sky, Scarlett knew they'd be relishing the pleasures of that argument for the rest of their lives.

* * * * *

If you enjoyed this story, look out for these other great reads from Jennie Lucas
UNCOVERING HER NINE-MONTH SECRET
NINE MONTHS TO REDEEM HIM
THE SHEIKH'S LAST SEDUCTION
THE CONSEQUENCES OF THAT NIGHT
Available now!

Also available in the
ONE NIGHT WITH CONSEQUENCES
series this month
THE SHEIKH'S BABY SCANDAL
by Carol Marinelli

MILLS & BOON®

MODERN™

POWER, PASSION AND IRRESISTIBLE TEMPTATION

A sneak peek at next month's titles...

In stores from 8th September 2016:

- **The Return of the Di Sione Wife** – Caitlin Crews
- **The Spaniard's Pregnant Bride** – Maisey Yates
- **Married for the Tycoon's Empire** – Abby Green
- **A Deal with Alejandro** – Maya Blake

In stores from 6th October 2016:

- **Baby of His Revenge** – Jennie Lucas
- **A Cinderella for the Greek** – Julia James
- **Indebted to Moreno** – Kate Walker
- **Surrendering to the Italian's Command** – Kim Lawrence

Just can't wait?
Buy our books online a month before they hit the shops!
www.millsandboon.co.uk

Also available as eBooks.

MILLS & BOON®

EXCLUSIVE EXCERPT

Dario Di Sione's triumph in retrieving his family's
earrings is marred by the discovery that his traitorous
wife Anais has kept their child a secret! But Anais's
return to his side casts a new light on past events,
and now it's not the child he just wants to claim…

Read on for a sneak preview of
THE RETURN OF THE DI SIONE WIFE
the fourth in the unmissable new eight book Modern series
THE BILLIONAIRE'S LEGACY

Dario froze.

For a stunned moment he thought he was imagining
her.

Because it couldn't be *her*.

Inky black hair that fell straight to her shoulders, as
sleekly perfect as he remembered it. That lithe body,
unmistakably gorgeous in the chic black maxidress she
wore that nodded to the tropical climate as it poured
all the way down her long, long legs to scrape the
ground. And her face. *Her face*. That perfect oval with
her dark eyes tipped up in the corners, her elegant
cheekbones and that lush mouth of hers that still had
the power to make his whole body tense in uncontrolled,
unreasonable, *unacceptable* reaction.

He stared. He was a grown man, a powerful man
by any measure, and he simply stood there and *stared—*

as if she was as much a ghost as that Hawaiian wind that was still toying with him. As if she might blow away as easily.

But she didn't.

"Hello, Dare," she said with that same self-possessed, infuriating calm of hers he remembered too well, using the name only she had ever called him—the name only she had ever gotten away with calling him.

Only Anais.

His wife.

His treacherous, betraying wife, who he'd never planned to lay eyes on again in this lifetime. And who he'd never quite gotten around to divorcing, either, because he'd liked the idea that she had to stay shackled to the man she'd betrayed six years ago, like he was an albatross wrapped tight around her slim, elegant neck.

Here, now, with her standing right there in front of him like a slap straight from his memory, that seemed less like an unforgivable oversight. And a whole lot more like a terrible mistake.

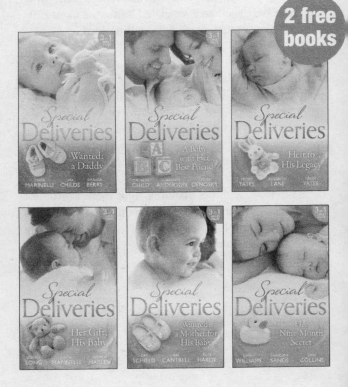